LILLIAN BOXFISH
TAKES A WALK

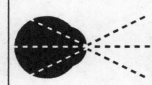

LILLIAN BOXFISH
TAKES A WALK

KATHLEEN ROONEY

THORNDIKE PRESS
A part of Gale, Cengage Learning

GALE
CENGAGE Learning®

Farmington Hills, Mich • San Francisco • New York • Waterville, Maine
Meriden, Conn • Mason, Ohio • Chicago

LIBRARY OF CONGRESS CATALOGING-IN-PUBLICATION DATA

Names: Rooney, Kathleen, 1980– author.
Title: Lillian boxfish takes a walk / by Kathleen Rooney.
Description: Large print edition. | Waterville, Maine : Thorndike Press, a part of Gale, Cengage Learning, 2017. | Series: Thorndike Press large print core
Identifiers: LCCN 2017001363| ISBN 9781410499660 (hardcover) | ISBN 1410499669 (hardcover)
Subjects: LCSH: City and town life—New York (State)—New York—Fiction. | Interpersonal relations—Fiction. | Older women—Fiction. | Reminiscing—Fiction. | Large type books. | BISAC: FICTION / Literary. | FICTION / Contemporary Women.
Classification: LCC PS3618.O676 L55 2017 | DDC 813/.6—dc23
LC record available at https://lccn.loc.gov/2017001363

Published in 2017 by arrangement with St. Martin's Press, LLC

Printed in Mexico
1 2 3 4 5 6 7 21 20 19 18 17

For Angela, my archivist always,
and
For Eric, forever my favorite flâneur

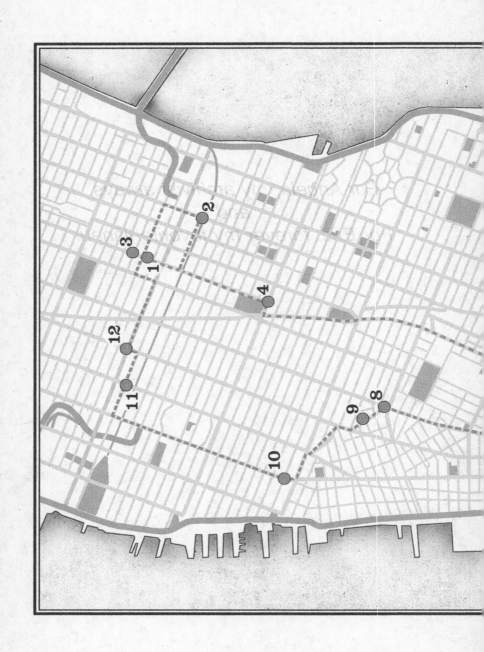

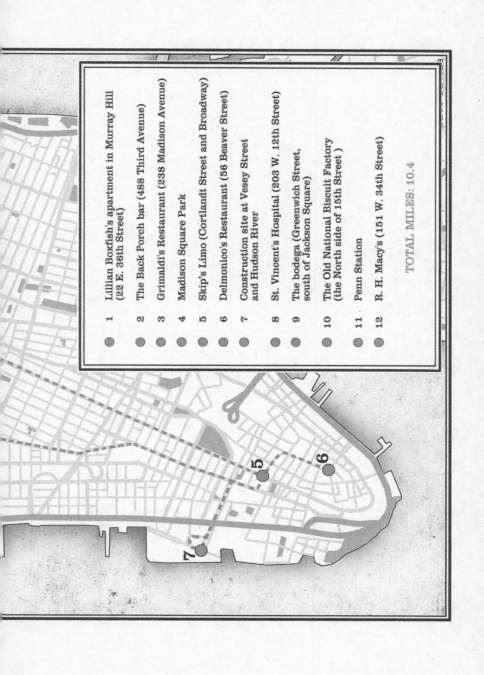

1 Lillian Boxfish's apartment in Murray Hill (22 E. 36th Street)

2 The Back Porch bar (488 Third Avenue)

3 Grimaldi's Restaurant (238 Madison Avenue)

4 Madison Square Park

5 Skip's Limo (Cortlandt Street and Broadway)

6 Delmonico's Restaurant (56 Beaver Street)

7 Construction site at Vesey Street and Hudson River

8 St. Vincent's Hospital (203 W. 12th Street)

9 The bodega (Greenwich Street, south of Jackson Square)

10 The Old National Biscuit Factory (the North side of 15th Street)

11 Penn Station

12 R. H. Macy's (151 W. 34th Street)

TOTAL MILES: 10.4

CONTENTS

ACKNOWLEDGMENTS

I extend more gratitude than I have the words to express to:

Anthony Antolini, Ann Greenleaf, and all of Margaret Fishback's extended family; Lisa Bankoff, Abby Beckel, Georgia Bellas, Logan Breitbart, Mitchell Brown, Hope Dellon, Sophia Dembling, Bob Drinan, Christen Enos, Elisa Gabbert, Meryl Gross, Silissa Kenney, Olivia Lilley, Angela Mc-Clendon Ossar, Dan Nielsen, Hannah O'Grady, Jen K. Olsen, Eric Plattner, Mitchell Rathberger, Beth Rooney, Martin Seay, Rachel Slotnick, Christine Sneed, Dori Weintraub, and Becky Wills; my family; all the poets who do Poems While You Wait; Lynn Eaton and everyone at the Hartman Center for Sales, Advertising & Marketing at Duke University; my students and colleagues at DePaul University; and anyone who has ever taken a walk with me, literally or metaphorically.

Skiddlee bebop we rock a scoobie doo.
And guess what, America? We love you!
'Cause ya rock and ya roll with so
much soul
you can rock till you're a
hundred-and-one years old.
— WONDER MIKE,
SUGARHILL GANG, 1979

1
THE ROAD OF ANTHRACITE

There once was a girl named Phoebe Snow. She wore only white and held tight to a violet corsage, an emblem of modesty. She was not retiring, though, and her life spun out as a series of journeys through mountain tunnels carved from poetry. I never saw her doing anything besides boarding, riding, or disembarking a train, immaculate always, captivating conductors, enchanting other passengers.

No, there wasn't. She was just an advertisement: the poster girl for the Delaware, Lackawanna, and Western Railroad. Her unsoilable Antarctic-colored clothes were proof that the line's anthracite-powered locomotives were clean-burning, truly — unlike their sooty and outfit-despoiling competitors:

Her laundry bill for fluff and frill
Miss Phoebe finds is nearly nil.

15

It's always light, though gowns of white,
Are worn on Road of Anthracite.

I was five years old when I first laid eyes on
her, on a postcard sent me by my dearest
aunt, Sadie Boxfish, my father's youngest
sister, daring and unmarried and living in
Manhattan. Sadie visited us in the District
of Columbia, but not very often. Her rare
physical presence she supplemented with
correspondence in snips and flashes. After I
scrawled back how much I adored Phoebe,
star of the story-poems, they became the
only kind of card Sadie ever posted.

The earliest ones my mother read aloud
(though I could read):

Miss Phoebe Snow has stopped to show
Her ticket at the gate, you know.
The Guard, polite, declares it right.
Of course — it's Road of Anthracite.

Mother clutched me in her lap, talking
about the image — Phoebe in a hat, Phoebe
in a dining car, Phoebe blue-eyed and mannerly chatting with the engineer — and
reciting the poetry:

Here Phoebe may, by night or day,
Enjoy her book upon the way.

Electric light dispels the night
Upon the Road of Anthracite.

In her clear contralto above my ears I could hear, in her neat bosom behind my head I could feel, her disapproval: not of Phoebe, but of Sadie. My mother — who was well-educated, read widely, passably fluent in German, conversant with the works of Freud and Adler, married at twenty, and never received a dollar of wages in her life — was also a woman who took difference as a slight. Anyone not living a life that fit the mold of her own — wifedom, motherhood — constituted a personal affront, an implied rebuke, an argument against. I thought Sadie quite bold.

"What a smart girl," my mother would say of Phoebe, who (I saw later) must have been so light and unburdened for having only air, and not one thought or care, in her golden head. Mother, stroking my own red-gold hair, meant only that Phoebe's frock was smart, or her little white gloves. Not Phoebe herself. Not smartness of that kind.

"Aunt Sadie's a smart girl," I said only once. To no reply. To my mother, gritting her small neat teeth, pearly and needle-like, reading that day's card more loudly than usual:

17

A cozy seat, a dainty treat
Make Phoebe's happiness complete
With linen white and silver bright
Upon the Road of Anthracite.

Sadie, career girl, and Phoebe, socialite, embedded inextricably into one another in my mind. Both of them expressed the inexpressible, suggesting that sex appeal existed but probably ought not to be named while one was living at home. Suggesting not so much a passenger train as speed and freedom, not so much a gown as style, not so much a hairdo as beauty.

Mother saw Sadie as wasting that last, working as hard as a beast of burden as a nurse in a hospital in New York City. Though now I know that Sadie can't have been living the life of Riley, I wanted to move there and join her. What a smart girl.

My mother resented Sadie like a stepsister resenting Cinderella, but she was polite. She did her no social violence. Was always hospitable and gracious on Sadie's visits, both as a point of pride and because my father would not have abided otherwise. Though he, too, a lawyer, thought Sadie's work beneath her.

My devotion to both Phoebe and Sadie has remained constant over the decades.

When I think of either, I also think of lofty mountain chains and cool delights.

The New York I moved to eventually was empty of Sadie, though I've since walked by St. Vincent's, the hospital where she worked, I don't know how many times. She died in the influenza epidemic of 1918.

Phoebe, deathless, simply faded from public consciousness like a once-popular song. Anthracite, needed to fight the Great War, was not to be used on railroads anymore. The world changed, and Phoebe disappeared forever:

On time the trip ends without a slip
And Phoebe sadly takes her grip
Loath to alight, bows left and right,
"Good-bye, Dear Road of Anthracite."

But I never forgot her. I didn't want to be her, so much as to have her — to create her.

Sadie led me to Manhattan, but Phoebe led me to poetry, and to advertising. So enrapt was I at her entrancing rhymes that when the time came to apply for jobs, I rhymed my letters and my samples alike:

To work for you
Is my fondest wish

Signed your ever-true
Lillian Boxfish

Fifteen inquiries. Five favorable replies.
Including one by telegram from R.H.
Macy's. This was the one I chose: my first
serious job in New York City. A job which
in some ways saved my life, and in other
ways ruined it. What a smart girl.

2
NEW YEAR'S EVE

The only man I ever birthed, though not
the only one I mothered, is on the other
end of the line, and he is giving me news
that is sad and bad and that makes me jealous. Julia, my ex-husband's second wife,
has been hospitalized after a heart attack,
her third. She will likely not survive. She is
much younger than I — fifteen years if you
go by my age as I've been lying about it
forever, sixteen if you go by my age as I am
pretty sure is correct. Either way, she is 68.

Either way, it is 1984, and she is with
them, and I am alone on New Year's Eve in
New York City, and it's too warm. I wish it
were snowing, but gently, gently, like sugar
falling on a great, gray cookie.

Unlike Julia, my health is and always has
been — physically — impeccable.

"She was struggling in all this Maine
snow, when there's none in California," says
Johnny, says Gianino, my Little John, says

my son, says Gian, as he asked to be called back in junior high school, when it occurred to him that he had the wherewithal. "She collapsed coming up the driveway after taking the kids to the library. It's pretty grim this time, Ma."

"Ma," he calls me — incongruous, ugly — but I enjoy it. Max, my ex-husband, taught him that: the harsh monosyllable sounding working-class, hardly our income bracket. But that was part of what I loved about Max. The blue of his collar to the white of mine. I was not entirely unmaternal toward Max. Of course when, finally, I needed his unconditional support, he could not afford the same care to me.

"Dreadful," I say. "I hope the ambulance didn't founder getting out to Pin Point."

Gian spends his time between semesters at Pin Point, the summer home Max and I bought in the thirties; perversely, he likes it in winter, too.

"No, they made it all right," he says. "I'm at the hospital now. Claire's mom took the train up from Boston to help out with the kids so I can stay here with Julia. The university's not back in session until the third week of January, so this honestly couldn't have happened at a better time."

This announcement that Gian is calling

from the hospital forces me to revise the image of him in my mind, an image I wasn't even aware of until I knew it was wrong. I picture him now in an overly bright lounge among grim institutional furniture, murmuring into an oft-disinfected courtesy phone. He rests his free hand atop his shaggy head in his distracted fashion — the absentminded professor, father of three, black hair threaded with gray at the temples, forty-three years old next month — and that imagined gesture recalls another, from what seems like yesterday: Gian placing a flat palm on the crown of his skull to measure his height against his bedroom wall.

The line goes quiet: He's stopped talking, and I realize I'd stopped listening. "How are the kids taking it?" I ask. I picture the three as last I saw them, the day after Christmas, bundled up like ornaments in red and green coats, and boarding the train north. I want to know how they will react when I die.

"They're upset. They're old enough to understand that this is it. That death is it. They're excited, though, that their aunt is going to fly in from California. We can't move Julia back there because she's too sick. She's going to be buried here anyway."

I imagine Gian's much younger half-sister,

23

the second child Max wanted, then got, standing graveside with him there in Maine. I'll be buried in that same boneyard. On Max's other side. It galls me to share. But where else would they put me? By then I won't care.

"If you want to send the kids back down here while you're dealing with this, you should," I say, knowing he'll never take me up on it, wishing he would. I only got to see them for a week at Christmas; there's so much more I could show them in the city, and I like when this apartment feels crowded — when they stay here to save money and avoid the fleabag hotels.

"I think they kind of ought to stick around, Ma, since their grandmother is about to die. They're grown up enough to go to a funeral."

"Step-grandmother," I say. I am interested in politeness; I am not interested in propriety. "And I don't know how character building a funeral is for a young person, or how much that will help Julia, past help as she'll be."

"Thanks anyway, Ma," he says. "How are you doing?"

"You just saw me. Healthy and hardworking as a Central Park carriage horse."

"Is that lady who comes to check on you

24

still checking through the holidays?"

"Vera moved to Texas with her husband when he got that oil-field job six months ago," I say. "I've told you three times."

"Who's taking care of you now?"

"Vera is my friend, not my caretaker. Rest assured that if I should drop dead I won't be reeking in the apartment for weeks, with the cat gnawing my carcass. There are a few people who would miss me. Not many."

"I wish you'd just come up to Brunswick for good, Ma. We've got the room. Murray Hill's not what it used to be. The city's not what it used to be. You're not safe."

I had hoped that the impending death of the false mother, of Julia, would have spared me another round of his entreaties to migrate permanently to Maine, if only because these efforts would be unseemly, would cast him in a bad light: my Gian, the Bluebeard of mothers. Once Julia's been in the ground for a few weeks, I'd reckoned, his Vacationland campaign would resume in earnest.

But no such luck. "I'm not leaving, Gian," I tell him. "The city has been unsafe for twenty years, and I've survived."

"Well, you're twenty years older now," he says. "And the city's getting worse. It's never been such a cesspool. The crime and disorder. The murders. The Subway Vigilante, Ma! It's out of control. What if you'd been on that train? What if you'd been on it with the kids?"

This, more and more, is Gian's attitude when I speak with him: a skittishness about the city's numberless perils. It strikes me as odd: He was never a nervous child. But as his own kids have grown older and more independent, his inventory of potential threats has steadily expanded — as, apparently, has his authority to give advice on such matters. Like many parents in middle age, he's quick to spot changes in the world, slow to note shifts in his own perspective.

That said, he is not incorrect. The city I inhabit now is not the city that I moved to in 1926; it has become a mean-spirited action movie complete with repulsive plot twists and preposterous dialogue.

Last week a man — neatly dressed, wearing wire-rimmed glasses — snapped on a downtown 2 express. Midafternoon, on a train full of people. Four teenagers surrounded him, asking for five dollars; people have been killed for refusing less. The paper says he says they threatened him with sharpened screwdrivers. The man pulled a gun from his waistband. *I have five dollars for each of you,* he is said to have said — as if he had practiced — before shooting them all. Two women collapsed at the end of the car in fright, and like a gallant gentleman, he helped them up before fleeing into the darkness of the tunnel at Chambers Street. Mayor Koch has said vigilantism won't be tolerated, and it seems he is right: Callers have been flooding the tips hotline the police set up, but their calls congratulate the shooter, thank him, offer to pay his bail if he turns himself in. The Subway Vigilante is not being tolerated; he is being idolized.

Gian just about about-faced the family back to Maine when it happened, even though we'd been uptown at the Museum of Natural History at the time, safe beneath the blue whale hanging by its dorsal fin, unarmed and pacific, silent as ever, a sentinel in the lurid tabloid nightmare this city's been dreaming.

"I *walk* everywhere, dearest," I say. And it's true: I like the exercise, and the subway cars are graffitied with so much text it's like being screamed at, like the voices inside my head and everyone else's have manifested their yelling outside, ill-spelled with spray paint. "And we *weren't* on that train. And he isn't shooting elderly ladies and adorable tots."

"But guys *like* the guys he shot are everywhere. Hoods. Gangs. Toughs. Whatever you want to call them."

"I would not resist if young thugs approached me for money," I say. "I would acquiesce. I agree with Governor Cuomo that a vigilante spirit is dangerous. Rude, too."

"Rude?" he says.

"Yes, Gian. Incivility is not incivility's antidote. I don't know whether I believe that vigilante really had reason to think those young men were going to harm him. It sounds to me like he planned to shoot someone regardless — like he'd seen those *I Want Death* movies one too many times."

"*Death Wish*?" says Gian.

"One of those young men is paralyzed. Eighteen years old. Never going to walk again."

"Maybe they deserved it, Ma. The city's a sick place. People are sick."

"This city may be a rotten egg," I say, "but I'll still be the last one out. What have I got to lose?"

"Ma, you sound depressed again."

"Of course I do. This time of year is depressing. New Year's Eve is a bigger thug than any mugger, the way it makes people feel. Being old is depressing. The Subway Vigilante is depressing. But I love it here,

28

this big rotten apple. I'm near my old haunts, my sycamore trees, my trusty R.H. Macy's."

"I will never understand," Gian says, "why living near Macy's is more important than living near your grandkids. You haven't written an ad for them in twenty-five years."

"It's not just R.H. Macy's, Johnny," I say, though I'd miss the department store like I'd miss a parent; the company gave me a life that I would not have lived otherwise. "In Murray Hill I don't have to drive. I don't have to rely on anybody. If I came to Brunswick, my brain would waste into a raisin and I'd break both my hips."

He goes on, and I listen, but he won't persuade me. I'm not leaving this city no matter how far it falls in its hellward slide. Over the years I have entertained the idea of moving. I adore my son, the kids, adore the idea of usurping the fake mother. And yet.

"Gianino, darling," I say. "I thought this call was about Julia, not your old ma. What will you do with the evening? I imagine this heart attack has quashed your plans?"

"We're going to let the kids stay up until midnight this year. They're all old enough. Even though I'll be at the hospital — just being awake will be enough of a treat for

29

them. What are your plans?"

"Same as always. Dinner at Grimaldi at five, and then early to bed with a book."

"Veal rollatini with green noodles?" he asks.

"As ever," I say. "Alberto's specialty."

The Grimaldis were family friends of Max's family. Max, whose full name was Massimiliano Gianluca Caputo. The restaurant is just around the corner on Madison Avenue, and I've been going there since they opened in 1956. Max and I had divorced — why say it that way? Max had divorced me — before then, but because I got to keep the apartment, got to keep the city, I also got to keep the restaurant and that set of friends. It's been my New Year's Eve standard since the late seventies, back before pasta became the rage of the age.

"Tell Alberto that Massimiliano Gianluca Caputo, Jr., sends his regards," says Gian. "Tell Al junior that I say ciao."

"I will to Alberto," I say, "but I can't to Al. He absconded to Palm Beach to serve tortellini to the snowbirds."

I think of my rollatini, and I don't feel hungry.

"I bet his new place won't require jackets in that Florida heat," says Gian.

I'd bet he's right, and though I'll never set

foot in Florida, I resent that, just as I resent our summertime tourists who underdress, who take no pride in looking any better than bovine, in their shorts and their neon hues and their fanny packs. Even were Alberto no longer to require it, I would dress for dinner.

"If I'm out when you have news, I'm at Grimaldi," I say. "So don't worry and just leave a message."

I used to use a service, but Gian and the kids set up an answering machine last week, one of their Christmas presents. The leave-a-message message speaks in the voice of Lily, my youngest granddaughter — my favorite voice, and not just because they named her after me, but because she's musical, a singer like her father. She's called me every day since they left, to record a reply to her own recording before I pick up and we talk a bit. Our new game: Lily ringing Lily, then speaking to Grandma Lillian.

"All right," says Gian. "Be careful out there. Love you, Ma."

I replace the Bakelite receiver in its cradle and look down at the kitchen table, where I've been sitting.

Dark, glimmering crumbs, like potting soil, are strewn across the tabletop beneath my elbows, my face. I have just devoured

31

half a package of Oreo brand cookies manufactured by Nabisco while on the phone
with Gian without even realizing it.

I never do that: Buy manufactured cookies. Eat that way, like an animal. I don't even
especially like Oreos. My mouth, which moments ago was obliviously munching, now
teems with their industrial-strength sweetness. My fingertips are greasy with creme
filling — creme so-called, as opposed to
cream, because it must be just powdered
sugar and lard, unless I miss my guess. I
suppose I must have been twisting them
apart, eating them disassembled, or how
else would I have made such a mess?

"Phoebe!" I say to the cat, creeping along
the back of the sofa, staring at me green-
eyed. "Why didn't you say something?"

Phoebe rotates her pert ears away and
plops to the floor, pretending she hasn't
heard me, in much the same manner a
cultured person responds to audible flatu-
lence.

I am, for the life of me, unable to fathom
why I even *had* the vile black sandwiches.
Did I buy them while the grandchildren
were here? I'm sure I did not. My week
prior to their visit was a Tartarus of sheet
pans, spent in the creation of a Christmas-
cookie fantasia; had the little goblins at any

point asked me for *packaged* cookies, I'm quite certain I would have shipped them back to Maine with stockings full of coal. Wherefore, then, this evil visitation? The episode is enough to make me fear the onset of a condition that until now I've mocked: this Alzheimer's disease that's evidently plaguing the aged. Or so I'm told; I don't often mix with the aged.

No time for such fretting now: Worst of all, I have only a little more than an hour before I'm to be at Grimaldi. I doubt I'll be famished again by the time they seat me, but I have to show up, or Alberto really will send a cop to look in on me. I couldn't abide that. Plus, I have my dinner attire picked out, and I don't want to stay in; I've been in all day. The weather, unwholesomely clement, dissuaded me from taking my usual stroll. The mercury hit sixty-five yesterday — December 30 in New York City — and the forsythia in Central Park thought it meant that they should bud. Tonight the low is supposed to be a more reasonable thirty degrees, so I can dress as befits midwinter.

Most days I don't see many people, per se, but in Manhattan, when I go for my walks, seven million sets of eyes — fourteen million eyeballs, potentially — stand to land upon me. Someday soon I may not be able to dress myself, so I intend to try to look stylish until I can't any longer. Julia in her blouses with bird appliques, in her colorful sweaters with knit pom-poms — such is not my way.

Phoebe follows me into the bedroom and watches as I dress. I used to always wear nylons — real pantyhose, nude — but my legs have grown pale and veiny. I put on a pair of mustard-yellow Coloralls. They are warmer than nylons, and I appreciate their optimism. But though the ads suggest treating them like hosiery and underwear all in one, I do wear underwear under them. I am a lady, after all; plus I don't want a yeast infection, and who cares if I have a visible panty line? I wore leg makeup during World War II because of the stocking shortage. I even helped advertise it: "As sheer and gauzy in effect as the most beautiful nylons, and so much more economical."

I like to think I do not dress like a typical old lady. I have some old pieces, yes, some classics that still fit me, but I like new clothes and have the money to buy them, so I do. I do not eschew the shoulder pads and jewel tones I see on the mannequins, silly though they may be. Everything in fashion these days seems so childlike and bellicose, bright yet aggressive, a cute positivity that recasts every woman as a cross between a majorette and a Sherman tank. My dress tonight is dazzling green velvet with long sleeves, pleasingly boxy.

I sit at my vanity. I am a vanitas. My hair of yesteryear was glossy red-gold. All the old photographs — from the society pages and the ad-industry trades — are black and white, so in those I look brunette, like film stars do in precolor films. But it was red-gold, friends, brassy and dyed though it is today.

I'll wear a hat, too, a wide-brimmed fedora of navy blue.

If you love something, know that it will leave on a day you are far from ready. I apply my Helena Rubinstein Orange Fire lipstick from one of the tubes I stockpiled in the 1950s. When I heard it would be discontinued, I bought twenty-five. One more reason, I'm sure, that Max thought me crazy. That lipstick fascinated me then, it fascinates me still: its color, its spiral stripes, its waxy fragrance and ineffable taste. No cosmetic has ever suited me better.

Women in my day spent $150 million on cosmetics annually. I helped get them to do it. Tonight on the street, under orange lights,

35

women will walk by, their arms through the elbows of their men in overcoats, their eyes lined in blue. The blue pencil I used in my day was to mark up copy, ad copy.

I finish with a bit of mascara, plain black, then sit back and gaze at what I've done.

I think I look all right. But who's to say? The insouciance of youth doesn't stay, but shades into "eccentricity," as people say when they are trying to be kind, until finally you become just another lonely crackpot. But I've always been this way. The strangeness just used to seem more fashionable, probably.

I pet Phoebe's fur of purest white and walk to the foyer.

Now for footwear. The snow's mostly melted following yesterday's freak heat, but I'm not going to risk a fall, not me. Not these hips. I put on my riding boots, from when I used to spend time on horseback in Maine. With some socks inside, between boots and tights, they're just right for me, a cold old lady.

I top it all off with my mink coat, obviously. The seams aren't done the way anyone's been working them for years, but I don't care. I bought it for me. Myself. In 1942. It was not a gift from Max. I used my own money. I have enough to buy another, but this one is the one.

In my girl-poetess days, I wrote the lines:

I'd rather have a fur coat now
Than crumbs at fifty anyhow.

Why is Ogden Nash remembered when I am forgotten? The funny thing is, I was closer to fifty when I wrote that than anyone realized. That poetic sentiment now seems very early twentieth century. The only century I've known. Or so I claim — born in 1900, I always say. I'm lying, though, because my real birth year, 1899, made me sound like a grotesque relic, even when I wasn't. A woman can never be too rich or too thin or too young, truly. So I revised.

I descend in the elevator, bid the doorman good-bye and return his "Happy New Year," and then I am out in the late-afternoon light.

In the air hangs the scent of dampness and birthday candles blown out, which I have always associated with the presence of ghosts.

Since Max and I moved here almost forty years ago, I have felt at home in Murray Hill. The name sounds like a person: Mr. Murray Hill. Cheery Mr. Hill, a living friend, stalwart Murray who has not yet forsaken me.

I have a little under an hour until my reservation. Perhaps I can walk off the abominable Oreo cookies I savaged and dine happily after all?

Off to traipse *the Century's corpse outleant* — or 1984's, at any rate — I head east on Thirty-Sixth Street toward Third Avenue. Maybe I'll walk by one of my old apartments, the second one I lived in after I first came to the city from that much duller metropolis, Washington, D.C.

That I was a success is not apparent now; that I would be a success was not apparent then.

Within a few steps, though, I feel that it's hopeless. I can't walk this fullness off by five. How am I still making stupid mistakes in my eighties? Whenever somebody says to me, "Maybe it'll come with age," I want to say, "I wouldn't count on it."

Gian is not wrong about the great decline. Even Murray Hill is shabbier than it should be. The sycamores looking sickly, trash gathered at their roots.

I have half a mind, next time we talk, to ask Gian to secure as my epitaph that most poetic of the signs planted in the parks back when I first arrived in this city:

38

Let no one say and say it to your shame
That all was beauty here until you came.

Let no one say and say it to your shame
That all was beauty here until you came.

3
YOUR BRAIN IS SHOWING

In my reckless and undiscouraged youth, I worked in a walnut-paneled office thirteen floors above West Thirty-Fifth Street.

When I arrived in Manhattan in 1926, I scrimped along on help from my parents and pittances from ballet performances until I landed the job at R.H. Macy's: Forty dollars a week as a lowly assistant copywriter.

From the first moment I took to my desk and touched a needle-sharp pencil to a steno pad, I felt a sense of correctness that I have never known before or since. I would look down at the streams of strangers moving up and down Seventh Avenue, at the fog of their breath beneath their black and gray and brown hats, and I knew by instinct just how to buttonhole them. In my little walnut nook I was like a human cannonball, snug and ready to be launched above the unsuspecting crowd.

By one muggy morning in hot, late August

1931, I'd become a salaried institutional copywriter for that great department store, and the highest-paid advertising woman in America.

I had a front-page article in the *New York World-Telegram* to prove it: "Personality, Understanding, Interest: Those Are Keys to Success Says Mere Girl Who's Found It," read the headline.

I carried it with me up to the thirteenth floor, lucky number thirteen, with my coffee in one hand and, in my bag, an apple that I'd bought from one of the apple sellers on the street. Lucky, truly, not to be one of them, tattered and desperate in Herald Square, in the midst of the Depression. Lucky to be cast as the plucky starlet of a human-interest puff piece, a spry and spritely gal getting over in spite of everything, making it sound so effortless — making no mention of the drudgery I sometimes felt, grateful though I was to have the chance to be a drudge.

That headline calling me "girl," even in my early thirties, made me think of my mother back home in Georgetown. I'd be sending her a copy later, because it would fill her with complicated pride: happiness that I wasn't starving, and disapproval at what she'd perceive as my being showy and immodest.

Quoth the subhead: "Lillian Boxfish, Who Upset Advertising Ideas to Win Executive Recognition Found Personality and Sense of Humor Helped Her to Goal."

I resolved, as ever, to maintain my good humor as I approached Chester Everett to ask for a raise.

The days the copywriters put in, 8:30 to 6, were long, but mine were usually longer, and I was there that morning before almost anyone else, which had been my plan. Chester, too, was already in; as I unlocked my office I could see him wedged behind his desk, morning light ablaze in the thick, white hair of the small, wide head that topped his former-football-lineman's frame. My boss's appearance, while not entirely unhandsome, evoked an icebox crowned by a cauliflower.

Chester was a good egg, by and large. He had no gift for writing copy but knew that about himself. He did, however, have an unerring sense of what would and wouldn't work: what approaches would attract, inspire, confuse, or offend our prospective shoppers. He was a good manager, too, in an environment resistant to being managed. Our office was a field richly seeded with volatile and mercurial temperaments, and

42

Chester's firm but gentle hand was adept at selectively pruning them such that they would flourish rather than wither. I liked him because he ran a tight ship; he liked me because I was both creative and even-keeled. Overall we got along well. Then again, overall I rarely demanded much of him.

I set down my things — all but the newspaper — and headed toward Chester's open door.

To my chagrin, he already had a visitor. Olive Dodd — simpering, unctuous, not-quite-evil Olive — was perched on one of his two visitors' chairs. Too late now to turn around and wait. I walked in.

"Chester, darling, good morning to you," I said. "Olive, lovely to see you, too."

Olive, with her prim posture, her ungainly manner, and her reliance on elaborate fashions inappropriate for the office, strongly resembled a fancy pigeon: a creature bred out of its dignity across many generations. Although pretty enough by the standards of the day, with a voluptuous figure and a pleasant if somewhat shapeless face, she always gave an impression of bigness, as if poorly fitted to any locale. Whenever I encountered her I thought I could detect an agitated quaver, as if she might be

43

on the verge of bursting into laughter or tears or, God help us, song. I hadn't yet been able to work out whether she was like this all the time or only when I was around.

My dim hope that Olive might let me speak with Chester alone guttered when I saw what was in her hand: the same edition of the *World-Telegram* that I held in my own. "Oh, Lillian," she said, "I was just showing Mr. Everett your wonderful news."

Olive was twenty-eight or twenty-nine if she was a day, but her cloying insistence on "mister"-ing Chester made her seem younger — not youthful, but simply unformed. Her early arrival to show Chester the story gave her the air of a tattletale, though I couldn't see how what I'd achieved might be punishable.

The store below us had just installed a state-of-the-art air-cooling system, but upstairs we still made do with oscillating fans. The one in Chester's open window riffled the edges of the newspaper that Olive spread before him.

Chester wiped his forehead with a monogrammed handkerchief as he scanned the page. "Congratulations, Lily," he said. "This is your finest write-up yet. And I'll bet you helped them decide to quote your air-conditioning ad. Getting that word out to

44

our simmering mass of sweaty customers seeking relief was a well-timed stroke. Particularly given that it didn't cost us a red cent."

The reporter had asked if they could run a sample illustrating my greatest innovation to the ad industry and the secret to my success. "Humor," read the story, "used judiciously, lifts Boxfish's ads above the pomp and routine of Macy's competitors."

Being funny — it was true; that was my innovation. Everyone took it and began doing it themselves, but nobody was funnier than I was, not for a long time, not for years. Mine was a voice that no one had heard speaking in an advertisement before, and I got them to listen. To listen and then, more importantly, to act on what they'd heard.

I'd given the reporter the image that Helen McGoldrick, true friend and crack illustrator, had drawn, an amusing cartoon of a deer sporting eight antlers with a hat perched on each, as well as my verse that had inspired it.

Chester read aloud from the newsprint in that thunderous voice of his, stentorian and clear as a Roman orator's, just as he'd done days before when I'd brought him a draft to get his go-ahead:

This reindeer finds Manhattan heat
A shattering experience,
For when he ventures on the street
He undergoes the great expense
Of weighing eight straw hats upon
His antlers, in the hope that they
Will separate him from the sun
And keep him cool despite the day.
Poor deer, his overhead is quite
Absurd. He should be told to go
To Macy's where the Fahrenheit
Is like the prices, sweet and low.

"It was also a not-so-subtle signal to the management that maybe they could pump some of that refreshing oxygen up here," I said, taking the seat next to Olive and thereby clearing her route to the door, hoping she'd take the hint.

To my utter absence of shock, she remained unmoved and unmoving. In recent months Olive, a junior copywriter, had emerged as my friend-rival. Not my friendly rival; rather, she was someone who pretended to friendship even as she was being boiled alive from the inside out by seething jealousy. My grinning enemy. Someone who, when Chester would approve my copy yet again, even after a tenacious fight, would smile — teeth gritting — and say, "Honestly,

46

Lily, you're undefeatable as always," resentful and obviously longing for my eventual defeat.

Olive was in the habit of saying "honestly" so often that even a child could see that she must be deceitful. I marveled at her mother's prescience in having named her daughter after a green — with envy — cocktail garnish: hollow and bitter.

"It's hotter than blazes," said Chester, "so I hope they listen. But look at you, Lily, fresh as a flower, like the heat can't touch you. Just like in the article." And he read again from the page: " 'A slim, copper-haired girl in a softly clinging yellow dress is bending over a great clipping book, studying the full- and half-page advertisements pasted there.' "

"Yes, yes," I said. "And 'green eyes that smile.' "

"Oh, but those eyes are not smiling now," said Chester. "What's the matter?"

Perceptive as always, that Chester. It was he who'd first seen my talent, calling me clever and breezy as he plucked me from the forty-dollar-a-week field in which I'd been toiling — where Olive was still hung down — and flung me into the stratosphere. I had no reason to think he'd accede to my request for more money, at least not easily,

47

but I had to make it. Not out of greed, I hoped he would understand, but out of justice.

"Chester, do you see what the lede of the article calls me?"

"The highest paid advertising woman in America," he said. "I should think that's correct and that you more than deserve it. We owe our loyal advertising readership to you. You're better than vaudeville."

"Thank you," I said, giving a stagey bow from my seat. "But *woman,* Chester. It says woman. Why not person? I've come in here to ask for a raise. We both know I bring R.H. Macy's more business than anyone else on the thirteenth floor, woman or man. Why not pay me what I'm worth?"

"Lil," he said, resorting to the nickname he always used when things between us became strained. "About that . . . I know it's been on your mind. But I'm afraid it's been decided that we really can't do that at this juncture."

"The passive voice, Chip?" I said, resorting to my counterpart to Lil. "The use of the passive voice to disguise one's role in the making of a decision is imprecise and obfuscatory. You're a better adman than that. Active verbs! Why not say 'I refuse to pay you fairly'?"

48

Chester picked up Olive's paper, folded it, and handed it to me, though I was still clutching the one I'd walked in with. I could tell Olive wanted to ask for hers back but was too meek to do so.

"In here," he said, tapping the article from behind his mahogany desk, "you sound so gracious and unassuming. I wouldn't have expected we'd be back on this again today."

He folded his shirtsleeved arms — too hot for a jacket — across his barrel chest, their cross echoing the barricade his desk seemed to have become.

"I love it here, Chip," I said, looking at him as I handed Olive's *World-Telegram* back to her. "I love working for you, and I would never speak ill of Mr. R. H. Macy or the store that bears his name. Not in print and not in private. But the two-track, male-female pay grades don't make much sense. While I'm at it, it seems as though Helen should be paid the same as the male illustrators, too."

Though I was fantastic at my part of the job, Helen McGoldrick's visual bravura pushed my words that extra mile into the contested territory of our audience's minds. Her technique was advanced, anticipating the jazzy, kinetic midcentury style, each stroke a smile, streamlined and forward-

49

thinking. Each image vibrated with such sheer American cheer that even my darker copy came off as droll, the perfect inducement to buy buy buy.

I knew that Helen, generously paid though she was, wanted to attain a male pay scale almost as much as I did. I also knew she'd never ask.

Olive, on the other hand, had never been one to understand that her own self-interest might be attached to the interests of others like her. She decided to offer her two cents, like an idiot pitching change into a well that nobody ever said was open for wishing.

"If you ask me," Olive said, picking at the corner of her paper, "I think you and Helen should be grateful for what you already have. Chester has given you both so many opportunities. There are plenty of people in this very department who would give a whole limb to be like you two."

"Olive," said Chester, "thank you, but would you mind letting Lillian and me continue our conversation in private?"

With the posture of one who actually would very much mind, Olive fluttered herself out in a flurry of certainly-sirs, shutting the heavy door behind her with theatrical effort.

Chester's transom remained open to catch

the trace breeze. I was sure that Olive could keep eavesdropping even after she'd relieved us of her physical presence, but I really didn't care.

"Lil, you know I think the world of you, and Helen, too," said Chester. "But that's just not the way things work around here."

"It hasn't been in the past, I know," I said. "But perhaps the time has come for R.H. Macy's to free itself from the yoke of historical precedent."

"Have you been consorting with those communists down in Washington Square Park?"

"Chip, my request is as capitalist as they come."

"Lillian, I'm sympathetic, but these fellows whose salaries you aim to match have families to support."

"Nobody asked these fellows with salaries to reproduce themselves," I said. "And were I ever to have a family, you wouldn't let me keep working here. Ladies get the boot the instant they show signs of spawning. Not that that matters to me, since I'd sooner die than join the wife-and-mother brigade."

Chester had a sign behind his desk — NEVER USE A SUPERLATIVE IN ANY AD HERE. IT MAY LEAD TO EXAGGERATION. — and he insisted that each of us copywrit-

51

ers have a facsimile hung behind ours. But he knew as well as I did that I was not exaggerating.

I was not on the hunt for my other half. Not only did I have no desire to find a husband, I had *negative* desire.

"Might I point out, Lil," said Chester, "that in fairness everyone does at least get an identical bonus at Christmas time? Pure egalitarianism."

"Chip," I laughed, "the Christmas bonus is a turkey. And I haven't got a wife to take mine home to so she can prepare it for me." Fortunately this made Chester laugh, too, though our laughter differed in character: his nervous, mine not without bitterness.

R.H. Macy's kept out labor unions. But among the female salesclerks in their dark blue or black dresses and the male ones in their stiff collars and dickey-bosom shirts, nuptial unions were common. Even in the upper offices like mine, institutional advertising, employees joked that the store's real name ought to be Macy's Matrimonial Bureau.

I made a point not to reveal too much of my personal life to Chester or anyone else from the office, excepting Helen, but I knew that he knew that while I liked to go out with men, they were never from Macy's, and

I was not on the prowl for a permanent connection. No taxidermy for me; strictly catch-and-release.

"Lillian," he said, steepling his fingers in that pose that bosses seem trained to do. "Please believe me when I say: I am truly sorry. But right now, in this Year of Our Lord 1931, this is just how it is. Maybe someday things will change. For today, will you at least let me take you to lunch to celebrate? I'll tell all the waitresses you're the beautiful lady in the papers."

Having already challenged him once on his grammatical evasion of responsibility, I let that one slide, but I was not a believer in things just changing. One had to try to change them.

"Sure thing, boss," I said. "What are you thinking? Horn & Hardart?"

"Nah, let's leave the automat to those overpaid guys who skimp on lunch to shore up Junior's college fund. We'll go to the Silver Room and have a real sit-down time."

And though Chester was an unflappable man, gifted at never seeming to try excessively at anything, I could tell that he was trying hard then to make it up to me. So I agreed.

"Well, goodness," I said. "Isn't that fancy? If living well is the best revenge, I've got to start living better more conspicuously. The Silver Room's a sterling place to begin."

Back in my office, settling into the day's work, I was trying to console myself with the thought that while I was usually good at getting what I wanted in life, I was not always so good at enjoying it, so maybe it was all right that Chester had denied me. Then Olive knocked her milquetoast knock.

"Are you busy?" she said, even as she walked in.

She seated herself in a manner meant as devil-may-care, but it failed to convince. Olive had an enthusiasm that was studied, forced. She was no giant intellect either, though she was far from stupid.

I thought of the day she'd debuted at the office. I thought of how I'd thought then that she and I could be friends. She started out as I did: assistant copywriter, forty dollars a week. But she did not climb the ladder. Could not. That had been almost four years ago. No one stayed in that job for four years. They either moved up or moved on to a different field.

Chester was a Harvard man, and Olive went to Radcliffe, which is how she got hired. But as skilled as she was at proofreading, she had no wit or sense of the place and could not write a quality, well-voiced ad at all. At all. But being an adwoman remained her fixation; she wouldn't let it go, and the company wouldn't let her go. Some murky connection, some muddled sense of Ivy League loyalty between Chester and Olive's father led her to be indulged, kept on in a way she wouldn't be otherwise.

I looked at her face, nearing thirty but with something babyish in it. Not fresh, but inchoate: something rudimentary that would never develop. Her sense of humor, I suspected. Olive was pretty, with velvety dark brown hair and huge eyes, but these she spoiled with excessive kohl, and her lipstick was too bright: a sad clown suffering from a lack of confidence. So far in the Macy's Matrimonial Bureau, Olive had been unlucky — which I would not care about, except that she herself so obviously cared.

We both had the age-old impulse to be attractive, though — or at least fashionable. She referred to my hair as silken, and tawny, and in abundance, and it worried me, this eerie connoisseurship, like she might sneak up behind me and snip it off. Yet because I found myself wanting, against my better angels, to be cruel to her, I forced myself over and over to be nice.

"Olive, is that a new dress?"

"Yes," she said, actually blushing.

"It suits you beautifully."

"Thank you, Lily."

"You're welcome. You got it here, didn't you? Women's wear? Summer clearance, to make way for the new arrivals?"

"I did," she said, looking at her lap. "No one knows the store quite like you do."

"Well, we are working on the campaign for fall frocks now, aren't we?" I said. "So I've been keeping an eye on the floor, making sure I know what's come in."

"That's why I've stopped by," said Olive, handing me a typewritten sheet, heavily worked over with strike-through *X*es and ink-pen cross outs. "I think I've written the ad you asked for. Fun and funny."

I tried to twist my anticipatory wince into a grin. I had only given Olive that assignment to make her feel better and to keep her busy, and I had to resist the urge to hold her attempt with two fingers at arm's length, like something disgusting. Stay, gentle Boxfish, I chided myself. Today may be the day she finally figures it out.

I looked at the sheet, intending to read her verse aloud, but got no further than the title before my jaw clamped involuntarily shut.

PARDON US, MADAM, BUT YOUR
BRAIN IS SHOWING

It's tactless to be too darn smart,
And hiding your brains is an art,
But if you'd attract
The boys, it's a fact
That <u>beauty</u> appeals to the heart.

Before I could say a word, Olive had snatched it back from me, saying, "Helen could work up some sketches that would really make it sing, I think."

"Olive, darling," I said, "our aim is not to antagonize the bulk of the customers who spend their family's hard-budgeted money here. If you imply that the frock-purchasing ladies of Manhattan aspire to be empty-headed, then it's likely they might make the logical leap that shopping at Macy's is itself not smart."

"That's not what I meant," said Olive, folding the sheet into the tiniest square. I was afraid she was going to cry.

"No, of course not," I said, trying to sound reassuring, "but that's how it might read." With anyone else I'd have tried to make it into a joke, but with Olive that was the whole problem. "Tell you what let's do. I'll keep thinking about this. In the meantime, I have all these proofs of ads that Chester's already approved, and they need to be proofread. Nobody's better at that than you are."

"I can do that, yes," she said, taking the stack and rising to leave. "I guess you just have sort of an advantage, Lillian."

"Excuse me?"

"At being funny, I mean," said Olive, blinking hard. "Happy people are just bound to be funnier. That's just how it is."

I thought about that, mildly awed by its wrongheadedness. I almost tried to explain what a mistake it was to take comedy for happiness, or good cheer for joy. But it was none of Olive's business how happy I was or wasn't, so I didn't.

If I had, I might also have told her that she had it backwards. It wasn't that happiness led to humor, but more that humor could lead, perhaps, to happiness — that an eye for the absurd could keep one active in one's despair, the opposite of depressed: static and passive.

Instead I walked Olive out, just as Helen — lovely, ingenious Helen McGoldrick — walked in, blonde as a sunrise and just as warm, lighting the lingering darkness of Olive from the corners of my office.

"Congratulations, sugar," she said in her

Alabama drawl, pulling a chair around to my side of the desk. "And thanks for getting that little drawing of mine in the paper."

Then she and I got to work, sprinkling each page of copy, mine and others', with irresistible little eyedrop-sized points of wit.

Then she and I got to work, sprinkling

4
GREAT WITH IMAGINATION

All my life, I have taken satisfaction in
finishing things in order that I may experience a sense of achievement, regardless of
whether the thing was really worth achiev-
ing.

Graduating from college, writing scores
of institutional advertisements for R.H.
Macy's, mowing the lush Maine lawn at Pin
Point, weeding, washing dishes, and writing
inferior verse — any and all of these have
given and can still give me this lulling feeling of accomplishment. So does finishing a
drink.

Across Park, across Lexington, I'm beginning to think I might as well stop in somewhere for one. I turn down Third Avenue
and head for the Back Porch. It's a bar in
my neighborhood, though I would not call
it my neighborhood bar. My relationship
with liquor has always been less regimented,
more improvisatory. Sometimes I have an

old friend or two up for cocktails, or walk to meet them somewhere just to get out and about. And sometimes, yes still, even still, sometimes I make myself a drink and have it alone, with no one else but purring Phoebe. What's the harm?

Death, I suspect, will likely be unsatisfying because I will no longer be present to feel the achievement thereof.

The Back Porch is clean and dim and almost empty except for that mellow bar smell of disinfectant and beer and lingering smoke, and as I walk in the bartender greets me. I haven't seen him before. Maybe the regular bartender will be in later for the holiday rush. By then I'll be at Grimaldi.

I hang my mink coat on a wall hook next to the stool I intend to occupy — I have my pick, apart from a couple at the opposite end of the bar — and as I do I see a television set. The Back Porch never used to have a television set. Now it does. I want to walk right back out and find another place, but there's not really time before my reservation and I badly want a drink, so I sit anyway.

"What'll it be, miss?" the bartender asks, and I like his tie and his mustache and the friendliness in his eyes that does not seem fake.

61

"Thank you for not ma'am-ing me," I say. "What's your name?"

"Sam," he says.

"You can call me Lily, Sam, and I'd like a Negroni, please."

"Coming right up, Lily."

I watch him walk down the bar and gather up the gin, the Campari. Then my eyes — what choice have they? — are drawn to that interloper, that damned TV. Sam has on some show that I don't recognize, but the program's going to a commercial break: a subtle thunderclap of increased volume and then that Wendy's ad that everyone on the planet seems gaga over.

There they stand, two-dimensional and flickering, the three little old ladies in a fast-food emporium arrayed around a preposterously large and fluffy bun. They open it up. Therein lies a meager amount of mystery meat. The ancient dame who comprises the right flank of the triumvirate appears to be wearing a doily around her neck. She bellows like a musk ox:

"Where's the beef?"

Not once, but thrice. Is that what we, the aged, are like?

I despise this ad, and the TV on which it plays with those flashing lights. I mourn the conversations murdered by their juvenile intrusions.

"Your Negroni, Lily," says Sam. "Bon appétit."

"Cheers," I say, and sip the bitter red liquid.

I am about to tell him that it's funny he should say bon appétit, because that's the whole problem, I haven't got much of one now, when another ad comes on.

It begins with the familiar image of a bespectacled boy who reminds me of my studious Gian when he was young. The pleasant recognition curdles and spoils as a folksy tenor sings, "O, O, O, bright ideas and an Oreo cookie!"

My nostrils flare. *J'accuse!* I think. *You* did this to me. Caused me to eat that half package of mediocre black-and-white sandwich cookies. Exhibiting exactly the kind of distracted-old-lady behavior that I've long prided myself on avoiding.

On the television an adorable black boy in a red shirt deftly removes a cookie from the middle of a stack of a dozen without toppling it. A blonde girl with a simpleminded smile unscrews the two halves of her snack, just as I must have been doing in my kitchen as Phoebe looked on in mute feline horror. The camera pans a cellophane package, and then the voice is spelling out "O-R-E-O,

63

goes great with imagination," and I could just about scream.

Imagination. I sip my Negroni.

I don't remember when I saw this ad before, but I certainly *have* seen it. I don't remember wandering the grocer's aisles with the idiotic jingle playing in my head, but no doubt I did. I don't remember lifting the cookies from their shelf — thinking wistfully of my young Gian as I did so, I'm sure — and dropping them in my basket, but nevertheless they infiltrated my pantry. A nutritionally nugatory Trojan horse. And I ate them. I ate them while on the phone with my grown son.

To sell a thing — goods, services, property — one tells a story. So we, the copywriters of my generation, were told, and it was true. Now, though, it seems the language of commerce has little use for stories. Stories take too much time. The span of attention — I see it like a bridge, a span of that sort — is shortening, shortening. Or being shortened.

In my career I always assumed that advertising communicates with people in order to persuade them. But these ads don't persuade; they barely bother to communicate. Why be clever? Why be novel? Why not simply find an asinine catchphrase and repeat it endlessly?

64

No longer is there a bridge to span, a walking across from either side, seller to purchaser, a meeting in the middle. There's just a stabbing at the base of the brain — so much the better if its targets aren't even aware that it's working. This seems to me like a great cheapening of all of us. Instead of appealing to my reason, my thrift, or my taste, those Oreos insinuated themselves into my unspoken desires and anxieties. My missing Gian back when he was young, still more my son.

I have a great many unspoken desires and anxieties.

Another commercial comes on, this one for Twix, clearly meant to be taken as happening in New York City. These ads are revolting and inaccurate, objectionable not just for being false but for being so much less interesting and vibrant than the city itself. The commercial shows an ersatz Jerome Robbins dance-routine vision of the city that is even less edgy than *West Side Story*. I do not see *my* city in it all.

I want to tell Sam, who is down at the end of the bar, chatting with the couple, that his new TV and his Negroni have helped me to see what is so repulsive to me in these ads: the way they depict, and thereby encourage, this infantilization of the country. Through most of this century most of us Americans were treated as — or were encouraged to behave like — grownups, proper adults. But now we have turned, or are being turned, into a tribe of incorrigible brats.

Given that the majority of communication to which we are subjected in a day consists of advertising, if nearly all of that advertising insists on regarding us as pampered children, what does that do to us? It winds us up with a godforsaken second term of smarmy granddad President Ronald Wilson Reagan for one. But I can't say that to Sam. Gauche to bring up politics.

Onscreen, a batch of housewives orgiastically fondle rolls of toilet tissue, then are instructed by a shopkeeper to "Please don't squeeze the Charmin."

Sam comes back to check on me.

"Sam," I say. "I would like you to answer for me just one small question."

"Sure thing, Lily," he says. "Fire away."

"Why has this establishment installed a television set?"

"Not a fan of it?" Sam says.

"Honestly not, no."

"Me neither," he says. "But I guess the owner just thought it was due. Almost 1985 and time to get with the trend. People come into a bar, they expect to be able to watch the game, see the news."

"But the Yankees are terrible, and the news is appalling," I say, and Sam laughs. "I don't hate TV, just so you know. For example, *Columbo* is an excellent program. That Peter Falk."

"I love that guy," says Sam, chomping an imaginary cigar and raising a hand to his forehead. "One more thing!"

"I also enjoyed him in that Cassavetes movie, that *Husbands*."

"Really?" says Sam. "You don't say. I heard it was depressing."

"Well, I think that was the intent," I say. "But, Sam, to return to *Columbo* and my point, what I mean is that I watch Peter Falk in the privacy of my own living room. I do not go out into public gathering places to ignore other people while I watch him solve mysteries."

"I hear you," says Sam. He nods toward the flashing box. "Seems like it's already making people less likely to talk to each other. Or to me."

"It hurts your tips," I say.

"It hurts my feelings," Sam says.

"I suppose there's no going back, Sam."

"Nope," he says. "Time only goes in that one direction. Or at least that's how we go

67

in time. You heading to Times Square later to watch the ball drop?"

I decide not to tell Sam that I dislike Times Square. Times Square, much like these TV ads, expects little of us, if not quite the worst. Instead of treating one like an overgrown six-year-old with impulse control issues and a huge piggy bank ready for the smashing, as the ads do, it treats one like an enormous genital. A penis with a wallet, if one prefers.

Rather, I say, still telling the truth, "I have dinner reservations at five, so I ought to be going. May I settle up with you?"

"Of course. Pleasure meeting you."

I doubt I'll ever come back here, so I leave a tip that's thrice the cost of the drink. Gian's kids will inherit most of my money when I die, but I might as well spread it around as long as I'm still here.

A Negroni is meant to be an apéritif, a little predinner something to whet the palate. This one was delicious but seems only to have filled me up more. It's a quarter to five, and I have to start walking.

I have enjoyed watching Sam for the same reason I think people enjoy watching sports: seeing someone in full command of what he is expected to do, doing it better than most would, and doing so with joy.

My work used to be like art for me: giving form to the world. I sometimes have a vague intimation that people were better read and smarter once upon a time. I could write a divisional ad for luggage with perfect anaphora and no one would doubt its effectiveness:

> If you are a man who is apt to decide at
>   eleven o'clock to catch the midnight
>   boat . . .
> If you are a woman with a penchant for
>   weekends . . .
> If you are a student about to embark by
>   Student Third Class . . .

It likely would have ended with something along the lines of: "One of Macy's wardrobe trunks will add to your comfort."

Now I don't work anymore, and the world is uncomfortable.

5
LUNCH POEMS

People didn't always hate pigeons in the city
— in fact, one could look up and catch
glimpses of homing-pigeon lofts atop a lot
of the lower buildings, owners doting on
the dear little things, circling on their wings
high above the rooftops. But people have
come to make a hobby of detesting the
birds, I think, because they've come to see
that pigeons are much like people: dirty and
murmuring, greedy and abundant, flocking
in a corpus of such shit and weight that one
fears they may permanently deface or crush
whatever they congregate on.

But ever since we learned about augury in
our advanced Latin class at Goucher College, I've had a fondness for them. The
omen I always augur from the rippling gray
waves of their massed flight is straightforward: If I am in a place with that many
pigeons, then it is probably urban enough
for me to want to live there and be satisfied

with the quantity of urbanity.

Manhattan has always been such a place, never more so than that day in early November 1931, when I was out walking among both the pigeons and the people. I was on my lunch break, on my way to my publisher's office to drop off a corrected set of final proofs for my debut book, *Oh, Do Not Ask for Promises.* My first poetry collection was coming out. It even had a birthday: April 5, 1932. A springy book with a springtime release, it had to go to press in time to send out advance copies for review.

I could have sent the proofs by messenger, but I wanted to walk south from my office at R.H. Macy's to E.P. Dutton at 300 Fourth Avenue, and though Broadway was the straightest route, I wanted to take Sixth Avenue. It would be just twenty minutes by foot.

I always took walks on my lunch breaks. That, in fact, was when I'd written most of the book. For me, a peaceful atmosphere devoid of noise and distractions is absolutely the *worst* place for poetry, likely to wind me up in a doomed attempt to stare down a blank page. My funny old brain, like those of many poets, has always done its best work sideways, seeking out tricky enjambments and surprising slant rhymes to craft lines

71

capable of pulling their own weight. Taking to the pavement always helps me find new routes around whatever problem I'm trying to solve: phrases on signs, overheard conversations, the interplay between the rhythms of my verse and the rhythm of my feet.

I was hardly the only poet in the city who worked like this, of course. Manhattan was full of lunchtime poets in those days, and stayed that way for many years thereafter. In the sixties, long after I had been forgotten, a clever young man even published a well-regarded book by that title — *Lunch Poems* — and although I wanted to resent him for jumping my claim, I could not; his lines were too full of the real sounds of people's voices and the vitality of the street. Even that seems long ago now. I wonder where today's lunch poets are, and whether I would know them by sight.

On that November day, however, I strolled in youthful, cheerful ignorance of the tradition in which I had been participating. This particular walk was like an early Christmas present to myself: the street beneath the IRT Sixth Avenue Line. The Sixth Avenue Elevated. Chow mein restaurants and diners with names like The Griddle. Cinders and ash and noise sifting down, shaking the ground, rattling the buildings. Above me, the commuters getting disgorged at one of the overhead stops dislodged a deposit of pigeons like a plume of smoke. I would not want to live there, but the walk was magnificent.

Do not think that I romanticized every moment of my life in the city. I cherished my work, but I worked so hard. Each day there'd come a moment when I'd be tired to death. Practically out of breath from exhaustion. A dull pencil, a dull mind, in need of a sharpener, in need of a drink, or at least an unthinking wandering down the hall among the other copywriters on the thirteenth floor. Outside crocuses flaunting their carefree colors, me inside and sunk with care.

The walks — morning, lunch, and home at night — revived me.

I thought at times that poetry might be an elegant way of screaming. Oh, that I could be a local swan in the park. Or the sparrow loafing on the window ledge.

But I never quite grew tired of being reliable. Even once I had money to burn — and it didn't take me long to have it — I still had to work. I wanted there to be something to do in life besides mate and reproduce and die, and advertising was that, or it was for a long while.

When I wasn't walking, I had a window and a rubber plant in the sun on a radiator. If I craned my neck, I could see a brief but valiant silver sliver of the Hudson River. I could make myself find window washers as serene as buttercups.

Irksome pedestrian behavior, I knew, but if I turned and looked behind me, I could see the Empire State Building, just completed. So I turned and looked behind me.

They'd cut the ribbon a few months back, in May. It had practically been a national holiday.

My mother would not let me forget that although the World's Tallest Building was in New York, President Hoover had pushed the button to turn on its lights remotely from my old hometown of Washington, D.C. She always wanted me to come back to stay, but I never would. One might be able to control the electricity of the World's Tallest Building from the nation's capital, but there one could not work, as I did, at the World's Largest Store.

I hurried on, among all the other workers out on their lunch breaks. The skyscraper was already being called the Empty State Building because of its lack of renters. And they couldn't land dirigibles there as they'd planned because of the updrafts caused by

74

the building's very height. But I thought that its beauty outweighed its folly, and that a little grandiosity in the Depression wasn't actively harming anyone, even if it wasn't necessarily helping, either.

In truth, I suppose I identified myself with that skyscraper, and my fortunes with its own, rising while others foundered and fell. Each new triumph that I achieved became at once more dear and more private every time I descended from my snug apartment or my bustling office to step into the desperate street, where a dog whistle of raw panic seemed to quiver increasingly in the air. The creeping disaster that had started on Wall Street — part sickness, part madness, like a peril from Poe — had come finally to infect the whole country. People lost jobs and stopped buying. Prices plunged. Those lucky enough to still be working hoarded their pay, reluctant to buy today what they knew would be cheaper tomorrow, until the contagion took their jobs, too, and they joined the crowds wondering where this year's Thanksgiving dinner would come from. Among many other things, the Depression changed how I felt about crowds: When I first came to the city, a line of people often helped me discover an exciting premiere or a big sale; in 1931, such queues more often ended at soup kitchens or collapsing banks.

The lines of automobiles on Sixth Avenue, however, still struck me as merry. It was pleasing to be alongside the stream of cars as they rushed uptown and down — or tried to rush. I have always been comforted by vehicle traffic, by being near but not in it. Taxis kept honking, trying to see if I wanted a lift, but I kept waving them away. What I wanted was that walk: slate and windy, the sky overcast but not threatening rain.

I enjoyed walking outside even in bad weather. I took my lunchly strolls even when the snow was hard and sharp — little ice pellets flying at one's face like fingernail clippings — as it had been that first year here, back in 1926.

I spent my first Christmas in the city alone. Alone, but not lonely; in the state of being solitary but not the condition of wishing myself otherwise. Solitude enrobed me like a long, warm coat.

Eating Christmas dinner by myself in a restaurant far from home and hearth, I wondered whether lightning would strike me if I dared to take mushrooms and a steak instead of turkey, cranberries, and buttered rolls. I ate the steak. I ate it rare. Mother could not care about what Mother did not know. Depraved, depraved. But Christmas was the copywriter's most frantic season — Saks and Hearns and R.H. Macy's, of course, all hitching their copy to the Star of Bethlehem. Profane, profane. On subsequent holidays I'd been able to head southward to the welcoming bosom of family once more, but that first year, a mere forty-dollar-a-week assistant, I'd wanted most of all to impress my employers, and impress them I did. What an extravagance that steak had seemed! And yet how meager compared to the bounty spread on nearby tables, where supped financiers and stock operators. Five years later those fellows were all gone, their capital vanished like so much cigar smoke, while I churned out the only commodities that still held their value: courage, poise, humor, and hope.

If I'd kept walking down Sixth, past the turnoff to my editor Artie's office, I'd have hit Ladies' Mile, the department stores which Artie, a sharp but nostalgic man, still called dry goods stores. Faint and fading, R.H. Macy's aging competitors. But of course I turned left at Twenty-Third Street to head for my destination: the sixteen-story Beaux-Arts building in which Dutton made its home.

I admired E.P. Dutton as a publisher

inherently, or else I'd never have sent them *Oh, Do Not Ask for Promises*. I also admired their current president, Mr. John Macrae, who embodied the sort of up-by-the-bootstraps narrative that is so appealing — and so vanishingly rare, when one actually considers who else has done it. My father found his rags-to-riches story of greater interest, or at least greater ease of understanding, than the basic fact that my book was to be published. So did my mother, as she disliked my poetry writing even more than my writing advertising. "You sound so unhappy in those poems!" she would say. My father was proud, my mother embarrassed.

Macrae had started as an office boy at the company in the 1880s and remained aboard in various increasingly lofty capacities until Dutton himself died in 1923, at which point Macrae ascended to the presidency. His commitment to taking the press in a more refined direction was why my books had a home there. I never dealt with him personally, but his staff was superb.

Artie was waiting for me, and I was happy to see him, his drooping, almost totally gray mustache betraying his age, which was better concealed by his Brilliantined hair, still abundant and mostly black. His mustache

78

and adroit civility reminded me of my father, though Father was an attorney and not a man of letters.

My editor's given name was Arthur Eugene Stanley, and he went by A.E. professionally. So Housmanian, I'd told him upon our first meeting, and he'd smiled at the comparison: It turned out he'd studied Classics with Housman, very briefly when he was a scholar abroad at Cambridge. But he was always Artie to me, even though in his formality he rarely called me anything but "my fair Miss Boxfish," courtliness being the gear that his engine idled in. He was as courteous to the office boys as he was to me, but he also managed to make me see that I was as dear to him as he was to my own heart.

There was a market for poetry then. My verses had appeared in *Vanity Fair, The New Yorker, Life,* and *The Saturday Evening Post,* and on and on — a list that had not only published but also paid me exquisitely. And yet Artie was the first editor who had believed in my verse as a body — an oeuvre, as he'd written in response to my query letter — and his assistance in editing and assembling *Oh, Do Not Ask for Promises* had proven invaluable. Starting from the moment he let me know that Dutton would offer me a contract, his assessment of my compositions was always praiseful, perceptive, and farsighted, even — indeed, especially — when we didn't see eye to eye.

"Remarkable," he'd called my poems at our first meeting. "So urban and breezy. So droll and cosmopolitan. It's rare to find such profusion of wit in a woman." This remark, I now suspect, was neither as thoughtless nor as innocent as it seemed at the time; it was an experiment, intended to see how gracefully I'd handle being patronized. I responded with what seemed an appropriate blend of honey and vinegar, suggesting that wit, like anything else, is rarely found where rarely sought, and that in my experience it was damned uncommon in men as well. Artie beamed; if it *was* a test, I had passed.

From the beginning Artie understood that my poetic career had as much potential to advance through the society column as through the book review — as much to gain by well-documented bons mots as by publications in prestigious magazines. The trick was to cultivate a compelling public persona — the Girl Poet — that was a simplified and amplified version of my best-composed self. I didn't squirm away from this initiative. *Au contraire,* I was all in favor, having arrived independently at similar conclusions: By then I'd grown skilled at crafting disciplined messages on behalf of R.H. Macy's, and I was eager to ply those skills on the product I endorsed most heartily of all — namely, me.

To be sure, ambition wasn't my only motive. The voice of the Girl Poet also let me say the things I most wanted to say, to whom I most wanted to say them. It set me up to play with popular preconceptions about girls, and poets, and especially girl poets, and to do so in a way that made people listen to me and remember what they heard. The day would come when I'd have second thoughts about this approach — or at least consider the degree to which playing with those preconceptions also meant embracing them — but as I laid the corrected proofs on Artie's desk, that day was still far in the future.

After the Great War it had become acceptable for women to smoke and to apply makeup in public. I avoided the latter habit as one best left for the powder room, but I'd taken up the former as soon as I'd come to the city. Smoking helped me think and calmed my nerves, which I had in excess.

Before I'd even gotten the cigarette from my engraved gold case — a present from a

81

beau of a few years back — to my lips, Artie was leaning over with a filigreed lighter. He smelled clean, like lavender and lemons, and was dressed in his typical fashion: tweed jacket, wool pullover, off-white Oxford bags, all slightly out of date and a bit too casual for the office.

"Thank you for coming by," he said. "So much more pleasant than an impersonal messenger."

"I hardly needed to get these back to you. By messenger or in person. The copy was sparkling clean."

"We do strive for excellence. Especially with such sophisticated *vers de société* as yours."

I liked that Artie never called my light verse "light verse," instead referring to it by its French name, *"vers de société,"* and doing so with the intention of giving it the seriousness the English had when they used that term — a nod to my work's dignity, he'd once explained: its epigrammatic and aphoristic qualities.

I wouldn't have minded if he *had* called it light verse. My verse *was* light — though I couldn't abide when anyone called it "light-hearted," as that seemed a poor reading and against my intent. My rhymes were not sappy, were meant neither to comfort nor inspire.

I also liked that Artie would garnish his speech with foreign morsels, much as I'd adorn my apartment with vases of cut flowers. I kept a list of them in my mind, and sometimes put them in my poems for him to find, which he did with delight: *caelum, non animum mutant,* for instance — climate may change, but not character — and *chacun à son goût* — people have their own taste.

"So is that it?" I said. "We send it to the printer, and then we wait?"

"That's almost it," said Artie. "Apart from one fairly minor thing, Miss Boxfish."

He had averted his eyes and was fully engaged in the important business of straightening the already very straight edges of my stacked proofs. His expression was sheepish enough to supply a Highland village with wool and milk.

I cocked a loaded eyebrow.

"It's about the title," he said, picking up a pen and holding it above the thing of which he spoke: the words *Oh, Do Not Ask for Promises* centered on my manuscript's top page. "The sales department and I think it might need to be changed."

"The *title*?" I said, trying to keep my question mark from shading into an exclamation point. Artie blanched, raising the pen slightly, as if he might need it to defend himself. "How embarrassing," I said, "after all these years, and so many verses written, to learn that I have been misusing the word *minor.*"

"Of course, Miss Boxfish, you're right. I misspoke," Artie said. "It's not a tiny thing. But if you'll permit me, I shall make our case."

"Very well," I said. "Fire away."

"Our concern is that *Oh, Do Not Ask for Promises* does not speak to the full range of your poetic flowering. Your emotional gamut."

"Maybe not," I said. "But it's catchy. It's perfect. It evokes Dorothy Parker by way of Edna St. Vincent Millay. The title matches much of the sentiment."

"Much," said Artie, "but not all, Miss Boxfish. That's the issue. You're still in the bloom of youth — hardly a spinster, and hardly such a perpetual cynic as that title suggests. While the persona is amusing and effective for a poem's length — just the thing for *Vanity Fair* — in assembling the book we've sought to hint at a more gentle, more vulnerable sensibility. A distruster of people, an eater of men: Is this really the narrow picture of yourself you wish to present to the world? You scoff at love now, but may yet change your mind."

"Artie, darling," I said, appealing to his status as a confirmed bachelor, one who perhaps shared with Housman more than just a pair of initials, "*you* may be more likely than I to marry someday."

Artie gave me a wary look. Then he relaxed, his abashed expression sliding away, another of who knows how many masks. "Aren't you curious to hear our alternate title?"

"Fine," I said, trying not to sigh. "Why not?"

"*Frequent Wishing on the Gracious Moon*," he said. "Isn't that pretty? Fresh and wistful."

"It's too tritely poetic," I said. "Too much of the sky. Not enough of the razor."

"I take your point. But speaking as someone who knows you, Miss Boxfish, you are not so wicked as you seek to appear. You know a thing or two about cocktail-lounge love, but that hardly sums you up."

Artie was right: I was not entirely like that. My poems were not entirely like that. Though I kept the effort off my face, my mind was racing to consider poems in the book that might supply a compromise title,

85

one that could mollify the sales department without mortifying me. One of my favorites was inspired by a wish I once made on a lightning bug I'd seen, operating improbably in East Fiftieth Street: "What makes you seek your fortune here / In Gotham? You must be as queer / As I am, and a million other / Insects far from home and Mother."

Still, a judicious capacity for wonder hardly invalidated my cynicism, which was no less sincere or profound. When it came to love — so-called — I considered myself particularly accomplished in the art of amputating body from heart. *Love makes the world go round,* Helen and I would often say, setting the other up to reply, *Then it makes the world go flat.*

"Of course there's more to the book, Artie. But that title's terrible. Boxfish is no moony girl sighing for her lunar love to find her on a silver-bathed balcony. Here, just look," I said, reaching for the proofs. "Just turn to any page, any page whatsoever, and you'll see what I mean."

"But *Frequent Wishing on the Gracious Moon* also comes from one of your poems, Miss Boxfish, as I'm sure you recall," said Artie, reaching across the desk to turn to that page, that poem, with startling accuracy. "So it too describes you. It's a beautiful line, I daresay. Hopeful, and bright — and romantic, at least latently. All fine qualities that you personally share with your wonderful poems."

In all my days I have rarely received praise with any sort of discomfort. Yet as this conversation drifted away from my manuscript and toward my character, I found myself reacting with an antipathy that was almost allergic. I did not want to talk about this. I particularly did not want to talk about this with Artie, whom I'd viewed as the gatekeeper to a world of letters free of treacly sentiment, a guide to a route around the tacky cobwebs that seemed fated to snare every promising or challenging thing and drag it back to some tedious norm. Hearing him advance an argument that I'd sooner expect from my mother was worse than disappointing; it was just shy of horrifying, catapulting me straight past self-doubt into crack-brained paranoia. Surely, he seemed to suggest, I couldn't really *mean* what my poems said. Could any sane person *really* oppose hope, romance, love, marriage, children, family: the most basic materials of human society? Was I — the cool and composed sweetheart of the smart set, the Girl Poet made flesh — secretly a

87

monster for entertaining such suspicions?

Polite intransigence seemed the best tactic. "Ah, inflation!" I said. "Personal inflation, that's the thing! I am so much pleasanter and more competent when I am being flattered. But nevertheless I must insist, Artie, on the original title. With all due respect to your expertise, I *do* know a thing or two about how to entice a customer."

"Are you sure, my dear, that you cannot be persuaded?"

"Artie, I'm sure. Please don't tell me that this means we've reached an impasse. I've already begun to spend the royalties in my mind."

"No, it's not an impasse," he said, leaning back in his wooden chair. "I told the boys in sales I'd give it a try and do my best. Now I have. I still wish you'd change it, but if it's the original title you want, then the original title you shall keep. I suppose you do have a certain hard-won reputation to uphold. Your more-than-passable vamp impersonation. Even if I'm not entirely fooled."

"Thank you, Artie, for seeing the good in me," I said, standing up and proffering a hand to shake. "Now I must do my best impersonation of a track star and dash back to remain in the good graces of R.H. Macy's."

"Good-bye, my fair Miss Boxfish. Dash with care. We'll be in touch once the reviews begin to roll in, and if any of them remark unfavorably on your title, then I promise not to say I told you so."

"Oh, Artie," I said, smiling. "If you want the last word that much, you can have it." He laughed as I shut the door behind me.

I did have to hurry, but I walked back on Broadway, the better to gaze for a moment at the Flatiron Building, like the face of a friend, and to sneak a glimpse at Madison Square Park, a trusty destination on other lunch breaks. I still managed to make it back before Chester noticed I'd been gone longer than usual.

My victory pleased me, but all afternoon, whatever else I was doing, Artie's alternate title kept rising to the top of my mind, like the fizzy little bubbles in a carbonated drink. Tickling my brain.

I remained sure I'd been right. But I would wonder later, much later, if I had done things differently — lots of things, even something as seemingly small as naming a book — other aspects of my life might have turned out otherwise. Then again, who doesn't wonder?

When the book came out five months later, under the title I desired, it was a smash, selling out its print run within the first thirty days and hurrying through four subsequent printings. The reading public, at least some of them, wanted a break from the Depression, and found repose in my pose, world-weary but still cheery.

Although R.H. Macy's was already paying me more than I could think to spend, I wanted to use my first royalty check for something celebratory. Symbolic. Thus I acquired — simultaneously, so as to let them get to know and learn to live with one another — two delightful little Hartz Mountain canaries to fill my apartment with song, and a red-haired kitten I'd named Tallulah — after Miss Bankhead — whom I fed on fish and cream.

The reviews glowed so hard they threw off heat; I could feel it on my face when I read them. They led to an avalanche of fan mail. Some went to E.P. Dutton, but most went to the thirteenth floor of the World's Largest Store, since the biographical note below my author photo, which Helen had snapped, listed it as my place of

90

employment.

One sunny day in late May of 1932, Chester Everett, in an unseasonably saturnalian disruption of the usual office order, brought me my mail. I thanked him and was about to set it aside to carry home with me to open that night, when he said:

"I'm curious — if it's not too forward — what do all these people have to say to you, Lillian?"

"Let's open one," I said, "and we'll see."

The letter, as I'd suspected, was from another male stranger, an admirer, one of the dozens I'd acquired since my book's birth date. I read it aloud:

"Dear, Sweet Miss Boxfish, I know I mustn't be the only man to have made this joke, but *Oh, Do Not Ask for Promises* has got me wanting to ask you for the promise of joining me for dinner. You name the time and the place, and I'll consider it an honor . . ."

"Is that what it takes these days to bring the poor boys a-runnin'?" said Chester. "For a single gal to sneer at love?"

"They can run all they want," I said. "They'll be rejected *and* exhausted."

"Make something seem difficult to get and more people want it, I suppose," said Chester. I noted something unsettled in his

91

expression: concern, or jealousy, or both; it was indeterminate in its precise character.

I decided to ignore it. "That's exactly it, Chip," I said. "A lot of these love notes seem to be from well-read and lovesick young men with literary aspirations. That type doesn't interest me in the least. They say they only have eyes for gazing at you and then end up gazing right back at their navels."

"I hope so, Lil, because I don't know what we'd do if one of those would-be Casanovas swept you off your feet and away from Macy's institutional advertising."

"Put it out of your mind, Chip. You needn't worry. And actually, I'm trying to finish the summer campaign, so if you don't need anything more, I'll get back to it."

"Actually, Lil," he said, "I do have one concern, more serious than love. I'll strive to be brief."

He shut the door — thereby providing a month's supply of grist for the office rumor mill — and took a seat. "It's just," he went on, "that your poems, well, they're as snappy and as fun to read as your advertising. And you know I'm happy for your success in publishing, but —"

"You don't want me to give away my best ideas?" I said. "To serve the muse before mammon?"

He looked relieved at my comprehension. "That's the crux of it," he said. "Your work has been finer than fine these past few months as the book's been coming out, but as your supervisor, I felt I'd be remiss in not sharing my concern."

"Chip, darling, I understand perfectly," I said, because I did, and because I'd considered it already myself. "Can I let you in on a remarkable secret? I find that the more ideas I let myself have, the more ideas I have. They just pour out of me. Poems for ads and poems for poems."

I was speaking the truth. My lunch-poem routine, my practice of poetry, was actually quite similar to and compatible with my working practices. One just happened inside the department store, and the other happened outside.

In R.H. Macy's I was a veritable stroller, too, taking the wooden escalators and roaming from floor to floor, surveying the displays, coming up with ads and writing them. Not so different from roaming the sidewalks around Herald Square after gobbling a sandwich or watching people — seeking faces or trees and greenery and then composing poems about them. That had become the way that I moved through the world, and the way that the world, in turn, moved my mind.

"Ah, Lillian," said Chester, "I can see that's the case. And it's a load off my shoulders to hear you say so. And the viewpoint in the poems is certainly more that of a scoffer at convention than the one in the ads is."

"But?"

"But," he said, "I have another worry. And you can tell me if you think I'm being a ninny when I say this. While I agree there's no sign of the Boxfish wit-well running dry, there's a danger that comes with *over*supply, too, isn't there? Till now you've enjoyed the element of surprise: Your readers have happened on your verses in the pages of a magazine — or, hell, in the even unlikelier setting of an advertisement — and been swept off their feet. It's like encountering some jungle beast on a stroll through Central Park. But this book —"

A copy of *Oh, Do Not Ask for Promises* — which had been lurking, I supposed, in my disorderly stack of mail — materialized in Chester's hand.

"— is like a trip to the Bronx Zoo. It's a delight, of course. I'm happy to give up serendipity in return for a chance to make a sustained study of your craft, and your sales

94

figures show I'm not alone. But doesn't this very success hem you in a bit? You're now subject to the admiring scrutiny of connoisseurs. Each new Boxfish poem is apt to be compared with other Boxfish poems, received as part of a body of work, and not simply assessed on its own merits. Doesn't this stand to lessen its impact? Now that you've become fashionable, are you in danger of falling *out* of fashion?"

His awkwardness had fallen away as he warmed to his own argument, and he summed up with the satisfied smile of a debate-society champ. It was impossible to tell how sincere he'd been about any of this.

"That is extremely prescient, Chester," I said, "in one respect: You *are* being a ninny. As for the rest, I am truly grateful for your concerns, but upon reflection I am inclined to file them in the drawer labeled *good problems.* Now, shall I get back to the copy?"

"Last thing, Lillian, and then yes, I'll leave you in peace," he said, handing me his favorite fountain pen, a gift from his wife, along with the book from his hand. "May I please have your autograph?"

Back at E.P. Dutton, Artie, needless to say, was spared any temptation to say I told you so as he'd threatened he might. No one could argue with the bottom line.

"*Oh, Do Not Ask for Promises* has delivered on its promise!" he'd written in the note he sent with my author's copies of the second printing.

Artie would end up editing all my books, or the poetry books anyway: *Notes Found in the Street* in 1933, *A Complaint to the Management* in 1935, and *All Right, You Win; or, I Admit Defeat* in 1936.

And my pride just went; there was no fall. Not for a long time.

But E.P. Dutton didn't publish my final book of original poems. That came out much later, in the 1960s, after Artie was long dead.

With the help of a new editor, one whom I did not like remotely as much, I'd settled upon the name *Nobody's Darling,* which by that point had become an accurate descriptor of my state of being.

96

6
A Sandwich at the Mission

I step out of the Back Porch bar and the streetlights come on. It feels like magic whenever I catch that moment. Like there ought to be a prize. What do I win?

The city is dazzling but uncompassionate. It always has been, but I feel it more now.

Winter, at bay for weeks, has taken sundown as its cue: The wind seems to clear a path for the dark as the chill the weatherman promised gathers in the unruly air. The end-of-shift sidewalk crowds have lost their common purpose and are on more particular errands, some suspect if not outright sinister. So it goes these days in my city.

A green Dodge on Third guns its engine to beat a light, startling me, although the Negroni has done much to calm my spring-loaded nerves. As it speeds off I notice that its stereo is playing a song I recognize, one that I've heard playing many times in recent years from other cars and apartment windows and portable tape players but that I've never learned the name of, a song about hotels and motels and hipping and hopping and not stopping, a song without any real singing in it. *Rap,* I gather, is what this is called. I wish the Dodge *had* stopped, so I could hear more of it.

I have always worked hard to keep myself up to date, to be mindful of trends. At first I did this in order to stay sharp at my two jobs, copywriter and poet, which both required me to know what my audience knew. Lately, since I retired, I do it just because I enjoy it, and because it keeps me from feeling old. I very much enjoy that MTV, for instance, those music videos, and I watch them often, though I still find that a long walk through an unfamiliar neighborhood teaches me more about what's new and exciting than any number of hours of television can. As ever, the street is the source of the latest things humans have invented — culturally speaking, at least. The last new things, maybe, that humans will ever invent.

These days, when I think of history, it occurs to me that maybe we have stopped moving forward, and are now just oscillating.

The last new art form I've seen was a

group of Puerto Rican teenagers on St. Mark's Place, jerking and spinning acrobatically and robotically atop flattened cardboard boxes. This, I gather, is called *breaking*. The last new art form I've heard is rap music. And I love it. It thrills me. The joyful mastery of language, its sounds and its rhythms. Rhymes and puns and nonsense, ranging from dumb and fun to witty and profound.

It troubles me that among my few remaining acquaintances there is no one with whom I can share my enthusiasm for these new things.

It wasn't always this way. In my youth, before I had made any of my most consequential choices — and isn't that what we always mean by *in my youth*? — in the days when my friends and I were the word-mad ones, earning our keep by saying things fastest and best, the new thing then was jazz. Without a second thought we'd ride the East Side Line to Harlem to listen to the bands and dance among the Lindy Hoppers at the Savoy on Lenox Avenue. It was new, but it wasn't a novelty: We knew it was important. We weren't tourists, or didn't think we were; we wanted to be part of it.

What happened was what always happens. The best Lindy Hoppers earned minor celebrity, became a draw. The ballrooms started paying them, and rightly so. They in turn became more serious, more competitive, more and more skilled, working out heart-stopping flips and spins and somersaults that no casual dancer could ever hope to duplicate without injury. It was amazing. It was also a show, and not — to lift a term from my son's teenaged lexicon — a *scene,* not the way it used to be. It put a barrier between us and the Lindy Hoppers, or it shored up barriers that were already there, of which color was only the most obvious.

So who was to blame? The dancers, for taking what they'd earned? The crowds of Midtown gawkers who brought the dollars in? Or we young bohemians who blazed the trail they'd followed? Maybe there's a natural order in all this: New things pop up at the edges, but the middle's where the money is. I did that dance myself over the years. I got rich doing it. And now here I am, an old white lady in a fur coat on a Murray Hill sidewalk, eavesdropping on passersby, wondering what I'm missing.

Nostalgia for what's new: The French probably have a word for that. In any case, there's precious little trace of the avant-garde in *this* neighborhood, which has been successfully staving off the advances of fashion since J.P. Morgan moved in a hundred years ago. I've come to prize its stodgy constancy.

I've lived in a total of six different apartments all over Manhattan — starting with the Christian Women's Hotel in Midtown that a friend of my parents found for me when I first moved to the city — but Murray Hill is where I first felt at home, and Murray Hill was where I figured I'd end up returning, eventually — and I did, though not for many years.

Murray Hill is where Helen McGoldrick and I lived — sharing the rent on a one-bedroom, crowded for the sake of independence — after we moved out of the hotel, and not an instant too soon, as that place had been stifling. Thirty-Third Street, between Third and Lexington. We moved in just after she'd begun working at R.H. Macy's, and so, thanks to her, had I.

Although it'll make my walk to Grimaldi ever so mildly longer, I want to pass by the old place — days of auld lang syne and all — and I have enough time. Typically neither closeness nor distance matter much to me on my walks. Neither convenience nor difficulty is my objective. Usually I'll accomplish about five miles a day, perhaps taking Saturday or Sunday off.

I am old and all I have left is time. I don't mean time to live; I mean free time. Time to fill. Time to kill until time kills me. I walk and walk and think and think. It gets me out, and it keeps me healthy, and no one on the street seems to want to mess with me, as they say on the street. All my friends in New York — back when I still had friends, before everyone moved away or died — had mugging stories, but I've never had trouble.

Once, a few years ago, while I was walking down Bowery, I was invited in for a meal at the mission. I don't fully understand how I might be mistaken for someone in need of a soup kitchen, so I suppose that's why I went in. It seemed rude to refuse, and I met some nice people. Some of those there were unmeetable: too far gone, either within themselves or on drugs or booze. I don't judge them, though.

Some of the other people I met were just having a bad year, and some of them were on their way to someplace worse, and I'm not sure that the volunteer who insisted I sit down and have a baloney sandwich was wrong about my belonging there. I am able to afford to feed myself, but I don't always remember to eat, and sometimes I go days without speaking to anyone but Phoebe — who is a good listener for a cat — and my

102

son on the phone. I stuffed some twenties into the donation box on the way out, and I still send that mission money every Christmas, anonymously.

A police officer walks by with a German shepherd. I used to be on the Murray Hill beautification committee, with a lot of other old ladies, some of them smart and some of them silly, and some of them — who were also on the board of the Morgan Library & Museum — obsessed with the area's declining wealth. I drifted away, though. Stopped going, and I think by now they must have disbanded.

I am not a believer, but I still go to services at the church around the corner from my apartment, the Church of the Incarnation, not so far from where I'm walking now. A free show. A museum, practically, with work by Louis Comfort Tiffany and Augustus Saint-Gaudens. Something to do, and some people who know me.

My son, my Gian, my Gianino, my Johnny, learned to play the stately and formidable Aeolian-Skinner pipe organ there. The AA meetings that happen in the basement during the week these days seem more popular than worship. But I don't judge them, either.

And here it is, the first place of my own.

Our own. Plain brown brick façade. Fire escapes descending like strips of black rickrack. Our apartment was on the sixth floor of six. Only the rapture of having escaped the mild and pious confines of the Christian Women's Hotel made climbing all those flights tolerable.

It was freshly built when Helen and I moved in, completed in 1926. The street noise then was different than now — everything was being constructed, going up, up, up. Progress is loud: riveters riveting, radios blaring.

The decay currently taking place is mostly quiet, a steady dissolution, almost inaudible. But everything was new then. So was I.

A damp wind from the East River blows steam from the subway grates: shiny ghosts.

7

FAST AND LOOSE

By the 1920s, American men no longer received invitations to call on women; instead, they took them out.

Or so they did in free society. Not at the Christian Women's Hotel in Midtown, though, a low-rise building on West Fifty-Fourth Street, where my parents had insisted on ensconcing me upon my arrival in Manhattan — for my safety, they contended. Thus those of us with an inclination to consort with gentlemen had to devise other schemes to avail ourselves of their company.

Helen McGoldrick, blonde and goddessy, shared that inclination with me.

There in the city, where the fluid and frenetic social jumble proved a challenge for my still-girlish brain to parse — so different was it from Southern, stately, structured Washington, D.C. — I'd acquired the habit of placing new acquaintances into handy categories: Ally, for example, or Enemy, or

Lover. Helen from day one was sui generis: Her category could only ever be Best Friend.

The daughter of a steel executive from Birmingham, Alabama, she'd come north after college at Newcomb in New Orleans, to seek adventure, she said, and the opportunity to be more than a dizzy ringing belle.

I thanked every star in the light-polluted sky for aligning to make Helen arrive in that girls' club on the same day as I did in January 1926, and also to place her in my class at the Metropolitan Opera Ballet, where we took lessons for a while — both of us stagestruck, like so many young things with the bee of New York City buzzing in our minds.

One Sunday afternoon in May, Helen stood in the first-floor parlor, which we'd converted into a theater, declaiming her lines in a velvety drawl.

"Nay, sister, reject me not, but let me die with thee, and duly honor the dead."

We were putting on *Antigone*. No Greek tragedian, I was sure, had ever spoken that way, but it didn't matter; our audience was rapt.

"Share thou not my death, nor claim deeds to which thou hast not put thy hand:

106

My death will suffice," I said in answer.

The cream-colored lace curtains blew back from the open windows as if in agreement with my defiance.

I was playing Antigone — whose name has been suggested to mean "opposed to motherhood," hence the casting. Helen was Ismene, Antigone's hesitating sister, though Helen herself would never be so quaking and cowardly. Creon was played by a girl named Ginny, a natural authoritarian; so, too, did she play the chorus, but a chorus of one, so we didn't have to split the house take too many ways. Ginny's shift between parts was a trick effected with masks and voices. Helen was also playing Haemon, Antigone's faulty suitor, transitioning between the role of sister and never-quite-husband by means of a nappy and timeworn beard.

These productions were fairly ridiculous, but that was beside the point.

Since February, Helen and I had been staging monthly shows in the girls' club's first floor, charging admission at the door for anyone not actually performing, whether they lived there or not. This balmy afternoon, the front room was lit honey-yellow by the sun, and packed.

Miss Bernice Lockhart, our matron, had

her usual seat of honor in the very front row, practically in the actresses' laps. Her posture, as ever, was erect to the point of pain, and gave the impression that she was trying to balance a book — the Bible, probably — atop her mouse-brown head.

The ballet was fun, and it kept us limber, and Helen and I even went on at the Met a few times: We'd don our flower crowns and throw our arms in the air amongst the other nymphs and sprites, and for that we'd receive one dollar a performance. Not so remunerative.

And so we'd devised these plays. If our amateurishness was a deterrent to some, the faintly illicit thrill of being admitted to our forbidden parlor proved irresistible to others, particularly young male others. By following a standard theater schedule — Friday and Saturday evening performances, and a Sunday matinee — with a single set of shows every month, we'd been building up our escape fund.

Miss Lockhart was a shining disciplinarian, but not the brightest coin in the fountain, and we'd had to convince her of the legitimacy of our theatrical endeavors. The Christian Women's Hotel had been built in 1920 for single professional women, but most of our fellow lodgers were professional

108

husband hunters. Therein hid the secret to our persuasion of the middle-aged Miss Lockhart: We framed our thespian undertakings as a sophisticated mantrap — a means of getting doctors and lawyers in the door.

Miss Lockhart missed that rebelliousness was the thrust of *Antigone,* seeing only that it was old, a classic, and Greek. To her mind, this kind of material would attract the right kinds of fiancés, men with college degrees and social mobility. The script had uplift and values, and had withstood the onslaught of time.

I gazed across the stage at Helen as she recited her Ismene lines, a bedsheet toga over her jumper of forest green gabardine. We'd both have preferred to have nothing between the white cotton and our skins — the better to be unfettered and authentic — but such costuming would be too risqué for the likes of Miss Lockhart, keeping our virtues under lock and key.

Both Helen and I had the men we were seeing — the men whom we let take us around town — in the audience: Dickie Prestwick, who worked in bonds, for me; and his colleague Abe Strong for Helen. In this way we could parade them respectably before the appraisal of Miss Lockhart, who would then permit them to take us out for dinner.

They'd met us at the ballet. They had wealthy fathers and money to spend on us, and aside from all that, we enjoyed their company.

Helen and I abridged the scripts ourselves so that the shows would not drag on, the better to have time for entertainment afterwards.

The end was nigh. Ginny was uttering her Creon lines, dooming me to death by being buried alive: "Away with her — away! And when ye have enclosed her, according to my word in her vaulted grave, leave her alone, forlorn — whether she wishes to die, or to live a buried life in such a home."

Typecasting was not always a bad idea. Ginny had been born for that part, a goody-goody girl prone to tattling. Like Helen and me, Ginny wanted a career of some nebulous kind, having also arrived at the Christian Women's Hotel to seek a profession and not just a husband. And Helen and I wanted to like her for being like us, for using the girls' club as a port of call for a trip that differed from that of most of our peers.

Trouble was, Ginny was annoying, obedient to rules even if the rules were stupid. Full, too, of rules of her own imposition, like "Make a friend of receptionists in big offices," as she'd told us once. "To have a friend, be one. These girls can help get the names of key executives, so your résumé will shoot the mark." Or "Make at least three new friends every day, and keep driving!"

Involving her in the plays and allowing her a cut of the proceeds was our bribe to keep her from telling Miss Lockhart how late we snuck back onto the floor we shared after seeing Dickie and Abe.

As I let my Antigone-self be led away to die for my transgression, I could not see for certain, because Miss Lockhart's watery blue eyes were behind the lenses of her spectacles, but I felt fairly sure I'd succeeded in bringing tears to them.

"Tomb, bridal chamber, eternal prison in the caverned rock, whither go to find mine own, those many who have perished, and whom Persephone hath received among the dead!" I cried to great applause.

We received a standing ovation from our fellow lodgers and their marriage-minded beaux, crowded though it was to stand among the makeshift theater seats consisting of every mismatched chair available in the Christian Women's Hotel.

Miss Lockhart swept forward, after we'd

taken our bows, to embrace and congratulate Helen and me.

"Another splendid run, ladies," she said, clasping her hands to her chest and beaming. "That Antigone is spun from such strong moral fiber. Even if, historically speaking, she must have been a pagan."

"Thank you, Miss Lockhart," I said, careful not to look at Helen for fear of betraying inappropriate mirth.

"And Helen," said Miss Lockhart, raising a hand to Helen's radiant curls, marcelled and flaxen. "I doubt the boards have ever been walked by a more pulchritudinous Ismene."

Helen answered with a curtsy at Miss Lockhart and a wink at me.

"Now what charity will we be donating the proceeds to, ladies?" said Miss Lockhart.

Then Helen looked at me with such mischief that I couldn't not laugh, because the charity was the same, of course, as always: The Get Helen and Lillian Out of the Damn Christian Women's Hotel Fund. But Helen, with grace, lifted the cash box from the matron's hands as gently as if it were a kitten, and said:

"We'll need to think about it. And possibly pray. We'll let you know."

Both of us had parents helping us, and both of us wanted badly to get out from under that arrangement: to enjoy the abundant fruits of independence that the flowering of financial solvency yields with its growth. We had both been applying for jobs like crazy, but neither of us wanted merely to be the confidential private secretary to a man of great importance, which, to date, were the only kinds of replies we'd been getting. And so we kept trying.

Abe and Dickie stepped forward then, greeting Miss Lockhart.

"Another commendable afternoon's entertainment," said Dickie, shaking Miss Lockhart's hand, causing her to blush and rustle, the scent of her lemon verbena sachets rising from the folds of her high-necked blouse.

"Thank you, Mr. Prestwick," she said, hewing to formality, though he'd told her last month that she could call him by his Christian name.

Miss Lockhart did not offer her hand to Abe, as she knew he was Jewish, a fact that her bigoted heart could tolerate, but only barely.

"May we help tidy up the performance space, while the ladies put away their costumes?" said Dickie, placing a neat square hand on the back of one of the folding chairs, beginning to collapse it. Abe did the same.

Strapping, I suppose, one could have called Dickie, his men's eights crew days at college still much in evidence in his shoulders, broad from rowing.

Abe was shorter, snappier, and had a goofy handsomeness that made me want to laugh whenever I saw him, which is what Helen said she liked best about him. He was a suave and competent clown whose curly hair rarely stayed stuck down no matter how he pomaded it. When we met them months ago, that first night after the ballet, I immediately liked Abe better, but was physically attracted to Dickie. There could be no resisting.

That night, after we'd folded our togas away and gotten Miss Lockhart's benediction, they took us to dinner, as was often the case, to a place in the neighborhood. I felt acutely aware of the passage of time.

"Alas, May is not a month that is spelled with the letter R," said Helen, gazing at the menu with a forlorn air only partly put on.

Since we'd begun seeing them in February, we'd dined almost exclusively on her favorite: oysters Rockefeller, awash in butter and parsley, chased with plenty of Champagne at a speakeasy.

Late spring, though, almost summer, and that old guideline for safely dining on shellfish necessitated a change. Now was the season of medallions of lamb or aiguillettes of striped bass, a datum which made me, that evening, as Dickie ordered roast duck with asparagus tips au gratin for me, unaccountably sad — not because of the foodstuffs, but the change of season.

Though I could tell that Dickie's and my couplehood was not long for this world, I ate mostly left handed, Dickie holding my right tight with affection.

Dinner was nevertheless delightful, full of bons mots from Abe and Helen. We waited on her, indulging her as always, as she got dessert. I liked sweets all right, but I never ordered them. I had a good metabolism then, but why test it? Besides, I liked to save room for my treat of choice: the cocktails we'd be off to later. Even then I could drink almost as much as the men, a capacity which wowed Abe but worried Dickie, though he tried to act as if it didn't matter.

Helen's confectionery weakness then was Venetian ice cream. She tucked into it with a dainty silver spoon, making her way through each melting layer with careful determination.

115

"One of these days I'll whisk you away to the actual Venice, in Italy," Abe said with admiration as Helen cleaned her plate with an efficiency that was both robust and lady-like.

"You know, Abe, I wish I'd thought of this sooner," I said, "but we should have told Miss Lockhart that we'd like to give the money from the play to the Brooklyn Federation of Jewish Charities."

"Wit of the staircase, Lily," said Abe, paying the check. "It's all right. I don't worry about people like her; she can't really hurt me. Just keep it for the cause of making it easier for me to see Helen without asking anybody's permission."

Sometimes they took us down to Chumley's in the West Village because Dickie knew that I scribbled poetry, and the place was popular with the drinkers in that set. I had not met with much poetic success yet, but I was flattered all the same.

That night, though, they took us to the Puncheon Club on Forty-Ninth Street in Midtown, better known as 21. We went there because it was closer, and because it had tables the size of small yachts and oceans of the best booze to be had in post–Volstead Act Manhattan.

Unprepossessing aside from a large iron

gate, 21 resided in a row of brownstones. It maintained a large clientele among the Yale men in the city, including Dickie. He was pals with Jack and Charlie, the proprietors. When the eyeball behind the peephole peeped upon us there in the May dusk, we were given immediate entrance.

We had told Miss Lockhart we were off to a tea room, but instead of tea, we ordered sidecars for Abe and Helen and whiskey old-fashioneds for me. Dickie's drink was the Barbary Coast, which contained both Scotch and gin, an admixture that caused me, silently, to question, as I often did, his taste.

"Olives?" said Dickie, passing around the small complimentary plate that came with each table.

"No thanks, but could you hand over that candied ginger?" said Helen.

Cosmopolitan — that's what Abe and Dickie were. Debonair. Dickie especially. His suits fit him like perfect plumage, giving him the look of a man who was going places.

And he likely was, being one of those people positioned naturally, in terms of wealth and family background, to be destined for success. Yet for all that — perhaps because of all that — Dickie had few significant long-term goals. He was gifted, rather, with a joyous irresolution that made him seem to live wholly, unlike anyone else I'd yet met, in the present. Even sitting there, munching the free salted nuts that came with the cocktails as an invitation to get thirstier, his presence felt momentous. Not as in big and important, though he did fill a room, but as in one who inhabited each moment as and by a moment.

The room was warm, the thick air blown by fans. Our cocktail glasses sweated condensation, leaving rings on the table and damp on our hands. I wiped mine on Dickie's pant leg, mostly as an excuse to touch his thigh.

There was live music, as ever and, as ever, we danced. Dickie was immaculate on the dance floor, but Abe, less polished and more improvisatory, was the better dancer. We danced to "Whispering." To "Linger Awhile."

"What do you say we linger a while elsewhere?" said Dickie, squeezing my waist and leading me from the dance floor.

Meaning what did I say we head back to his place and go to bed together.

"I thought you'd never ask," I said, though he always asked, just as Abe asked Helen, and we both said yes, and would meet up back on our floor of the Women's Christian Hotel later that night.

Dickie's apartment wasn't a far walk from 21, but in our tipsy haste, we took a taxi, Dickie paying. Windows down, hair gently blown, I could hardly wait to be alone in private.

One might find such wildness shocking. But people had sex even back in those days.

True, I had been brought up in strict, Victorian style. Reading books and dreaming dreams, drinking chocolate sodas, and spending summers at the broad Atlantic. Mother, in my youth, made me eat my daily stint of Cream of Wheat. Anti hand-holding, pro girlish pride. "Girls should always turn aside," she'd say, reminding me of the protocol for a boy attempting a kiss. "Anything you love is a joy and a care," she'd say. And, "Dinosaurs are gone, but fleas persist," when I spoke of my ambitions — her way of making a point about the dangers of wanting to be too immense.

But I didn't listen, not really.

Self-taught, I learned how not to hang around the front stoop too long waiting to be properly kissed. Not to say I kissed promiscuously. But some desires could not be commanded.

I had first gone to bed with a boy when I

was in college at Goucher: a philosophy student from the University of Maryland. Physically attractive but mentally pedantic, he was forever explaining some pretentious point about Kant. "I Kant stand it when you talk that way!" I said once, but humor was lost on him. He drew out the old saw about puns being the lowest form of humor, which struck me as idiotic. Puns require the minute manipulation of language on its most fundamental level! A pox on John Dryden, or whomever, for saying that in the first place, and a pox on that philosophy student for being so full of received ideas. He and I did not endure. And sleeping with him had not been all pyrotechnics and roses, to be honest, as both of us had been ardent virgins.

But I knew that, like anything I set my will to, I could get better at it. And I did.

In those handful of years between Goucher and Manhattan, I lingered in Washington. Or rather malingered.

A classmate told me of an opening in a publicity firm. Slightly vague as to what publicity actually was, I walked into the office and demanded an interview with the president. The surprise was that I got one, and the following Monday started work. Luck, pure and simple. My first assignment was to make a speech before a group of women I was supposed to organize for a fund-raising drive. I was scared to death, but I ended up being a natural. Plus, I learned by working there the best way to be stylish — stocking seams always straight, nose never shining, lipstick never faded, coiffure always in curl or wave — without being one of those women other women are prone to hate.

I passed three years there, jotting poems in my free time, cherishing with pride a few clippings and the memory of what sweet things the professor in English composition had said about my college themes. My boss was a blowhard who grunted and snorted and stripped his gears over every little thing, but was ultimately harmless.

The next boy I went to bed with was a law student from Georgetown, an assistant to my father. We were involved. For a while. It would have been a match to make my parents proud — someone following my father in his chosen vocation, someone to keep me close to home in Washington — but I couldn't.

What's bad in a sweetheart becomes unbearable in a husband.

I'd become so bored that I bored myself. I broke it off with my law student, who quickly found an aspiring housewife to embark on the becalmed seas of the life he desired. Bully for her. At the end of 1925 I at last resolved, above parental protest, to send myself off in my Aunt Sadie's wake to Manhattan.

Off to the Empire State's bright diadem. A charming and perceptive woman ready to charm and perceive.

Romantically, I arrived unburdened by propriety, no blushing maid. One could say I was "fast," but the pace felt right. One could say I was "loose," but I never felt myself far from the tightest self-control. I would have liked a companion-spouse, maybe. I would have considered that possibility of a mate for life. But they, all of them, to a man — even and maybe especially the ones who fancied themselves urbane, like Dickie, like Abe, or the most rebellious — secretly or not-so-secretly aspired toward a middle-class ménage.

Dickie had decided recently that, in the interest of being chic, he ought to wear cologne. That evening his bedroom smelled like citrus and spice.

"Very nice," I told him. "What is it?"

He handed me the bottle, and I stood before the vanity, watching him undress me in the dim ochre light of a single lamp. We wanted to see each other, but not to let people outside see in.

"Du Coq?" I said, reading the label and laughing, thinking that I had to tell Helen, who would appreciate that my lover would wear a perfume so aptly named.

"What's so funny?" said Dickie, kissing my neck; necking was then a popular *terme d'art.*

"Nothing," I said. "I just like that your perfume is so cocky."

I removed the cap and put my nose to the sprayer, finding to my dismay that up close it had an almost urinary note. I felt grateful that Dickie hadn't chosen to wear it that night.

"It's not perfume," said Dickie. "It's cologne."

I ignored his concern with being manly and slipped his suit jacket off his rowing-team shoulders and onto the floor.

After we'd finished, I had to hurry home. I was never able to stay overnight. Dickie understood, obviously. Walking me back to the Christian Women's Hotel, he kept a hand on my elbow. He spoke what might be considered pillow talk, but upright and ambulatory and without the pillows.

"Maybe one day we can stay together

longer," he said. "When you get your own place."

And that is how that night went, and how all our nights went, until we parted, inevitably, not with enmity, but with incredulity on his part: He, like the rest, could not believe that I really was not on the prowl for permanent union. Or he thought that he would be the one who made me realize that deep down inside, I surreptitiously was.

I kissed him quickly, for an instant, on the lips, then rapped my knuckles on the glass of the Christian Women's Hotel door once he was down the street and out of sight. Helen and I were friends with the doorman, who let us enter by this method instead of ringing and getting in trouble over curfew.

The last time I saw Dickie was at the first party that Helen and I threw at our brand-new place: the sixth floor of the six-floor walk-up in Murray Hill. He came bearing booze. He did not stay the night. I did not want him to. It would have been impractical, for one — the place being too small, with Helen in the bedroom and Abe in there with her, and I in the room designated for living. But that aside, I could feel it was over, and I told Dickie so.

He explained to me calmly that he knew I

was only saying that because of the upheaval of moving to a new place and because of my mistaken ideas about where my "career" — he sneered semi-intentionally as he said that word — might take me.

"You'll call me up again, Lillian," he said, placing a hand at my waist as we stood in the doorway, me trying to see him out, him seeking to stay. "I bet you will in under a week's time."

But I didn't. I was too busy. Doing new things — writing new poems and learning a new trade and meeting new people. New men eventually.

In the month prior to that party Helen had gotten her job in advertising illustration at R.H. Macy's, and thanks to her, I'd gotten mine there, writing advertising copy.

When Helen had told me to apply that June, after she was hired on, I had been leery. I had not entirely enjoyed the PR work in D.C. But advertising, I found, was a different and entirely more rideable beast.

With the pure driven vision of Phoebe Snow glimmering in my mind, I sent out my rhyming application letters — not only to R.H. Macy's, but all over the place, just in case. Thanks to Helen and some mild exaggeration on my résumé — or a bit of finesse, as she suggested I call it — R.H.

Macy's took me on on a trial basis, and I tried and tried until they agreed to keep me.

Ginny had moved out of the Christian Women's Hotel that first weekend in July, too. Independence Day indeed. She became a journalist, and we invited her to that first party, as well, full of goodwill and gratitude at being so free. A few years later Ginny would have to return to Kansas City to help her parents after the crash and through the Depression, settling in to work for the paper there. But Helen and I, we stayed in the city.

We couldn't stay that way forever, Helen and I, living together, but while we did, everything was charmed. We never fought, we never felt crowded. We gave one another everything we required by way of fun and friendship, and the only necessity either of us could not get from the other was male companionship.

Before that party, we stood together on our fire escape, smoking and waiting for the guests to show up. The ravines of the city as seen from that vantage were sublime: Some of the other fire escapes strewn with shirts hung to dry, and clouds shifting overhead, dyed red by the sunset.

The following Monday I came home from

work and paused to get the mail, our first delivery there.

I looked it over in the lobby — two letters for Helen and two for me. One was from my mother in D.C., expressing her worry at my ability to maintain an income steady enough to support this excursion into independent living, insulting as ever without meaning to be. "My darling girl," she called me, and "my beloved child," making me feel somehow even older than my twenty-six years.

The other, to my surprise, was from Abe. Seeing his return address and fluid handwriting, I thought at first that there must be a mistake and that he'd meant to write Helen, whom he was still seeing, even though Dickie and I, as of the last forty-eight hours, were officially uncoupled.

But no, it really was for me.

"My Dear Miss Poisonfish," he addressed me, good-humoredly. Then, "In all seriousness, Lillian, Lily, most appealing Miss Boxfish, I fear you've broken poor Dickie's heart, and poisoned the well of his zest for life, at least temporarily. I do not think this will make much difference, but since I hate seeing my pal so crestfallen and downcast, and since selfishly I adore the pleasure of your company on our double dates: Reconsider?"

The lobby felt stifling, and I crumpled both letters, one per fist, thinking to throw them in the trash bin near the stairs before I walked up, reluctant to carry such burdens to our rented heights.

Then the feeling passed and I felt all right. I loved them both, but neither Abe nor my mother had any purchase on me. They could say what they liked, and I would love them still, but I would not change my behavior, would not change my mind. I smoothed the letters flat again, replacing them in their respective envelopes, and kept them.

So for that first year of freedom, until the lease was up and we each had enough money to acquire our own places, Helen and I lived like happy cliff dwellers with our kitchenette and our combination shower and bathtub.

We had all we needed: work to do, vegetables and fresh milk and money to pay for them, even though they weren't cheap. I think they would've sold autumn leaves for fifty cents a bunch if they could have found a market for them. It was a bandit city then, as it would always remain.

But the sidewalks were clean and the

garbage was collected and I gave no thought as to where it was hauled or burned.

Up there in my snug sweet tower, I felt I'd made landfall in the shoals of shifting clouds. Far enough from the crowds to relish the crowds.

8
THE PEARL ANNIVERSARY

You would think that food — its ready command of our senses granting it immediate
access to our hearts and minds, our ap-
petites and memories — could be trusted to
speak for itself.

Not so, apparently. In the 1950s, when I
was freelancing, I was often enlisted as a
grocery-aisle Cyrano, a ventriloquist for the
new and improved, repeatedly making the
case that the way Mother did it was not, in
fact, best.

Sometimes clients would send me samples
of the product for which I was composing
copy. Sometimes they would also request
that I build the ads around recipes, or at
least let me know that the ads would have
these recipes embedded within them. One
unforgettably repellent-sounding one was as
follows:

2 cups of roast beef, ground

3 tbsp Karo syrup
3 tbsp vinegar

Take the gravy from the roast and cook all together about 5 minutes.

A little salt may be necessary.

Suggest serving this with pickled peaches.

Fortunately, the food at Grimaldi — Northern Italian cuisine of a superior quality — is nothing like that. Unfortunately, I am still full of damnable Oreos when I arrive. Yet I find the garlic smells and the clinking knife-and-fork-on-plate sounds a welcome greeting. Even the Sinatra recording that's playing — that tired Italian restaurant cliché that I've never liked — feels right tonight, just because it's familiar.

Alberto, the owner, is at the front of the house, standing next to the hostess, going over the evening's reservations. Shoulders slightly stooped but still natty in his charcoal-gray suit, he hails me as if I were family.

"Lillian, *mia cara,* right on time," he says, embracing me. Then he says to the hostess, "The reservation is under Boxfish. I'll take her to her table, don't you worry."

Alberto moved to Manhattan from Lombardy in the early 1950s — born in Milan, like my ex-husband Max's parents. He still has the accent, tuneful and rhythmic. Max's accent was pure New York: dropped final Rs and nasal diphthongs.

Alberto installs me in my red leather banquette, the same one I sit in every New Year's Eve.

Most of what we consider beauty is manufactured, but the fact of that manufacture does not make it unbeautiful. Grimaldi as conceived by Alberto is like this: garish paintings that one early reviewer said looked as though they'd been purchased by the square foot and gleaming reproductions of classical bronze statues.

"What'll it be tonight?" he says. "We got anything you like."

I hate that I have to tell him that I don't want anything.

"Alberto, I'm afraid I haven't got much of an appetite tonight," I say, without saying why.

The white tangle of his eyebrows rears back, and he's about to start persuading, insisting, but then he intuits my mood and stands down. "Mind if I take a load off for a moment and join you?" he says. Younger than I am, he is still categorically old, and he lowers himself into the seat with caution. "It's not because you are too sad, now, is it?"

"Not exactly," I say.

"There is something about the year's end that leads to a taking of stock that can lead in turn to melancholy. Isn't that so?" he says, candlelight from the red votive holder on the table flickering over his wrinkled face. "There is at least for me."

"It *can* tame one's appetite," I say.

"For me, a way to handle that sadness is by being a Catholic," he says, and I laugh. "I know it sounds maybe crazy," he says, "but here is what I mean: The turn of the year is the time of resolutions, yes? Makes me feel like a confession. Like the sacrament of reconciliation. The examination of conscience, the contrition, the admission, and — eventually, maybe, if you're lucky — the feeling of absolution following the penance."

A waiter comes by, and I order a glass of Chianti. After he's gone, I say, "I'll drink to that, Alberto. And that was rude of me — should we have ordered you one? To toast?"

"Nah, Lillian, I'm working," he says, waving a hand to brush the suggestion away. "But you, you celebrate."

I do not say that I feel uncelebratory.

133

Rather, "It's also a matter of personality, right? That feeling you're describing. Important to, and practiced by, those who are already predisposed to lists and rituals."

"Ah, Lillian, Lillian, exactly, exactly," says Alberto. "You and me, we've always been simpatico."

"Haven't we?" I say. "You've always made the city feel even more like home — almost thirty years now. It's the year *after* next that's the big one for you, isn't that right? What will you do to celebrate? Thirty years is the pearl anniversary, if memory serves. Oyster specials, maybe?"

"It won't be me who decides," says Alberto, eyes down at the white tablecloth, not meeting mine. "I didn't want to tell you, Lillian, but I won't be here for that. We're selling the place. To my nephew, so it's not going to close. But we're leaving this summer. Me and Fabiola are moving to Palm Beach to be near Al."

"But Al's running the restaurant down there just fine by himself, isn't he?" I say.

"Of course he is," says Alberto, looking up at me with brown eyes that seem faded, like mud that's turned back to dirt in the sun. "I taught that kid everything he knows. He's expanding the Grimaldi empire. But he's expanding it to places we actually want to spend our twilight."

"New York City is the place to be," I say, blindsided, sounding like a ludicrous tourism bureau.

"Lillian, it was, but it's not anymore," says Alberto. "How to put it to a poet? It's like in Dante. If he'd lived up to now, and wanted to add a Tenth Circle to Hell, he could call it New York. And the first ones he could throw in would be that Subway Vigilante *and* those guys he shot. Let 'em rot together forever."

"Forgive me, Alberto," I say, "but that decision sounds a little bit irrational. Are you sure?"

"Rationally, Lillian, business hasn't been so great lately. There aren't so many three-martini lunchers anymore. The businessmen with their fat expense accounts and their Diners Club cards are thinning out."

"But what about your loyal regulars?" I say, gesturing around at the other tables, slowly starting to fill with patrons, like grains of sand in an hourglass.

"Not so many of those, either, as there used to be," he says, then smiles. "Even you aren't ordering dinner."

"But I do have this wine," I say, making myself take a sip of the Chianti, making myself smile back. "And I'll leave a gargan-

135

tuan tip."

"You always do. You're a peach, Lily, a true friend. It's not personal, you know that. It's just time."

"I know," I say. "I hate time."

"Me too," he says, lifting himself from the table, putting a sandpapery hand on mine. "I have to go see about the other tables now, but you come find me before you go, Lillian, yes? And I'll see you out."

The betrayal I feel as he walks back toward the hostess stand is crimson and grand and unjust. How could he? How could Fabiola? How could they? But they are not mine to keep. Nothing is mine.

I drink my Chianti and watch the other diners, none of them alone the way I am. And isn't this key to the feeling of being alone — the sense that no one is like you?

I didn't used to be this way. I went to cocktail parties with friends and advertisers, with entertaining experts and houseware and furnishing designers. I rubbed elbows — literal elbows! — with Mary and Russel Wright.

I watch the waiters and wonder whether anyone but me will notice a change after Alberto decamps. Whether his nephew will surrender to the dictates of fashion — introducing "blackened" entrees, a chocolate dessert with a menacing name, even, God forbid, a television — or keep the place the same, preserving its strange indulgences, like zabaione, a frothed concoction of egg yolks beaten with sugar and wine, poured over fresh berries, prepared tableside. The booth next to mine has just ordered it. It is all I can do not to say to the couple, fancy and middle-aged, *Enjoy, because it won't last.*

I've met the nephew, I'm sure, though I can't remember his name. Younger than my Gian, certainly. Maybe younger than this restaurant. When Alberto and Fabiola are gone, no one here will know me any longer as the ex-wife of Massimiliano Gianluca Caputo. I'll only be myself. Whatever that means. A strange old lady from around the corner. Orange Fire lipstick wiped off a wineglass.

I sit awhile, watching the tables fill up. Trying to think of an Italian lullaby that Max used to sing, but with Sinatra's relentless crooning I can't recall the tune.

True to my word, I leave a tip proportionate to my sense of betrayal. Alberto, meandering among the other tables like an ancient river, checking in with the newcomers, the regulars, sees me rise, excuses himself, and comes to my side to bid me good-bye.

Like the old man he is, he shuffles his feet in their shoes of Italian leather, so I have to slow my own stride as he walks me to the coat check.

"Safe walk home, Lillian," he says. "Take good care, and sleep well, and happy 1985."

"Same, Alberto, same," I say, as he helps me into my coat.

Alberto hands me a salmon-colored rose — long-stemmed, no thorns — of the variety given out to every female guest, just as he has done for decades. This may be the last one I ever get from his hand.

What I do not tell him — because he would worry, and because it would wound him — is that I have decided that I am neither tired nor ready to go home for the night.

Instead, one last adventure to round out the year. I have mapped it out in my mind to go to Delmonico's, the legendary steakhouse at South William and Beaver, near Wall Street and City Hall, way downtown. And I have resolved to walk there, because the calculus of exertion plus time should add up to my finally being hungry.

Institution though Delmonico's is, I have only been there once, and my memories of the occasion are entirely negative, except that it was a great restaurant with delicious food which I lacked any capacity to enjoy at that time.

I put on my gloves. I adjust my hat. I kiss Alberto once on each rough cheek as he kisses mine, and off I go, into the night, into the last hours of 1984, with his customary "Ciao, *bella*!" rasping after me.

9
SLAMBANGO

Can any telling ever be so thorough that there is no more story left to tell?

My husband — ex-husband — Max seemed to think so. Wanted his version of our dissolution after twenty years to be the one of record. I would not permit this, though our divorce was uncontested; by then even I could see that there was no contest, that I had lost. As for the story, however, there was his version, and there was mine. There was more to say, and we were saying it, over lunch at Oscar's Delmonico's, early October, 1955.

We had finalized our divorce after a short court appearance at City Hall. Delmonico's was nearby and seemed a fair setting for discussing final details — mostly having to do with our son, Johnny, then thirteen — and for saying good-bye.

I was conscious of making this decision — to go to the restaurant — but then somehow shocked to actually find myself there, amid the soft bustle of the noonday crowd. It was as if the span between the notion and the action had simply vanished, like events follow each other in dreams — an experience that I had often in those days, I'm afraid.

Walking into Delmonico's on Max's arm felt like a ride in an ambulance, or the moments just after a car crash: an overwhelming rush of detail diamond-etched itself into my brain, as if I'd remember the scene forever, though of course I forgot almost everything right away.

"Those columns at the entrance," I said as the maître d'hôtel seated us, just for the sake of saying something. "They look freshly dropped off by Caesar Augustus himself."

"Indeed, madam," he said. "The lady has a discerning eye. They were imported in the 1830s, from the ruins of Pompeii."

At the mention of Pompeii, my scant appetite shaded quickly toward nausea. "Oh my," I said. "How unusual."

"We've been to Pompeii," said Max. "We saw columns just like those, all covered in ash."

Max was referring to our honeymoon trip to Italy in 1935: our purest moment of wedded bliss, now disfigured by our unhappy end. If he detected any irony in the advent of this reminder, today of all days, then he didn't show it. I suspect it never occurred to him. Max had no sense of irony. Most hypocrites haven't.

The maître d' evinced the appropriate degree of regard for our worldliness. He and Max — who was always brutally casual, without even realizing the brutality part — chatted in affable generality on the subject of Italy, Max's parents' homeland, the place where Max had been stationed during the war. Watching him speak with this stranger made me think of my own first impressions of him — before I'd learned what did and didn't lie behind his brassy vitality — and envy how little he'd changed: hardly thicker at the middle, wavy hair still black.

As for me, I felt like a ruin. Still extant but not intact. A plaster effigy cast in the shape of my old incinerated self. A wreck one could contemplate as an object lesson in one's own potential to become a ruin one day. It could happen to anyone. It could happen when one expected it, or when one did not.

I placed my napkin in my lap and accepted the menu from the hands of the maître d'. His were steady, mine shaking, I hoped not perceptibly.

Back then, in the divorce's immediate

aftermath, my mind briefly became even more bent and misshapen than it already had been, circling around revenge, wearing a track in the carpet to the alla breve march-beat of "retaliate, retaliate." But I didn't really want to. I was more hurt. More sad. I still loved Max, though he had proven himself by that point to be quite an ass, and callous.

His birthday — the last one he'd have while we were still married — had passed while I was in the hospital. We likely would not have celebrated anyway, but I'd made him a card, original, hand-crafted, and self-composed, with what I hoped was recogniz-able — no Helen McGoldrick, I — as a pink tropical bird on the front. I handed it to him.

"Lillian," he said. "You shouldn't have." He sounded sincere, like I really shouldn't.

"Go ahead," I said. "Read it out loud. It's the first new poem I've shown anyone in a while."

"All right," he said. "Here she goes: 'By jingo / The flamingo / Joins our fandango / For your birthday slambango.'"

Our waiter arrived to take our drink order, saving Max from having to comment fur-ther. I asked for a glass of Amarone. Max did the same, then said to me:

"*Vino,* eh? You sure Dr. R would think that's a wise idea?"

"I can't very well toast to your birthday with water, now can I?" I said. "That would be unlucky, and I think we've already enjoyed enough bad luck."

"Fair enough," he said, setting the card aside and opening the menu.

The slight lowering of his head as he perused his choices afforded me the opportunity to see again what I already knew: His thick black hair was still truly black, almost no gray. I wanted to reach across and run my fingers through it one more time.

What else can be said about Max? I loved him so much, even though doing so had become stupid and pointless.

He had a hoarse laugh, but not a horse laugh. Had sex appeal. Most men I'd met would clearly have starved me emotionally, but Max was a feast. Max was too much. After I met him, all other men came to seem plug-ugly. He was dominant, but never a bully. A courtly salesman. How did that happen to attract me? When we met, way back in 1934, I was tall and graceful, but I willingly became his Little Woman. Proverbially: We were the same height, he said — and I let him — but in fact he was at least a full inch shorter than I. But he was as dashing in his daytime suit of blue serge as in his broadcloth evening clothes, when we still went out evenings.

He rarely played in a minor key — not until these past few years. Back when we lived in the now-foreign land of our happiness, he would give the bottle to the baby and wash dishes with agility, if only occasionally. Change some diapers. Spend some evenings at the club and some Saturday afternoons in golf foursomes. No college reunions because he went to college in Switzerland. Rarely in his cups. Unlike — I know he would say, and justly so — me.

The waiter returned to take our food orders. I sat there mute as he looked at Max, then at me, and I realized that Max wasn't going to order for me. How could he? I hadn't told him what I wanted, and I was not his wife anymore. He ordered for another woman now.

The other woman. Julia. His second bride to be. Younger, conspicuously, merely thirty-nine, and easy to be around — *just happy, so happy,* Max had said when he'd given me the news of their impending nuptials. And I had to agree; she had a beautiful smile, if you like people who have thousands of teeth and no evident capacity to ever be sad.

"Madam?" the waiter said, prompting me.

"Steak, please," I said. "Medium well."

I'd meant to say "medium rare." But who cared? I didn't correct myself. It had been awkward enough to place an incorrect order.

I watched Max ask the waiter which of three popular options he'd most recommend, and I thought how young he seemed. Not boyish, per se, but not old. Not like me. I wondered how the waiter saw me. Did my pause strike him as doddering? Did I register to him at all? He was in his early thirties, probably, and I suspected that I had for him the relative invisibility of a woman of a certain age and face. *I used to be beautiful,* I wanted to scream. *I used to be quick.*

Once, shortly after I moved to Manhattan, I accompanied Helen to the Met; she was looking for exemplars for her own sketches, bulking up her illustration portfolio in the hope of being more hirable. We were saturated, supersaturated, with art that day: so much craft and artifice all in one place. But the piece I remembered most indelibly — at the time, and ever after — was called "A Speedy & Effectual Preparation for the Next World." It was an etching of an old woman applying rouge at her dressing-table, oblivious to the approach of skeletal Death behind her. A tiny funeral cortege drawn by racing coursers coasted down her architectural eighteenth-century hair. She was a figure of satire; as an on-looker, one was meant to laugh at her vanity. But I did not laugh: Even at twenty-seven, I didn't find it funny. Even then I'd begun to think — and to push away the thought — that committing oneself to being fashionable was simultaneously committing oneself to being perishable.

I thought of that image as I was looking across the table at Max, at him looking back at me, old me, much older me: fifty-six. Max was born in 1906 and thus had always been — would always be — younger than I, by six years if I lied about my age, as I always did, or by seven if I was honest, which I was only in the privacy of my mind.

He still looked as handsome as an Italian-ate statue. His few wrinkles brought out the deeper character of his face, as verdigris did on aging metal. Me, though: I was well dressed and thin, but because I'd just got-ten out of the hospital it was a sagging thin-ness, not sharp but haggard. Unfair, unfair.

At least the light in there was flatteringly dim. Lowish ceilings decorated with wedding-cake moldings, everyone dressed to impress upon the eye the ideas that yes, they had money and yes, they had style. Chandeliers and wooden chairs.

"So," said Max. "I don't mean for this to be too much of a business lunch, since most things are sorted. But I guess we ought to discuss what we've got to discuss."

"Of course," I said, reaching into my pocketbook. "I typed up that letter you asked for. The one for Johnny's orthodontist."

"That bastard orthodontist," said Max. "Thanks."

Despite our split and my recent incapacity, Max still relied on me to perform certain tasks for our son, almost all of which were really tasks for Max himself. Correspondence was one. I didn't mind — or if I did mind, I didn't hesitate. Partly because it was gratifying to still be adept at something. Partly, too, because I didn't want Johnny to be harmed by Max's indelicacy. But mostly, at least in this case, because I could scarcely bear the thought of incivility occurring anywhere it could be avoided.

"Shall I read it?" I asked.

"Yes," he said. "I always like hearing you perform your work."

"All right," I began. " 'Dear Joel. We have been friends for many, many years; hence, I feel that I can be perfectly frank with you to state my displeasure in suddenly receiving a bill covering three years of orthodontia work on Junior in the amount of $415.00. Now Joel, it must be obvious to you that you do not suddenly sock a guy with a $400 bill for work going over three years and never submit an interim bill. Without being facetious, what I should say to you is: If it takes your staff three years to bill me, it will take my staff three years to pay you. It will be paid. Have no concern, but I do not like surprises of this sort. I feel assured that you will agree with me that pay as you go is by far the best principle. Signed, Massimiliano Gianluca Caputo.' "

"That's perfect, Lillian. Pitch-perfect," said Max. "Thank you. That's exactly what I wanted to say. I couldn't figure out how to make it —"

"Forceful," I said.

"Forceful, yeah. But still with the right amount of —"

"Grace," I said. I folded the letter and passed it to him. "I left the signature blank for you, obviously. And I typed up the envelope, but you'll have to get the stamp."

The judge had decided that Johnny should continue to live with me for most of the year, being as I was the mother, and being as he'd soon start high school and moving would be disruptive. Plus Johnny did not want to leave me. While I did not want him to stay out of pity, I was in no position to be choosy, so if pity was what motivated him, fine: I'd take it. I couldn't bear for him and Max to both abandon me. Summers he'd spend with Max and Julia, an annual three-month absence I was already dreading, though it was only autumn. Not to mention my preemptive jealousy that they'd get Johnny when he was totally free and would therefore enjoy his company uninterrupted.

The waiter returned and set Max's lobster before him and my Delmonico steak before me. Almost two inches thick and shot through with delicate marbling, it was delectable. But I did not feel like delecting. A small, shapely mountain of Delmonico's potatoes lay on the side — mashed, covered in grated cheese and buttered breadcrumbs, gently baked — but I could scarcely scale it.

We talked — about the logistics of sharing our place up in Maine, holidays, saving for Johnny's college, and so on. I picked at the meat and moved the potatoes around the plate, hoping Max wouldn't notice. He did. The same eagle eye for detail that had made him so effective as the head rug buyer at R.H. Macy's never failed to set itself upon any and everything in his line of sight.

"I thought you said you had your appetite back," said Max. "I thought Dr. R put you on a program."

"Please don't be critical," I said. "I'm trying."

"Lils," he said, using the nickname only he used. "You've got a fine mind. Don't let's confuse criticism with concern."

"I'm not confused, Max," I said. "But surely you can understand that this cuisine is a bit more robust than the dining options I had in the hospital. I'm still adjusting."

"All right, all right," he said, with that gesture I'd come to hate: two open palms facing me and patting the air, as if pushing me away, pushing me down, pushing any tears I might be preparing to cry back into their ducts.

Max had ordered Lobster Newburg, a sea bug drowning in butter and cream and eggs and cognac. As he ate, I could practically see a future heart attack peering over his shoulder, licking its fatty chops. But it was not my place any longer to remark upon ways he might extend his life.

Things between us had always been light and witty; we realized too late how grave life could be. By then I found I had no effective means of being serious, and the needle of my personality flung itself all the way over to crushing sadness and debilitating ennui. Now I was the kind of person who said things like:

"You know, Max, you could have been a lot more decent about all this. Writing to me in the hospital, asking if I could leave long enough to fly to Reno and get it over with faster?"

"Look, Lils, I know that. I admit it and I'm sorry," he said. "But you could have been a lot more decent about a lot of things too. You're not being fair."

"What I'm driving at isn't fairness," I said, "but honesty. If, for example, you'd been earning more money, I wouldn't have needed to write that letter to the orthodontist. The judge said that you're responsible for those incidentals, but we both know you're not good for it right now. Let's be frank about that."

"If you were being honest, you'd admit what you've been like these last few years," he said. "How difficult. Unfunny. Not the girl I married."

"If *you* were being honest," I said, "you'd admit what you've been like, too. And no one stays a *girl* forever, Max. Time doesn't work that way."

"You're a poet, Lils," he said. "Therefore I fail to see your need to be so literal minded all of a sudden. That's not what I meant."

"No?" I said. "I just want you to admit — honestly — the realities of Julia. Much more girlish, yes? Fifteen years more girlish than I. And you took up with her almost a year before I got sick. She wasn't just your employee at the import-export for all that long."

The Amarone and my otherwise empty stomach had helped make me righteous but reckless: Even as I felt the reins slipping, I heard my voice regaining youthful force. Though I was in the right — the injured party, near Christlike in my magnanimity for not having shared what I knew of Julia with the judge — I had until that moment avoided confronting Max about her fully. He would know that my information could only have come from one source. While it was clear that Johnny was destined to become simultaneously the referee and the playing field for a stupid, degrading, protracted scrimmage between Max and me, I had intended to delay the starting whistle a bit longer.

"Listen," Max said, "let's drop it. What's

done is done. I'm leaving New York. Johnny's staying. I wish you well. Enjoy the apartment."

"Of course I'll enjoy the apartment!" I said. "It's mine. I paid for it. And don't try to pretend that I'm taking it from you, or that you even want to stay here. You're moving to Chicago because Julia's uncle can get you a job in the Merchandise Mart."

The sad and wounded expression that Max had been wearing finally failed, becoming apparent for what it was, a mask. He balled his napkin up and threw it on the table. "I don't have to sit for this if that's the way you want to play it," he said.

"I'm not playing, Max. I just think we should tell the story straight. We owe it to Johnny, if not to each other."

That was an underhanded move on my part, and to no end. If Max recognized it as bait, he didn't take it. He was a hard, brash, handsome man to the day he died. "The story's been told, Lillian," he said. "The story's over."

"Yes," I said. "Between us it is. And your next story is already well underway. You're going to be the suburban lord you've always wanted to be."

"Sure. Will it make you happy if I agree? Julia's my mulligan. My do over."

154

"Right," I said. "Because this is all as consequential as a round of golf to you."

Then there was the maître d', hovering tableside in a vaporous cloud of solicitousness. "Is everything quite all right here?" he asked, leaning in and speaking quietly.

"Yes, everything is perfectly sane," I said, standing. "Perfectly *fine.* I was just saying good-bye. The gentleman will pay."

And I walked out alone, out of Delmonico's, into the dime-gray light of Wall Street.

It seemed so long ago that Johnny had been the first to mention — furtive on the sidewalk, staring at my feet before we walked into our building, one late afternoon after his singing lesson — that Max had been spending time with another lady, the lady from work. Prior to that I had had my suspicions, but I hadn't pursued them, primarily out of inertia. I could barely keep going at that point as it was, and even one more thing to contend with would have laid me out completely. Max's extracurricular fun could go ignored and undealt with so long as Max didn't know that I knew, and so I thanked Johnny for telling me and told him not to worry.

But a few months after that, my knowing became public, and I had to decide how to respond. Max's friend Frankie, a fellow import-export man, was in town from Boston, visiting us at our place. I'd never liked Frankie — bluff and loud, with little sense of when he might be wearing out his welcome or inconveniencing his hosts — but we'd put together a little party for him anyway with a few of our friends. There Frankie sat, in the middle of our sofa, duller by the moment, this strange, well-meaning malefactor, too merry, too mirthful, telling us all to join him in having another, never mind that he'd make us late for dinner, never mind that the next day most of us were expected to get our children to school or ourselves to the office. A cocktail pig hysterical with joy at the sight of free booze, that was Frankie, setting his cup wherever while rattling on. I had fairly freckled the face of the living room with coasters, but darling Frankie simply could not connect the dots.

I was whisking his martini from tabletop to more hospitable cork when he turned, quite drunk, to Max, and said, "Where's that little gal of yours, that Julia, the one you introduced me to last month? She really knows how to have fun."

And just like that, Max's infidelity was laid out before me, and before others. I could no longer proceed in the semblance of sweet obliviousness. I had to do something. React. I hated the situation, and I hated Frankie, and I hated Max, sitting there gasping after mis-swallowing his drink, and I hated how embarrassed and humiliated and absurd it made me, cast suddenly in some cinematic melodrama where the score hits the unflattering key of the woman wronged. We carried on as normal that evening — dinner, the theater, good-byes to Frankie — and afterwards Max swore that Julia meant nothing to him and he was sorry about Frankie bringing her up, but that I was the one for him and couldn't I find it in my heart to forgive.

I loathed him all over again for filling our bedroom with those shrill clichés, but I didn't fight him. I had no appetite for it; I lacked the strength. I said okay, okay, let's patch it up, and we set out on the circuitous scenic route to our inevitable destination of divorce.

I wrote Max I don't know how many letters and cards over the years after that last lunch — and he often wrote back. But I only saw him in person three more times: once apiece at Gian's graduations from high school and Bowdoin, and last of all at Max's funeral. He succeeded in dying before I did, too, preceding Julia on my list of fortunate people felled relatively early by heart attack.

I was the renowned wit, but it was Max, ultimately, who proved to have the better sense of timing.

10
BENEFACTORS

Why lie? In the days when I was an item on the society pages, I craved the light of those eyes upon me.

But I also wasn't sure whether I was happy with how they saw me. A hopeful symbol of wealth and success during the Depression years? A vain one? Hairbrush in hand, transfixed by my own reflection in the mirror?

Now, walking south from Grimaldi toward Delmonico's on a stomach full of Oreos and a head full of Chianti, I see my faint reflection in the glass of the dark windows I pass, and I want neither to stare nor to look away. I am just Lillian Boxfish, eighty-four or eighty-five. No one still alive can correct me.

If I wanted to take a shortcut from Madison Avenue to Broadway, which I can follow almost all the way to my destination, I'd diagonal my way through Madison

Square Park. But that place is in greater disrepair than I am. While I frequent it by day, at night it fills like a horrible candy box with pimps and hookers, with drug dealers and their clients. I do not know the means by which such suppliers handle their institutional advertising, but they clearly know what they're doing, for they never appear to have any shortage of business. No doubt having a motivated customer base helps.

By day, while on my walks, I still stop in Madison Square Park to take my lunch breaks, even though my breaks are entirely self-assigned. When I worked at R.H. Macy's the park was magnificent, a spot to sit and compose my verses on city life. Now, even by day, it comprises nasty little bites of the unsavory covered with litter, its lawn mostly bare. Teeming with the pigeons I can't help but love, prolific and filthy, cooing stupidly, reproducing, pooping — hopping fearlessly, oblivious among the hypodermics.

Whenever I eat my lunch there these days, I always think of and hope to see Wendy. About half the time I do. She and I met last summer, mid-July, hot and hazy, the air like a gauze bandage, tight and stifling.

Until that humid afternoon when Wendy spotted me, no one had told me I was beautiful for a long, long while. I noticed her first, actually, though I hadn't planned to say anything to her; rather, I meant simply to sit on my bench and watch her.

Even in a city populated by outsiders with bizarre magnetism, she felt extra compelling, stalking the edges of the park in a feline fashion that made me think of Phoebe, of the way a house cat hunts, so that one can't tell whether it's serious or only playing, or if it's sure itself.

Wendy was obviously a woman, but had a lean androgynous look, flat-chested in a white tank top and torn-up jeans. Her thick black hair, choppy and cropped at the nape, looked less styled than chewed on. She wore a huge Nikon camera on a strap around her neck, and she held it to her right eye with veiny hands, their fingernails painted a chipped black, taking picture after picture. But she was no tourist.

She saw me seeing her, and I, never one to feign shame in my interest in others, waved to her with my own hand: well-manicured in classic red, gold watch on my wrist. A summer linen suit encased the rest of me — because no one wants to see these arms and legs uncovered, least of all me. I wore sunglasses, Dior, from the 1960s, because by then I had come to prefer my

161

face half-obscured.

Wendy strode over and introduced herself, shaking my hand, very direct. When she spoke, her demeanor — forthright, Midwestern — contrasted with her feral appearance, and made me laugh.

"You're beautiful, Lillian," she said. "Especially when you smile like that. May I take your photograph?"

"Maybe," I said. "First, have a seat. Tell me, why would you want to do a thing like that?"

"Well," she said, perching on the edge of the bench, almost as a prelude to a pounce, "I'm a photographer. Professionally. I work in a studio, as an assistant, just south of here. But I'm also an artist. Trying to be, you know? I'm working on my portfolio. And to do that, I'm operating under the motto, 'I'm seeing beauty in less-obvious places, and that makes me a more interesting person.'"

"Ambitious," I said. "But your motto also damns me with faint praise, doesn't it?"

"Oh my goodness," she said. "No! I just mean, like, society's idea of beauty is really warped and limited, and you —"

"I'm joking," I said. "I'd be honored. Where are you from, Wendy?"

"Garrettsville, Ohio," she said, shrugging

in apology. "But I live in Chelsea."

"You're looking at a long-term resident of Murray Hill," I said. "I haven't been to Chelsea in ages. And I've never been to Garrettsville, Ohio, but I've heard of it. Hart Crane was from there. Do you know him? His work? He was a poet. Killed himself in the 1930s by swan diving off an ocean liner."

"I've heard of him, but I've never read his poems," she said. Then her eyes got wide and she asked, "Lillian, are you a poet?"

I liked the way she asked that — not "Do you write poetry?" or even "Do you *like* poetry?" but "Are you a poet?" For Wendy, one's art was one's identity, and everything else one did simply amounted to getting by. She was still quite young, I realized, and she hadn't been in the city very long.

"I am," I said. "But not a poet like Crane. Though I do admire his work. You should read his first book, *White Buildings* — although *The Bridge* seems more the fashion these days. I only understand every third word of his, but it doesn't matter. Me — my verses are less opaque."

"I'd love to read your poems sometime," said Wendy.

"That won't be so easy, I'm afraid, as all my books are out of print."

"Books?" Wendy put her hand — pale and

163

sturdy — on my linen sleeve. "Lillian, you write books?"

"I did," I said. "In my prime I was even a bit of a celebrity. Everyone read me. But in the latter-day world of poetry it seems that nobody wants to read somebody everybody reads, as Yogi Berra might put it. So I'm quite forgotten now."

I was pleased with that bon mot, but Wendy sped past without sparing it a second look. "Well, *you* must have copies," she said. "You could loan them to me, couldn't you?"

"I could, yes. If I ever see you again. But what would a young go-getter like you want with an old lady like me?"

As it turned out, she'd want plenty — and I can't say I'm displeased. Wendy is now one of my best, if most improbable, friends.

I round the corner of Madison Avenue to East Twenty-Third Street, skirting the south edge of the park, taking the long way to connect to Broadway. As I do, I can't help looking over my shoulder to see if Wendy might be in the park. She's not, of course; she has enough sense not to go there after dark.

And tonight, I remember — I know because she invited me — she and her husband are hosting a New Year's Eve bash for all their artist friends at their apartment in Chelsea.

Wendy is like that, now that she knows me. She treats me as if I'm not actually sixty years older than she. Her insistence on including me — her idea that an odd old woman might have any business ringing in 1985 amid her chic bohemian demimonde — is sweet and silly and fantastic. I'm quite touched.

When Gian and the grandkids were visiting last week, I had Wendy over to meet them, over coffee and hot cocoa. After she'd gone, Gian had remarked how happy he was that I had her in my life, and how she must seem almost like a daughter to me. That's a pretty sentiment, so I did not correct him. But the truth is, that is not what she feels like, and of that I am glad. She is my friend, not my child, and thus our rapport has been unfraught and egalitarian, unburdened by guilt or disappointment.

Gian, on the other hand, is my child, not my friend. I love him more than any other human who still breathes upon this planet, but one child — one constant emergency, one ritual madness, one wrecker and re-maker of myself — was and remains enough.

Crossing the street to continue south on Broadway, I don't even have to wait for the light, there's so little traffic. I jaywalk with impunity.

If something happened to me, who would see it?

If the Subway Vigilante were out and about on these same sidewalks, who would know it was him?

Wendy and I ended up going to lunch together the day we met. I invited her, and she hesitated, and I thought that maybe, as I had suspected, she didn't want to spend her years as a young artiste in the company of the aged. When I said as much — blunt, I know — she said no, it was because she didn't have any money. My treat, I told her, and still she shilly-shallied.

"What's the harm in a free egg salad sandwich?" I asked. "I'm going to take us to a deli, not the Ritz."

"I don't want to take advantage," Wendy said. "My husband — he's a painter — is always saying that we need to find patrons. Benefactors. People with money to collect and cultivate our art, you know? And that seems so sleazy to me."

"Accepting one free meal from a lonely old has-been won't put your integrity in peril," I said. "And your husband is right. One must hustle to make money, don't you think?"

"Lillian, you're hysterical," she said. "But what'll you get out of it?"

"Attention," I said, and off we went.

Wendy, whose Ohio parents raised her to be too humble, in my estimation, but just the right degree of courteous, worried that we should go somewhere nearby so I would not have to walk too far. I assured her that while I am not much of what I used to be, I am still a walker — that since everything else in my life is mostly gone, I just *am* in the city. I just like to *be* here.

As I pass the string of photography studios that line this block of Broadway — located here because it's decrepit and therefore cheap — I find myself imagining her New Year's Eve party in Chelsea. Loud strange music. Skinny youths in Dumpster-plucked clothes. Various substances stashed upon my arrival. Suspicious neighbors, in one or both senses of suspicious. And her husband, charming and venal. Or brilliant and petulant. Or moony and narcissistic. Wendy's husband.

I think her invitation was sincere.

But whom is she kidding? An octogenarian staying up until midnight to hoot ecstatically at the onset of another year?

Then again, what else have I got to do? It's not as though I have to wake up early tomorrow.

On Broadway the damp wind is cooler

and more assertive, and I laugh a little because I realize that this is exactly how I've been imagining Wendy's husband: cooler and more assertive.

She doesn't wear a wedding band, I've noticed. Then again, I do, and I haven't been married for almost three decades. Symbols, or their absence, do not always mean what they seem to symbolize.

Nevertheless, I suppose they always symbolize something.

I like presenting myself to Wendy — presenting myself as I want to be presented, and being received as such. Maybe I *will* stop by her party. We'll see.

168

11
FLEURS DE ROCAILLE

In my day I was great at parties. And let me say, there were great parties.

Even after the crash, a number of us in Manhattan just kept smashing along. We all had jobs, and thus a need to unwind and the money to burn in the unwinding. The skyscrapers to which we would all eventually become accustomed were either new then or still going up, getting high, getting higher, with some of us getting high along with them.

But me, I lived in a low neighborhood — in the low sixties on the Upper East Side. The neighborhood, long ago the site of the old Treadwell Farm, built up quickly after the Civil War, filling in with corny Italianate and French Second Empire confections, including mine, a four-story townhouse. I had the top floor. The place had no river view and no doorman, but it was a small oasis all the same, the street quiet and tree-lined. I'd been there since 1930, and although it was gorgeous, I was almost ready for a change. I'd move to Greenwich Village the following year, and that move would alter my life in ways I had vowed up and down never to let my life be altered.

One night in late August 1933 I threw an unforgettable party, maybe the best I had when I resided in that particular apartment. It was the party that caused Olive Dodd, my archrival and colleague at R.H. Macy's, not to speak to me outside of professional contexts for almost a solid year.

I invited Hattie, the downstairs neighbor, of course, to avoid complaint, and because the more the merrier. She worked at the main branch of the New York Public Library, and luckily for our harmonious neighborliness, she got all the peace and quiet she needed while laboring amid the stacks: A little racket on the weekend was fine by her. She certainly wasn't shushing anybody present that night.

I had pulled down the ladder so my guests could avail themselves of the stars and the streetlights and the breeze off the East River. Prohibition would end, finally, later that year, but that evening — just as anyone who enjoyed the night life had been doing since 1920 — we were filtering the booze in

170

through the loopholes.

My gentleman caller, for example — a square-faced man named Benjamin, who went by Bennie — had a physician's prescription that permitted him to take a pint of liquor home from the pharmacy every ten days. He arrived with one tucked under each arm, each package labeled "Jim Beam: For Medicinal Purposes Only."

I'd met him the week prior, while being interviewed by a society reporter about my ongoing reign as the highest-paid female advertising writer in the country, a story that journalists seemed never to tire of. Bennie had been the photographer.

I was happy to see Bennie's liquor, if a bit disenchanted by its packaging. The prescription trick worked, but it always struck me as smug, inelegant, the wrong kind of clever. Most of us preferred to get our booze from honest crooks, who tended to be nicer and more interesting. It's hard to deny that a willingness to risk prison imparts a certain magnetism in social settings.

Helen McGoldrick, ever golden, was in the kitchen, one of the thirty or so people who'd shown up to my flat. Though none of the guests was fat, they almost seemed so for being crammed into so small a space. I'd just taken a pass through the other rooms to encourage anyone whose dexterity and anxiety would allow them to pioneer the less populous territories of the fire escapes — mine and Hattie's, as she didn't mind.

As it was crowded, so was it convivial: friends and friends of friends gently embalming themselves in alcohol, curing themselves like wild game in cigarette smoke, being made astringent, citrused with grapefruit juice from cans — little fang marks on opposite sides to permit them to pour.

Helen's husband stood beside her, can opener in hand to do the vampiric puncturing. Helen, using the gin they'd brought, doled out generous drinks.

"With oranges and lemons more expensive all the time," she said, "there's nothing to do but mix the cocktails stronger."

She and Dwight Zweigert had gotten married in 1931, when she was thirty-one and he forty-seven. I liked him immensely, and I liked them together.

He had been married before, but his first wife had died. He had two daughters, seven and nine when he and Helen got hitched. Now eleven and thirteen, both girls were at the family abode that night, the Zweigert brownstone in the Village, babysitting one-year-old Merritt. Named for Helen's Southern patrician father back in Birmingham, he was the first and only child Helen would ever have to have. She doted duly upon him, but had no desire to spring off any further offspring, nor did Dwight want her to; the family budget and his middle age made three the limit.

When they'd first gotten involved, or rather when they'd first gotten serious, Helen gave each of his daughters a tick in the "pro" column of the list she always totted up in her head. "One and I'm done!" she'd said the night she told me that he'd proposed and she'd accepted. "That's all he'll want. All we can afford. I can deliver that."

Dwight was a left-winger of a committed, considered, not especially specific sort. He routinely broke bread with a hodgepodge of romantics, pacifists, communists, and Roosevelt liberals in an era — brief — when it seemed they all might find common cause. Such were the circles in which Dwight circulated. Such was the political butter of his daily bread. I found these pursuits silly, but harmless and not without charm. He worked as an art critic for *The Nation* and assorted little magazines. A still-sizeable though slightly melted berg of postcrash family money made the fees earned by his writing live-off-able, especially with Helen working, too.

R.H. Macy's, like all employers, did not permit women time off to push the next generation of little workers and customers into the world. So now Helen freelanced, cartooning and illustrating for women's magazines, many of them the same ones that published my verses.

A number of the writers and editors — and their dates — whom we knew from that world were in attendance that night, along with some of the snappier copywriters from R.H. Macy's, newer girls who worked under me who grasped the effervescence of the in-house style, and who had the joie part of joie de vivre down pat.

Though not among their number, also present — owing to my having been mannerly — was Olive Dodd, hangdog and predictably unescorted.

Early on, before I realized how joyless and jealous she had it in her to be, I had invited Olive to such gatherings as these, thinking we might hit it off outside the confines of the office. She was young and reasonably pretty, and she'd read all the right books, so I thought, sure, let's give this a go. She drank and she smoked.

But it turned out she was a narrow-minded prig. She decked herself in bohemian trappings because she felt she needed to; there was nothing genuine about it. As Gertrude Stein — whose writing Olive pretended to like — said of the city of Oakland, there was no there there.

I couldn't very well exclude her, though — not without being more hurtful than I meant to. Plus I couldn't very well go on decrying her affectations if I weren't prepared to stand by my own notions of propriety, could I? So invite her I did.

And Olive, to be sure, could have mustered the finesse to simply say thanks and then not actually inflict herself on the party. But there she was, wearing an evening dress of periwinkle blue and sipping a ginger ale that must have been half gin.

Extending hospitality to all, even to the most cloddish, truly is the basis of civilization. The fact that the most cloddish, having nothing better to do, always show up and spoil the party for everyone else probably spells civilization's ultimate doom.

Olive was a clod, and I was loath to suffer clods. To do the kind of ad writing that I did, and to be good at it, you couldn't just echo conventional opinion back at itself; you had to catch people by surprise. You had to bring something more to the party, so to speak. R.H. Macy's institutional advertising was not the height of the avant-garde, certainly — not like Olive's favorite desk prop Ms. Stein, for instance, or the artists whose work Dwight championed in the pages of his little magazines. But it wasn't the Sunday homily, either. That calibrated understanding was what Olive lacked, and that lack was what made her seek — and fail — to copy me. And it was sinister.

That evening, as ever, Olive had made herself up quite too much like the vamp. Unspeaking, she leaned against the kitchen counter watching Helen mix drinks.

In Olive's earshot, one of Helen's magazine friends, waiting for a cocktail, remarked, "It is true most men dislike looking at a drippy, blood-red, oleaginous pair of lips during dinner."

An office mate of Olive's and mine replied, "And prefer nails that don't remind them of Dracula, even when crimson claws are fashionable."

"It simply reminds them," said Helen's friend, receiving her glass tumbler, "of our old hot primitive instinct to trap ourselves a man."

And our colleague, receiving her own,

176

clinked glasses with her in a sarcastic toast, saying, "Ah, we women are savages at heart."

They went giggling to the living room to rejoin their dates. Bennie, mine, passed them on the way in, as Olive, happy to have been wounded, wound her way toward me to complain.

"The character, Lillian, of some of your guests leaves something to be desired," she said.

I could have apologized, but I was so tired of Olive.

Instead I said, "I prefer witty friends to friends of character."

That was a lie. I preferred friends who were witty *and* had character. But I wanted Olive to shut up, and the quickest course was to simply throw myself upon her poniard, knowing it to be sharp as a wet noodle. If shock was the way to stopper the drivel always rivering from her mouth, well, fine.

"This type of atmosphere is all right for a while," she said, gesturing around the crowded kitchen with sham nonchalance, "but eventually you won't find it so homey."

"Nothing ruins a good thing faster than a family atmosphere," I said.

She gave me a look that was meant to be cool and appraising — probably something she'd seen in a film. "You're a queer thing, Lillian," she said. "Surely every girl dreams of her wedding day."

I could see why she thought this; the desire was endemic to our set, though I did not share it. But I also thought she ought to try thinking for herself. The walls around the main portion of R.H. Macy's thirteenth floor went just partway to the ceiling, so all day, whenever I left my own office — which had a proper door — to walk through to find someone, I heard, as Olive did, the steady drone of colleagues' lives lived by telephone: ranting to husbands or raving to beaux.

"Sure," I said. "Lace and satin and showers of rice. Nice if it stops you from thinking of the years ahead, when you'll be boiling that rice into mush to feed a screaming infant while your husband's out on the town, trying to find someone new."

Something changed in Olive's face; all her studied mannerisms drifting in different directions. When she spoke again, her usual breathy coo was gone — gone low and harsh. I thought that, for all her yapping, I might be hearing her real voice for the first time.

"I don't buy it," she said. "That you don't want a family. Is this all there is, Lillian?

Drinking on fire escapes? It's frivolous, I think. It's just childish. The most successful woman in advertising, the red-headed poet princess of Midtown — cold comforts when you're fifty and dried up and have no one to show your clippings to, don't you think?"

Here's a secret about me: My entire life, whenever I've found myself under attack by a relative stranger, or someone who means little to me, my reaction — which I gather is uncommon — has been to grow calmer, more controlled. I would have made a fine gunfighter, I suppose. Born too late! As usual.

"You don't have to buy it, Olive," I said, exhaling a smoke ring to the side of her head. "We're not at the office. I don't plan on selling anything until Monday morning."

She tore the smoke ring with her index finger, nearly losing her balance in the process. "Everyone thinks you're so smart," she said. "*You* think you're so smart. You're so funny. But the truth is that you're the biggest cynic of all time."

"I think you've had enough to drink, Olive," I said. "Maybe you don't quite re-alize what you're saying."

"I know what I'm saying." She took an-other sip and smeared a lurid lipstick glyph down her chin. "You think you're so precious, living here in the city. Scoffing at love."

"Love, Olive, is not what I scoff at," I said. "What I scoff at is rank sentimentalism: the silly, simplistic idea of love that advertisers — including us — use to sell everything from soup to soap to subjugation. As for the city, Olive, I live here because I like it."

"You like it because it's fashionable."

"No, Olive," I said. "I like it for the *same reason* that it's fashionable. Namely, that it's pretty swell."

I was exasperated at having to explain myself to her, but unable to stop. I suppose in a sense I was happy to be fighting with her, freed from the need to hide my dislike and glad at the chance to voice thoughts I'd long harbored but never had the call to speak — because no one ever challenged me. Everything Olive was saying, I knew, was something that my mother also believed but had long since lost the temerity to say. But Olive — poor Olive. She was like one of those miserable dogs that it takes more effort *not* to kick than to kick.

"This may be hard for you to understand," I went on, "but I'd rather live here in the city, in a microscopic apartment — like, for instance, this one, my home, where, as you might wish to recall, you are a guest — than ride a train to and from the suburbs. If you enjoy living with your parents out in Westchester County, then what do I care? And why should I do the same?"

"You'll end up there one day, I'll bet," she said. "You'll have a house in the country and a husband and a baby bouncing on the lawn, and you won't remember a word you said to me tonight."

"Olive, do you know the meaning of the term idée fixe? Because you, right now, are practically illustrating the textbook definition."

"Stop being so witty," she said.

"All right. I'll be direct: Live in the suburbs if it makes you happy. But you're *not* happy, Olive. All of us can see that. And might that be due at least in part to the fact that the suburbs put young ladies at a cruel disadvantage where fun with the local boys is concerned? Here's some free advice: Make an honest assessment of the choices you've made before you look askance at somebody else's."

I had it on good authority that Cornelius, one of the male copywriters at R.H. Macy's, had asked Olive to a movie recently, and she had refused. She had used the suburbs as an excuse, when really she was merely waiting on a juicier plum to fall her way. In addition to an excess of parental chaperon-age, Olive suffered from the condition of being a snob.

"I *like* it there!" she said, raising her voice even as I'd been keeping mine level. "Any boy with proper intentions will respect me enough to come see me there."

Boy? I thought. Olive, you must be every minute of thirty years old.

But I didn't say it. By that point, of course, everyone else in the kitchen had fallen silent to listen, including Bennie, who was now at my side. I could feel him tensed, ready to join the argument on my behalf — *Now see here . . .* — and I didn't want that. "Let's just wrap this up, Olive," I said. "You love your bucolic daffodils and buttercups. I prefer my flowers in proximity to cement. Agree to disagree, yes?"

I offered a hand, but she refused it.

"You can't even for one instant stop being cute, can you?" she said, slamming her empty glass on the counter, its forlorn lime wedge leaping from the rim to the floor. "It's disgusting!"

With that, she flounced from the room in a cloud of crumpled periwinkle satin, leaving a wake of mouths agape behind her.

"Oh my stars," said Helen. The room felt flabbergasted, but sympathetic to my side.

"What an outrageous outburst. She'd been bottling that up for quite some time."

"Are you all right?" asked Dwight.

"Quite," I said, to him, to the room. "Chalk it up to a free show. Stick around now that it's over. Don't feel that you have to go home, especially as it just got a bit more roomy in here."

"Let's get you some air," said Bennie, taking my elbow.

I didn't feel embarrassed, but I felt a little strange, so I let him guide me to the roof and its relative privacy. He put his arm around my shoulder, and we looked out at the sparkling city.

"So," he said, changing the subject with delicacy, "when you did that interview for the *Times*, you may recall that I and my camera came in at the end. Therefore I missed the most interesting parts. Your career achievements. Your biographical particulars."

"Well," I said, "you *could* just read all that in the paper."

He grinned. "Given the state of journalism I thought it better just to ask you. What kind of advertising do you do, exactly, for Macy's?"

I didn't feel too keen on talking about work, as it reminded me of Olive, but I did

183

appreciate his taking an interest, so I explained.

"Institutional advertising," I said. "That means ads dealing generally with store policy and service and amenities, et cetera. Timely ads arising from hurricanes, Labor Day, spring, July Fourth, et cetera. Promotional ads dealing with assortments of merchandise for various departments, and also all magazine ads, et cetera. I'm the voice of the store. But the store's voice is not my voice. I help everyone under me to also sound unlike themselves, but rather like R.H. Macy's, and then to step back and disappear so the store stands alone at center stage."

Most men were not impressed with my career but rather saw it as a diversion — a novelty that I would cease to find novel once they were done wooing me. They'd seek to give me the gift of not having to work anymore, not realizing I'd abhor few gifts more than that.

But Bennie, looking out at the lit windows of the newly sprung skyscrapers, said, "Ah — the way a crane creates and then erases itself from the skyline."

And I knew then that I'd be going to bed with him that night, after the guests had left us in quiet.

■ ■ ■ ■

The following Monday, on my walk to the office, when it was already so sticky that it felt like being underwater, I was not hungover, exactly. For one thing, I didn't get that way. For another, the party, obviously, had been on Saturday. But even my shoes felt glum and protesting. When I thought of arriving at R.H. Macy's and having to see Olive, I felt tired and flat down to the arches of my feet.

To my surprise, the thirteenth floor of R.H. Macy's that day ended up sounding like a symphony from which the conductor had struck one discordant and out-of-time instrument dumb. The fight seemed to have marked the merciful end of Olive's and my laborious attempts at friendship. From that point on, she left me alone — watching me from afar, but not bothering me, aside from whatever minimal communication was required to get our jobs done.

"What neighborhood cat has absconded with Olive's tongue?" asked Chester, an astute boss of the kind who would notice such changes.

"If I knew that," I said, "I would have brought a tin of salmon for it."

■ ■ ■ ■

Olive and I didn't have another run-in until just under a year later, June of 1934, when Bennie was but a distant, albeit pleasant, memory.

It had been a wiltingly busy spring at R.H. Macy's, and I felt in need of a present to perk myself up. I settled on a new perfume for summer. As soon as I could, as soon as it came out on this side of the Atlantic, I bought myself a bottle of Fleurs de Rocaille, a well-blended explosion of blooms with a solid wooden base — cedar and sandalwood and musk at the core. A composition that at the time was not unlike my own: feminine, but hard.

The day after I got a bottle on my lunch break and came back to the office wearing it, my grinning enemy Olive — though she could ill afford it — did the same: purchased a bottle on her lunch break and came back to the thirteenth floor of R.H. Macy's having practically bathed in it. I recognized it in an instant — though it smelled, on her, sour, like the sour grapes she feasted on daily.

She saw me smelling it. Her reaction, flushed and flustered, was that of a plain girl caught in flagrante delicto with the beau of the homecoming queen. A circumstance any civilized person would regard as an occasion for shame was, for her, a tiny triumph — what my profession, years after I left it, would come to call a "peak experience."

"I couldn't resist," she said, breaking the silence she'd held for a steady ten months. "I didn't get it because of you. I read about it weeks ago. That it was coming here, to America. And I knew I had to have it. Just for the name. Fleurs de Rocaille."

Eyes closed, dreamy sigh heaved.

"Just for the name?" I said. "No other reason?"

"Lillian, really," she said, eyes rolling skyward. "That was just an expression. I don't need to defend myself, but if you *must* know, *first* it was for the name. Next it was for how lovely it smells on me. Third is because the bottle is so pretty. And fourth is just because I felt like it."

"The rule of threes, Olive," I said, "does not just apply to writing copy. Always limit your reasons to three, the number of greatest credibility. Cite more and people will assume that you're fabricating. Often correctly."

"Hey, Lily," said Chester, coming up behind me. "Where's the damn copy?"

"Right here, you sweet-talker," I said, grateful that his good-natured question had interrupted our conversation, giving me the last word and an occasion to return to my work.

As Chester and I walked away from Olive's desk, I could feel her eyes on the back of my suit, like a child with a magnifying glass trying to set ants on fire. I ignored her and felt the fire grow hotter. I breathed in: floral, woody, aldehydic — a smell I would always associate from that point on with rosy serenity in the face of irrational hate.

As I sat in Chester's office and listened to his revisions of the work I'd done that morning on our new campaign, I thought about how Olive, even after years, still did not understand the most basic principles of what we did. Good advertising had to be genuine, joyful, unforced. To write informal copy, we had to *be* informal — to forget motives and mechanisms for a moment and simply speak to the public in the voice we might use to greet an acquaintance encountered on the sidewalk. The instant Olive took pen in hand, she stiffened up. She wrote drafts that left her humiliated because she permitted herself to be humiliated, revealed as fundamentally phony. As Chester tore through my first drafts with abun-

188

dant blue-pencil edits, I felt no humiliation. That was the process. Nobody's first cracks were perfect. Olive thought mine were, but she didn't see how hard I worked. How I loved this job, but how it wasn't easy for me.

Especially — though I hated to admit it to myself — lately. My mind was on other things, like my upcoming move to the Village. I was excited about that, truly. But increasingly I'd come to wonder if this was it. Though my achievements — professional, literary — were sweet, it was hard not to be conscious of the gaps between these successes and what I'd imagined of them, and hard, too, to see what route to take now that I had won almost everything I had wanted. From the peak, of course, all paths lead down.

I was still at the top of my advertising game. Still making plenty of money. And it was a glorious summer, so far, in the city, with liquor once again flowing freely.

But recently, even on the hottest nights, I couldn't fall asleep without being covered up, couldn't quite rest without at least the lightest sheet settled lightly over me. In my mind, I'd come to see it as the physical remedy for a vulnerability I'd begun to feel — a material attempt to ward off my own

189

light sheet of anxiety, ever-present, ever-covering.

12
A FIREMAN'S AXE AND A
DRACULA CAPE

In certain instances, walking alone in Manhattan is actually safer at night.

Passing by the Strand, for example, at Twelfth and Broadway. I usually walk past that bookstore with intense ambivalence: delight because I have been frequenting it since the 1930s, when it was over on Fourth Avenue, just one among nearly fifty similar shops; dread because on more than one occasion in the past two decades I have found my own poetry collections derelict on the sidewalk carts, on sale for mere cents, and with no one watching over them because if they get stolen, well, who cares? At night, at least, the carts have been rolled away and there's no chance I'll be confronted with evidence of my grim literary fate.

The Strand is something like two miles behind me now. I am making good time, nearing Lower Manhattan. Feeling the simple satisfaction of a well-executed plan, as I am close to Delmonico's and beginning to feel peckish.

Broadway takes me west of Little Italy, but among my fellow pedestrians I find many hints of its closeness: dapper hats and open collars, boxes of pastry wrapped tightly in twine, a brash and urgent music in voices — both Italian and Chinese, who increasingly are the actual inhabitants of the neighborhood. I think of how many times I came here with Max to meet his parents — when we were first involved, and also when they'd visit the city on weekends to see Johnny, their only grandchild. Back when I met Max, I was surprised and disappointed that his parents didn't reside in Little Italy, but, rather, in New Jersey — Rutherford, where they'd been for years, Max living with them. Little Italy, I learned, was really Little Naples, and Max's parents were northerners, Milanese. They also had the deeply held, received idea — received from friends and neighbors, and the parents of friends and neighbors, who remembered a time when Mulberry Street was the worst of Manhattan's slums — and also, to be sure, received from advertising — that success meant to pass through the city quickly and settle in the suburbs.

Within a couple of blocks, the foot traffic

has thinned almost to nothing. This part of the walk — approaching the financial district, emptied for the holiday — feels like passing through a ghost town or the backlot of a movie studio. I am the only moving figure in sight.

Passing the grand French Renaissance exterior of city hall, I am reminded of good manners. Max and I got married there. He was a Catholic, I an Episcopalian, and it was easier just to do it that way, civilly and with a nondenominational party for both of our families after, rather than trying to unify the two faiths. Plus we were able to save the money that a more stately wedding would have cost and use it to take a boat to Italy.

The funny part, the manners part, is that I was working on an etiquette book at the time: a guide that I had been invited by the publisher — thanks to the success of my verses, and to my prominence as a writer for R.H. Macy's — to compose. Helen was illustrating. We called it *Little Better than Beasts: A Guide to Rudeness and How to Avoid It,* and all of her drawings were of anthropomorphic animals. In the chapter on weddings, I advised blushing brides such as myself to work hard to reconcile the families but also to recognize — as I had — when such a reconciliation would not be possible, and to navigate the differences with grace.

For though I was raised Protestant, my true religion is actually civility. Please note that I do not call my faith "politeness." That's part of it, yes, but I say *civility* because I believe that good manners are essential to the preservation of humanity — one's own and others' — but only to the extent that that civility is honest and reasonable, not merely the mindless handmaiden of propriety.

I suppose I came to hold this belief for the same reason I came to work so hard: Civility and work gave me, respectively, a rationale and an opportunity for evading my family, my mother in particular. Work always provided an excuse not to see them when I didn't want to, and work always kept me from being indebted to them.

My mother understood the world to be a place where one's behavior was determined by rules, and rules determined by beholdenness. That understanding is not mine. If there are to be rules, they must be articulable and defensible, like etiquette. I do not do anything simply because my family did it. I do things because they make sense, and because they are elegant. Solutions of style have a greater moral force than those of obligation.

You could, of course, read all about this in my preface to *Little Better than Beasts,* were that book not long out of print. If fortune smiles, perhaps one day you'll come across a cheap copy on the sidewalk outside the Strand — one mute tirade among many.

About six blocks from Delmonico's I pause at Cortlandt Street, because Cortlandt Street always gives me pause. It used to be small and dense — full of trade — until they shut it down to build the World Trade Center.

It went by the name of Radio Row before the Port Authority — that practically paramilitary factotum of the odious Robert Moses — demolished it all in 1966, citing eminent domain. Social priorities are always changing, but these changes sadden me even when they don't affect me directly. Good-bye, Radio Row. Good-bye days when men — mostly men — came down to Cortlandt Street to comb the wholesalers in search of replacements for broken components that might Lazarus their radios, resurrect the dead machines. Max used to bring Johnny down here. But people don't repair very much these days.

By now I have come to appreciate the Twin Towers, even though I thought them ugly at first, boxy and rectangular and need-lessly huge. While they were being con-structed, somebody, I can't remember who, called them soulless and inhospitable to hu-man use: a pair of glass and metal filing cabinets on a colossal scale. In spite of myself, I have always found their gigantism majestic, and now I esteem them, too. If some latter-day Moses ever displaces them — their current tenants' arcane shifting of cash and commodities someday rendered as quaint as the radio scrappers' labor, sup-planted by robots, satellites, who knows what — then I suppose I would feel their absence much as I do that of other already absented parts of my city. Dully but not quite fully gone. A pair of phantom limbs.

I am standing there, north of Liberty Park Plaza, looking up at the Towers, when someone barks at me.

"Excuse me, ma'am," he says, in a bass-drum boom. "Excuse me. Hey, lady!"

The voice is close, but I don't see anyone on the street, and for a beat I'm confused — a feeling I hate for its resemblance to senility. Then I see he's yelling from the rolled-down window of a long limousine.

I have Mace in my purse — a Christmas present from Gian — but I do not bother to reach for it. The man looks harmless. He

196

pulls his heavy car to the curb, clicks on a light above his head to better show himself, and we regard each other through his open window. He is black and has a mustache as dapper as Dashiell Hammett's, and his eyes are wide, brown, and kind beneath his chauffeur cap. He is wearing a tuxedo, out of professional obligation, of course, but I admire how put together he is, all the same.

"Didn't mean to scare you," he says over the idling engine.

"I'd hate to see what you'd do if you did," I say.

"I just thought you might be looking for a cab. Are you?"

"That's thoughtful of you," I say. "But no. No, thank you. Besides, you look more like an extravagance than a cab. Very fancy. And strange to see you out here tonight — I can't imagine many people are working late on New Year's Eve. Isn't the stock exchange closed tomorrow?"

"It is," he says. "But my guy, the guy I just dropped at his office, is a commodities trader. I guess there's some shit going down in Tokyo, and he's got to be on top of it. That's a quote. Excuse my French."

"That's all right," I say. "What's your name?"

"Skip," he says. "My real name's Paul, but

nobody except my Aunt Kitty calls me that. How about you?"

"Lillian," I say. "And thanks again. But like I said, I'm not looking for a ride. Also, don't you have to take your trader home? Or to some New Year's Eve orgy?"

"As a matter of fact, I thought I would," he says. "But he just sent word that he'll need a few hours, so they're sending me uptown. He'll call the service later. Now it seems kind of wasteful to drive all the way back alone."

"I thought wastefulness and greed were the driving engines of Wall Street."

"I can't dispute that, Lillian," says Skip. "But please bear in mind that just because I am *on* Wall Street does not mean I am *of* it."

"Fair enough," I say. "I'm sorry to disappoint you, Skip, but I'm doing fine on foot."

"Well, maybe you ought to be looking for a lift," he says. "It's getting colder out, finally. And the city's dangerous. Just over there is the Chambers Street station, where that Subway Vigilante fled to. And you, well, you're —"

"Old?" I say. "That is a fact. But I'm all right."

And I pause, torn, as I often am, between wanting to tell the truth — to impress Skip

198

with my self-sufficiency — and not wanting to be perceived as crazy: some nutty old lady too far around the bend to care for herself. Erring on the side of truth and pride, I add:

"I've walked all the way from Murray Hill, and I'm almost to Delmonico's. I'm not ready to give up the satisfaction of making it there under my own steam. At my age, I need to take my thrills where I can."

"Murray Hill," says Skip, shaking his head. "Damn."

"Yes," I say, and decide I might as well toss in a lie, just in case. "I'll be right on time to meet the people I'll be dining with. My family. We have an 8:30 reservation."

"Come on, Lillian," says Skip. "You remind me of my Aunt Kitty. She's tough — can't tell her nothing. You've practically made it. Why not call good enough good enough? It's so close, I'll take you there for free."

"Has anyone ever told you how persistent you are?" I say.

"I've just seen some freaky things in this city, Lillian," he says. "I wouldn't feel right if I didn't try to help you out. The other day — check this out — the other day, up on the south end of Central Park, I saw a seven-foot-tall dude with a fireman's axe and a Dracula cape. He ran right into the park. Broad daylight. Families around and everything. The cape was from a kid's costume. Looked like a dishtowel tied around his neck. He wasn't wearing anything else. The city's getting fuller of degenerates by the day."

"That is an excellent story, Skip," I say. "But we are nowhere near Central Park. I'll be okay. And besides, how do I know you're not a degenerate yourself?"

He gets out his livery license and holds it out the window. "Seriously?" he says. "A degenerate with his own limo?"

"A very motivated degenerate," I say, and he laughs. "I don't really think that, Skip, but hopefully you see my point, yes? That I am somewhat sharper than you thought at first?"

"Point made, Lillian," he says. "Good talking with you. I hope you have a good dinner."

"Thanks, Skip," I say. "Thanks for stopping, and for trying. Happy New Year."

"You too," he says, rolling up the window, driving slowly away.

As I make my way south on William Street, the final block before I turn onto Beaver, I don't know how triumphant to feel about my victory. I could count my conversation with Skip as proof that I haven't lost it; that I can still be persuasive. Or it could just be that I'm stubborn, and that Skip — sizing me up in my blue hat, my mink coat, my mustard-yellow Coloralls — decided there's just no effective way to persuade the insane.

I have blind spots, like anybody. My biggest one is myself: how people perceive me. I suppose that's a common enough affliction — otherwise shops would stop stocking mirrors — but it's one that particularly galls me, because I'm generally quite good at guessing what people think. My fastidiousness of dress, my on-going attention to fashion, my occasional panic buying of discontinued cosmetics: These could all be taken as hyperawareness of my appearance, but in fact they signify its opposite.

A gust of wind blows over the Hudson, intensified by the jet effect of passing between the Towers, and it carries the night's first hint of real cold. I march on toward my destination, recalling a fight I had once with my mother, back in the 1940s, when Johnny was a baby, and she was up from D.C. to help me take care of him.

She accused me of having a thwarted sense of superiority. Said that was the cause of all my present unhappiness. I had a high degree, she said, of linguistic mastery, as well as an intuitive understanding — nuts and bolts, nontheoretical — of psychology.

"Those qualities are like two great swords that just cut away anything in your path, Lily," she said. "You're *different* from everyone else. All the rules and emotions and obligations that guide most of us through life — they're invisible to us. They're natural, like breathing. But they're visible to you. And you use that to manipulate people."

I couldn't argue. For years, that was how I did my work at R.H. Macy's: If I understood better than you did yourself why you thought or did or wanted something, then I could control you. Not in any kind of dramatic way — like something out of *The Manchurian Candidate* — but enough to get myself and my employer into your head, to give us a slight edge, enough to turn a profit. That was my job. You would find yourself in the department store, and you would not necessarily know *why* you had come there, but only that you were going to buy some merchandise that was going to make you feel better.

My mother did not make this observation as a compliment. But that skill — and it *is* a skill; not, as she suggested, some mental defect or weakness of character — was not something that I could simply turn off, even after motherhood ended my tenure at R.H. Macy's and left me with few productive uses for it. I still can't. Everywhere I look, I see people being manipulated: wheedled out of their cash through their vulnerabilities and anxieties. The problem, as I started to notice after I'd had Johnny, was that I had always believed myself to be exempt from that sort of manipulation. But I wasn't — as the empty package of Oreos in my kitchen waste bin will testify. And for a long time, that made me very angry.

It happened only rarely, but I always found it so frustrating whenever my mother was right.

13
A FLAW IN THE DESIGN

It is possible to stay indoors during a storm and end up struck by lightning all the same.

Generally, I went outside on my lunch breaks at R.H. Macy's, especially in the summer, to walk and to write. But this particular August day it was raining, an absolute torrent, so I opted to stay in and run a small errand in the store. I still wound up practically knocked down by the thunder outside.

I needed a new rug for my new Greenwich Village apartment, and I ended up acquiring the salesman, as well. That day, Friday, August 3, 1934, I met and fell in love with Max, with Massimiliano Gianluca Caputo, with the head rug buyer for R.H. Macy's, with my future husband and the father of my child.

My new place was on the top floor, the only floor I ever wanted to live on, not having upstairs neighbors being the key to a long and happy life of city dwelling. But to *have* a courteous neighbor, of course, one must *be* a courteous neighbor, so I wanted to cover my living room floor with a carpet — beautiful enough to stare at every day, thick enough to deaden my and my guests' footsteps over the heads of the tenants below.

The rug department was on the seventh floor, and I took the stairs from the institutional advertising department on the thirteenth, the weather slapping and rattling the windowpanes all the way down.

The electrified air reminded me of a performer I'd seen months earlier, at a down-at-the-heel circus that some down-at-the-heel newspaper had thought would be amusing to send me to. She was a whip cracker, Austrian or German, wearing a sagging sequined corset that I feared would not sustain her modesty for the duration of the act. As she went to work destroying a succession of increasingly tiny paper targets at increasingly improbable angles, my skepticism waned until I was transfixed, until the tension was such that I thought I might cry out in terror. For her finale she took up a whip in each hand and knit herself into the middle of an earsplitting maelstrom that I was certain could only end with her maimed or collapsed. And then it was over: She curtsied and made way for a clown and three dingy poodles. I had missed it. My question remained unanswered: how to stop?

The rug department — with its large, flat wares all either stacked on the floor or dangling from the walls — presented itself as a clearing in the jungle of R.H. Macy merchandise, and I felt oddly exposed as I walked in. Nevertheless, I got swiftly to business: My eyes fell on a hand-knotted Algerian rug, patterned and vibrant and seemingly made for the space I needed it to fill. I asked the clerk the price, certain that my salary put it within reach. But the figure he quoted halted me.

"Well now," I said. "That's steep enough to worry my hardworking-girl conscience. What can you say to convince me?"

"Nothing, I'm afraid," said the young man, thin and pale, his slicked-back hair the wan color of straw. "But we've got a guy who can tell you any and everything you'd ever want to know. Just one moment, please."

He walked off toward the back, calling "Max? Max, you back there?"

I didn't believe in love at first sight. In fact, as I would soon be reminded by seem-

206

ingly every literate person in New York, I had written and published more than a few poems lampooning the very idea of it. But one need not believe in something for it to happen anyway.

That was my first thought when the clerk returned with Max. Handsome. About my height, and I was tall. A strong-jawed, tan, and beautiful man, polished and attractive, but not too perfect. His suit was impeccable, but his hair — thick, black — and his tie shared a slightly rumpled quality, like an unmade bed. An invitation. Touchable.

He extended a hand, warm and strong, and his shake was like a glove — not too tight, not too lengthy — and I didn't want to let go.

"Max Caputo," he said. "Head rug buyer. Miss — ?"

"Lillian," I said. "Lillian Boxfish. I work upstairs, in advertising."

"You're Lillian Boxfish?" he said. Not standing too close, but still I could smell him, the best-smelling man I'd ever smelled in my life, like black tea and orange rind and something spicy.

"My reputation precedes me?" I said.

"Indeed it does," he said, holding out the in-house newsletter that had just been released for August. "I was just reading about you — I was in the back, sitting down for lunch. Have you seen this yet?"

I was about to tell him that I had — that in fact I'd done two rounds of edits for the folks in personnel — but he was already reading aloud. I was charmed by this: He seemed somehow to sense that this would not mortify me. Or perhaps it just never occurred to him that it might.

"Listen," he said. *"Time was when advertisers didn't jest about such sacred things as merchandise. But Lillian Boxfish of our Advertising Department thought that a pea sheller was a funny little contraption, so why not joke about it?"*

"That's me," I said, cheeks pink at his enthusiasm.

"They should have run a photograph," he said. "So everyone could see that you're as pretty as you are hilarious. But listen to me, running on. You had a question?"

I didn't especially care anymore about the carpet, but I wanted to hear him keep talking in his raspy New York accent; I made myself say, "Yes, I did. This carpet here is a dear little thing and the price reflects that. Can you tell me why?"

"Your taste, Miss Boxfish, is right in line," he said, stepping closer; I had to fight the urge to lean against him. "That's the one

I'd pick. In fact, I picked out that merchant on our last buying trip to North Africa. It's a Berber. Sheep wool mostly, maybe a little goat, maybe a little camel, all with an eye toward high durability. Entirely handmade, and it traveled all the way here from the sands of the Sahara. It's from a town called Malika where the carpets are the thickest and most colorful. Other cities have product of equal quality, but they're more mono-chrome. I can assure you, this carpet will last you a lifetime."

"Thank you, Mr. Caputo," I said, im-pressed at his knowledge, impressed at his travels, and impressed at how unpretentious he seemed about both. "And you can call me Lillian. I'm almost sold, but what about this?"

I pointed to a small but unmistakable break in the geometric design.

"Lillian, I don't think anyone's ever noticed that without my pointing it out," he said. "Each one is woven with a flaw."

I looked up at him, skeptical, but his bright black eyes were guileless. "If each one is woven with a flaw on purpose," I said, "then we can't really call them flaws, can we?"

Max smiled. "The mistakes aren't on purpose," he said. "The mistakes are mis-

209

takes. Choosing one flaw to leave uncorrected — that's on purpose. It's so that the weaver can't be accused of excess pride in his work."

We stared at each other for what seemed like an indecorous interval. "Well," I said, "the pride you take in your work, while not excessive, is certainly contagious, Max," I said. "I'll take it. With whom should I speak to arrange the delivery?"

"You're speaking with him," he said.

"Really?" I said. "The head buyer also flies around with the magic carpets?"

"Not generally," he said. "But you just bought the rug of a lifetime, which I know is not something you're likely to do every week. So I can't just let you walk out of here — I have to see you again. Beauty and humor have intruded upon the path of duty."

"Is that a fact?" I said, unable to conceal my enchantment.

"It may be forward of me," he said. "But when something feels right, it's right. And it feels right to ask: Are you seeing anyone?"

"No, I'm not."

"Would tonight be all right to schedule the delivery?" he said. "And then would you do me the honor of letting me take you to dinner after?"

I was just as astonished as Chester, my boss, would be later, saying this had to be the first time a rug buyer was given away free with the purchase of an R.H. Macy's rug.

Max was my favorite type of person: He was funny, and he had character. He was also something else, which was a type of person I never encountered, or maybe never encountered anymore, not since my ways had become — if I admitted it — rather set. In an instant I'd caught myself imagining what my circle of friends might make of him, which prompted me to realize how small that circle had become: small and getting smaller with each wedding invitation and birth announcement. And now here was Max, a living reminder of the city I once knew or never knew, a city of accidents, a city that gathered the world to itself.

So what else could I do but say:

"Yes, that would be wonderful. I'm at 25 Fifth Avenue. In the Village. Top floor. See you at seven?"

We had one of those Friday dates that turned into an entire weekend, and by the end of it I loved him so much my larynx ached. Vulnerable love, incorrigible love. Love in which he was both the nausea and the sodium bicarbonate.

I arrived home at six and stripped to my slip so as not to get my dress dirty as I moved my furniture to the living room's perimeter, the better for Max to lay down the carpet.

Then I dressed again, reapplied my Fleurs de Rocaille, and fixed my hair so it was, as Helen always put it, as shiny and tidy as my bank account. And then I waited. I sat on the davenport shoved against the wall and tried to read a book of poems I had picked up in the stacks at the Strand. It was *Harmonium* by Wallace Stevens, and I had been relishing it.

But my mind was like a puppy that wouldn't remain on the sidewalk, and I got tired of tugging the leash to bring it back. I closed the book and looked out the window at the sky, now clear, washed by the rain, and let the breeze through the screen rush against my face. I resisted getting up and pacing.

Lucky for me he was punctual, and the buzzer sang out at seven o'clock sharp. Lucky for him the building had an elevator — the first such one I'd lived in — so getting the rug up all the way to my floor was not so horrible.

"Lillian," he said. "You look lovely. And

212

smell like a garden of exotic flowers. I hate to seem a brute on this occasion, just having met you and all. But would you mind awfully if I took off my suit jacket and dress shirt? Just so I can work."

"Mind? I'd be sadder if you didn't," I said, and he laughed and set about the task in his bright white undershirt.

He was quick but not reckless, controlled but not deliberate. He was *decisive* — a man who didn't doubt himself. His prowess came from grace as much as brawn; he had a boxer's build, not a strongman's. His doffed shirt revealed at his chest and armpits what I judged to be an entirely reasonable quantity of hair.

He saw me looking; he meant for me to watch him, and I didn't turn away. I just bided my time with a few mildly provocative and entirely unnecessary adjustments to my makeup and wardrobe, returning the favor by giving *him* something to look at — and reminding him that while it might have been his rug, it was still *my* apartment.

"There we are," he said, looking down at his handiwork. "Rolled out flat in no time flat. Want me to put the furniture back?"

"Sure," I said, preferring an orderly room to a disorderly one, and also preferring to watch his muscular arms moving the pieces

213

into their places rather than doing it myself. "I've always written ads about R.H. Macy's' outstanding customer service, but I had no idea how right I was."

Afterwards he took me out for Italian food in Little Italy. He knew a place. Of course he knew a place — all our time together he knew a place for everything, and I adored that about him.

I told him what I wanted and he did the ordering.

As we ate pasta and drank red wine, I thought of the etiquette book I was writing and had to remind myself of my own advice to love-struck misses: "Do not gush or drape yourself about his neck. Do not engage in an excess of rosy diffidence and delicate reserve, but also do not engage in too brash or suggestive a deportment."

His parents were from Milan, he said, but he was born in New Jersey. After finishing at the Park School in Rutherford, he graduated from the University of Florence in 1924 and the University of Switzerland in 1926. He had been with R.H. Macy's for eight years, entering the rug department of the Manhattan store three-and-a-half years ago, having previously been in charge of the firm's foreign buying offices in Italy. Unbidden, my mind did the arithmetic and found

214

that I was seven years older than he: thirty-four to his twenty-seven.

It may sound gauche, but one reason I liked him so much was because so many people would think him a little beneath me. I was constantly being approached by men who were securely set in the world: soon-to-be titans of industry, and famous actors. *I would deign to pull you up to my level, hardworking girl,* was a theme they all played in one key or another. I always had a complete revulsion for that.

What was so appealing about imagining a future with Max was that I stood to do as much for him, if not more, than he stood to do for me — at least financially. We could live well in the city and take trips and have a summer home, and he would not only let but quite likely need me to keep working, and I would revel in that.

And I *had* been imagining a future with him, even as he'd worked shirtlessly in my apartment. I suppose it was something I'd done before with other men, but never so readily. It was as if his very unlikeliness as a match — young, striving, freshly American — made it easier to contemplate: less of a trap, more of a game. What would Mother think? It was delicious.

"My dad's in the import business, too,"

said Max, wiping his lips with a napkin. "Owner of Caputo Company, Inc., over on Hudson Street. Dad would really like your selling style, I think. The way you're so funny."

"That's sweet," I said. "Do you want to know the trick? This is a trade secret, so I hope you can be trusted. The trick is that you can't joke about merchandize indiscriminately. Inexpensive items can be treated with a tongue placed more freely in the cheek than expensive ones can. It's all right to say something smart about a nice homey shower curtain, while it wouldn't seem quite decent to joke about a Chippendale chair. You don't see banks waxing whimsical about trust funds, or Tiffany growing elfin on the subject of emerald rings. But a double boiler is something else again. Or a package of prunes. Or a baby's undershirt."

He folded his napkin on the table and laughed.

"Lillian, you're too much," he said. "I could listen to you talk all night."

"Oh, let's don't do that," I said. "Enough about work. Shall we go?"

On the way home we stopped and picked up some gin.

We took the elevator back up to my floor. I knew what I wanted to have happen, but

216

I didn't know if it would.

"Kiss me quick before I close the door," I said.

And he did.

"I don't want to leave yet, Lillian," he said.

"Well then, come in," I said.

And in he came.

Dinner had been such a din of jokes and easy rapport that I could hardly eat for just wanting to talk to and listen to and look at him. He let me be funny, let me be a poet, and he didn't try to overexplain my own interests to me.

He was the same as we sat on the davenport, drinking our drinks: martinis he'd made, meticulously mixed.

Harmonium still sat on the coffee table, and he picked it up and flipped through.

"Huh. 'Le Monocle de Mon Oncle,' " he read aloud. "I can see why you'd like this guy. He's serious about what he's doing, but he can kid around."

"I love that one," I said. "I'm only partway through, but I also really like 'Metaphors of a Magnifico.' "

And I reached over to show him, and he put his arm around me.

"Strange coincidence," he said, "but my father's named after a poet. Dante."

"I think I've heard of that guy," I said.

Then we looked into each other's eyes, and I dropped the book atop the newly laid rug, and we kissed some more.

I felt intoxicated — drugged by his presence. We went to bed. An infant moon, an evening start. A night as throbbing as any metropolis. He was magnificent.

My clothes on the floor had never looked so right as the morning after he spent the night: chiffons and crepes mixed with his soft gray trousers and navy socks.

The outdoors beyond the window had never been more polished: a mackerel sky over a misty dawn. Even my cat Tallulah liked him, and she didn't like anybody but me.

We passed the entire weekend that way, only saying good-bye after lunch on Sunday.

Nothing felt the same after that, nor did I want it to.

Before I met Max, it had begun to feel like the heretofore gentle maw of work had grown little mandibles and begun to gnaw at me. But afterwards, the teeth dulled and then fell out completely, and I was fresh and happy all over again.

Before I met Max — though I wouldn't admit it to myself — every morning when I punched the time clock, and every evening when I crept out to smack it another feeble blow, I'd get to coveting a different life, maybe, than the one I had. A motto of mine had long been, "When the heart isn't in it, all zest in the job is destroyed," but I could not acknowledge that perhaps my zest had diminished. How could I, when I had to keep working? Had to keep hiring all these new Little Bright-Eyes, the way I used to be, for whom life was just one potentially enriching experience hot on the heels of the last?

Before I met Max, I had still been working. Not tirelessly — you bet your baby I was tired — but unceasingly, even as everyone around me ceased, at least from time to time. They went abroad, they wed, they spawned, they got appendicitis. But me, I never stopped.

And there'd be days when, as I came home from work in the drizzle, even the food stalls on Third Avenue looked weary: limp parsley, worn cabbage, forlorn spinach. I'd think of sandwiches — rye with a spot of mustard — and how I'd give my left eye to eat them under a sunny rural sky in the company of someone fascinating.

Hence my new apartment. But that alone would not be enough to revive me — so I had begun to realize, now that I had met Max.

He had come along at just the right instant and revivified me without ever being patronizing. He was manly — maybe even the type some would describe as a man's man, if they didn't really know him — but also awake to the world in a way that few men were: childlike without being childish.

Before I met Max, I'd been giving my time to undependable and hence absurdly charming men. But Max proved to be both charming and dependable.

We didn't keep our relationship a secret. Couldn't: Though R.H. Macy's was the Largest Store in the World, it was quite like a small town when it came to gossip. But Max was unfailingly discreet and refined.

Waiting for him on our second date, when I had him over for dinner, I still felt those proverbial butterflies, close as we'd grown that previous weekend. I polished the silver and laid out the savory tart, very smart, from a bakery I liked down the street. Opened the strawberry jam, plumped the cushions, powdered my nose and powdered it again. Still felt utterly uncomposed. Then the shrilling of the doorbell. Then Max, looking like an old-fashioned Valentine with his little box of candy tucked under his arm. Other times it would be sherry. Or brandy.

Peppermint patties and twelve-year-old Scotch — high and low, that was Max.

We played and replayed this scene many times through that late summer and fall.

We bought each other gifts. I'd seen an ad in an Altman window, for instance, over and over, on my walks at lunchtime: "He'll be a perfect panorama in silk pajamas." I got them for Max to keep at my place.

Max knew better than to get me only flowers and went instead to a Fifth Avenue florist run by a Mr. Schling who sold potted four-leaf clovers. Never a man unable to emote, Max had said, "Because the day I met you was the luckiest of my life, Lils" as he handed them to me.

"You're more fun than anyone in the world," was the best compliment he ever gave me.

When he would stay over — which was every weekend — I'd think of the etiquette manual I was writing. "A lady is wise to leave her host's apartment long before cockcrow," I advised, which was certainly true, and advice that I myself had always followed with other men, never staying the entire night — honestly never wanting to. But Max lived in Rutherford, so that was not an issue, and he could stay at my place as long as he liked. I relaxed better beside him than I ever did alone.

Max would prove — years hence, at the bitter end — not to be addicted to monogamy. I might have known it even back then, but I did not care — or I failed to predict how much I'd come to.

He'd come over for cocktails, and we'd have cocktails, often Manhattans, which taste best when one is in Manhattan. Sometimes we'd go out to places I knew, places Max loved — places that my residency in the city had helped me discover, in the neighborhood, or uptown to Fifty-Second Street, or far uptown to Lenox Avenue — but more often than not we'd stay in. The stars would fling themselves across the sapphire sky, and below our voices would run the rumble of cars on Fifth Avenue. The air would be humid with hints of the sea, and somewhere from the floors below, Armenian cooking smells would creep their way in.

"You love me a lot," I said to him one Saturday morning in early October when we were still in bed. "But I love you more than you love me."

He laughed and denied it, but I said it again, for I knew I was right. It was the sort

222

of statement that might, if spoken within my earshot by one of the office girls, have caused me to grimace and retreat to my desk and shake my head at the varieties of silliness to which modern womanhood subjected itself. But now the concern seemed reasonable and necessary: Who loved whom more? How much of myself I could expect to lose?

We'd have a breakfast of toast and ginger ale, coffee and tea, and go back to bed, and then out again, for lunch down the street. Hungry from exertion. We'd be so tired in those days from staying up late, but I didn't mind. Sleep no longer rated.

His laugh was a merry roar, and his sartorial excellence was unmatched. Later, much later, after we'd been married for a time, I'd even come to like the cool, astringent style with which he put me in my place during fights.

We found we traveled well together when we took a late-autumn weekend in the country, in Maine: a rural dell well full of truculent birds, a rented farmhouse. Fresh and tasty lungsful of air. I was not much of a bird-watcher, though I did prize the simple birds I could recognize: doves, sparrows. Max knew them all, both by call and by plumage.

And that is how we passed those months.

Then, just after the New Year, January of 1935, when I'd returned from a holiday visit to my family in D.C., Max came over to my apartment and proposed.

Tallulah rubbed her auburn cat head against his ankle territorially as he went down on one knee.

"From 1935 on, Lils," he said. "If you say yes, this'll be my happiest New Year. I don't want another twelve months to go by where I'm not married to you."

I said yes without question and felt stupid with happiness.

Once our engagement was announced, of course, others did question it, so at odds was this turn of events with my heretofore strident bachelor-girl pride.

Why, the papers asked, why would I get married when I stood alone as the undisputed queen of the world — for even then Manhattan had taken to calling itself "the world" — when all impediments had been removed, and everything was wonderful?

"Sneerer at Love Engaged to Wed," said the headline in the *New York World-Telegram,* followed by the subhead, "Lillian Boxfish, Poet, to Marry Rug Buyer." The lede read, "Man bites dog — or, even more incredible, love bites Lillian Boxfish. The young lady who writes books of verses putting the sneer on the tender emotion has got herself engaged. Miss Boxfish has another set of poems all ready for publication. It should be titled *Eating My Words*."

Truth be told, I *had* branded myself as the scoffer at love — but the expectation that I scoff vocally at love every time some society-page scribbler buttonholed me at a function had grown oppressive. As had trying to explain that the love I scoffed at was not the genuine article — the visceral and untidy relations between adult humans — but rather the flat simulacrum thereof deployed by advertisers less imaginative than I to sell things that nobody needs. Worst of all was a suspicion, one I could neither dismiss nor explain, that my scoffing had done nothing to check the stupid sentimentality that it took as its target, but had actually strengthened it somehow, amounting in the public eye to a few rounds of witty banter prior to the taming of the shrew. I had been typecast in a bad role; my best option was to break character. Paradoxically, I figured, I would be *more* free to live and work and write the way I chose if I did so while married to someone I truly loved.

For I truly loved Max. And I would continue to do so for decades, even after we were no longer a couple.

The spring leading up to our wedding, the spring of 1935, proved that the life of a self-styled poet sophisticate and crack ad copywriter about to marry is not a tranquil one.

There was the telephone jangling all day with queries from friends who wanted to know "What about that sunny spinster's life now?"

Even Helen, though supportive, was stunned when I told her. She kidded around, throwing a hand to her lovely high forehead, pretending to feel faint and asking for a chair to collapse in as she absorbed the shock.

I didn't want to talk to anyone about it, actually — no one in the press, that is — but Helen wisely persuaded me to give some interviews, if only because the society columnists were going to go crazy at the news regardless.

Even as "How dare they?" became the mental counterpoint to all my activities in the days that followed our engagement announcement, outwardly I went along with the reporters' questions, sweet and buttery as a lamb, because in the end: Live by the sword, die by the sword.

The strangest profile of all ended up being the one in the L.A. *Times.* "This beguiling young lady is going to be married," it said. "So her picture is printed for that and various other reasons. First, she is a remarkably intelligent young woman, in addition to being beautiful. She writes *real poetry* and sells it for *real money.* Not every poet can do that. In addition, this remarkable young person can and does write advertising, a talent that makes her at least twice as rich every year as two members of the United States cabinet combined."

I might have been gratified, once, at this piece's emphasis on my earning capabilities. And I did get a small frisson from thinking of Frances Perkins, secretary of labor, who earned $15,000 per year when I was pulling down over $30,000.

But the stories about it had begun to seem vulgar.

I won't even quote the article about the engagement that ran in my hometown paper, in Washington, D.C., under the disgusting headline of "Love, Women's Greatest Role."

Indeed, it was my mother who really sent me over the edge. I read that clipping because she mailed it to me, of course. In doing so, she was the only one in that ecstatic, albeit beleaguered, time who set me to sobbing. It happened one night after getting off the telephone with her, alone in my apartment, reading over old drafts of antilove poems, thinking: *You know you have done something horribly wrong if your mother is saying, "I knew it. I told you so."*

I had been so sure when I told Max yes, but the public uproar had shaken me more than I thought it might, causing me — just slightly — to doubt.

Should I do this? Why was I doing this?

But then Max would come over, and I'd know why.

So I did it. And for a few years, I was as happy as I had ever been — as happy, it turns out, as I would ever be again.

Even after our divorce, twenty years later, he'd still sign the notes he sent with his child support checks "love."

14
MULLIGAN

The golden Ds on the scarlet awnings — surrounded by laurel wreaths in heraldic style — seem to stand not merely for "Delmonico's" but also for "do over."

The restaurant lofts steak smells over the intersection of William and Beaver, and as they waft toward me, I feel, finally, famished. I should be, I suppose, after a three-and-a-half-mile walk.

During our marriage, whenever Max was away on business, which was often, I missed him terribly. What I did not miss were my evening dates with pots and pans. I rejoiced in rest from rump and roast, from spuds and the suds of dishes washed. Max taught me to cook, but it brought me no joy without him, so I kept the food simple when I just made it for me, for me and Johnny: fragrant coffee, honest stew.

We had a cook, too, a few nights a week, to help me then while I was freelancing. She made hearty food: roasted chicken and creamed potatoes, oysters and grilled tomatoes, squash or scrambled eggs or scrod.

For the second and last time in my life I step up the three steps and stand in the doorway where I last stood almost thirty years ago. Whether and how the place has changed I can't say; I have no memory of the entrance. Despite my damned good health, I do take note of things like steps — and hips, and trips, and falls — differently now than I did in my fifties. Thirty years! I was in sorry shape then, but I was younger, younger, younger.

Alone this time, free from entanglements, I can pay closer attention, see the place for the institution it is and not just for what it means to me. So many ubiquitous dishes were invented here: eggs Benedict, Manhattan clam chowder, chicken á la King, and baked Alaska. The Delmonico's that served Max and me our final meal together, Oscar's Delmonico's, closed in 1977, but the restaurant reopened under new management in 1981. The posted menu appears to include all the classics.

Not that it matters. I'm getting a steak. A make-up steak. A steak to compensate for the spoiling of my last one by the one true love of my entire life.

I place a gloved hand on the brass handle of the wooden door and step inside. Into a crush of people that makes the restaurant lobby resemble a rush-hour subway car.

The harried woman at the hostess stand greets me with shell-shocked solicitude.

"Dinner for one, please," I say, raising my voice above the clamor.

"Do you have a reservation?"

"Actually," I say, "I haven't a reservation. This is a spontaneous undertaking. One last great adventure for 1984."

"I see," says the hostess. "I'm afraid we're quite packed."

"So I noticed," I say. "Very good to see such a good business doing good business."

"Mm-hmm," she says, eyes down, scanning her list.

Mild dismay — I feel it, for not having thought of this: a popular restaurant on a massive holiday. Of course they're overrun. But I also feel as though I should be able to talk my way in. I've rarely been unable to persuade.

"Surely," I say, "you might have an out-of-the-way space for an out-of-the-way old lady? A crate or two in the wine cellar, perhaps? It can be tiny. Just big enough to hold a steak."

"That seems deeply unlikely, ma'am," she

231

says, theatrically turning the paper over to reveal a back that's as scrawled with names as the front.

"I had very much hoped —" I say, then pause, brought up short by the complexities of what I *had* hoped. Clarity! Focus! The keys to any successful appeal! But my message is undercut by all the things I've wanted, all the people I've been.

"I hate to tell you, ma'am, but it cannot be done," says the hostess. "We have a wait of three hours at this point, and even then there's no guarantee."

"I ate here once before," I say. "It was terrible. The *circumstances* were terrible. The food was superb. Or I imagine it was. It's difficult for me to say. That's why I've come back. I was here with my husband. We'd just divorced. Now he's dead. This all happened thirty years ago. The divorce, that is. And the dinner. In that case it was lunch, actually."

The hostess's face is shading toward desperation; her gaze has grown distant, measuring the crowd as it fills in behind me. One small delay occasioned by a senile woman could breed a calamitous chain reaction on a night like tonight. "Ma'am," she says, "I'm really very sorry. I hope you'll visit us again soon."

I don't know what else to say — a formerly rare state of affairs, happening these days with increasing frequency. Boxfish in her prime — late twenties, this young woman's age — would be seated by now, probably drinking on the house. Times have changed. But not times only.

"Well," I say. "Thank you for trying."

When I turn, I am facing the face of a woman about Johnny's age, dark hair with some stately gray at the temples. Her expression says she's overheard our exchange, witnessed my failure, and I can guess what she's thinking: *I hope I die before I'm old and pathetic.* Would that I had, madam! Would that I had.

I feel a rush of heat under the skin of my cheeks, beneath my ridiculous mink, and I turn away, lest these people see me cry. Spoiling everyone's fun. Behavior I'd expect from Olive, frankly. I work my way back toward the vestibule, stopping for a moment to collect myself, using the glass front of a bookcase to reapply Orange Fire to the mouth of my spectral reflection. Through the front doors, between the twin Pompeian columns, I can see steam rising from grates and tailpipes in the all-but-unpeopled five-way intersection. I could take a cab back to Grimaldi, I suppose. Or find a hot

233

dog stand. On New Year's Eve. Somewhere in Lower Manhattan.

A do over. Max's phrase — a bit vulgar, but charming, like the man himself. Julia was his: Julia who buried him, whom my son will shortly bury in turn. Apparently marriage can be done over, while a steak dinner cannot. And yet steaks *are* often overdone, which seems like a significant paradox. I have overdone a few in my time, being no master chef. I have overdone any number of things. *Don't overdo it, Ma,* Gianino always cautions. But so much of my life was overdoing. Overdoing it at raging dos, quite often. Creating big to-dos, not always on purpose. Doing my best, over and over. Much ado over nothing. In Shakespeare's day, Helen learned during our brief career as thespians, "nothing" was pronounced the same as "noting," which, it's worth noting, vastly increased its punning potential. *How sour sweet music is, when time is broke and no proportion kept!* With nothing shall I be pleased till I be eased with being nothing.

In what time remains, very little that is broken can be fixed.

A light hand on my shoulder: I barely feel it through my heavy pelt. It's the dark-haired woman again.

"Forgive me," she says. "I wasn't trying to spy, but I couldn't help overhearing. That's a shame about them not having room. But, if it's not too brazen, my family is about to be seated for our 8:30 reservation, and we have an extra spot."

I track her gesturing hand to a party of four others: a bespectacled man I take to be her husband, another middle-aged couple, and a copper-haired girl of maybe ten or eleven. "My goodness," I say. "That's very kind, but you can't really want an elderly stranger to impose on your holiday."

"Oh, but we can, though. My name is Kathy," she says, and she extends a hand to shake.

"Mine is Lillian."

"Well, there you have it. We're not strangers anymore."

The young girl wanders over, friendly and quizzical. "Listen," Kathy says, "I should probably mention right away — just because I'll be thinking about it all night — that my mother was supposed to join us tonight. Penny's grandmother," she says, squeezing the girl's shoulder. "But she's in the hospital with pneumonia and couldn't make it."

"Oh no," I say. "I'm very sorry to hear that. How is she doing?"

"Well, at her age there's no such thing as

a minor illness, but the doctor says she'll be fine. It's sad, though, to be away from people you love on New Year's Eve. I hope you don't think it's strange that I asked you to join us."

"Not at all. It does seem a waste to throw away a choice seat at Delmonico's and a chance to get to know one another," I say. "You've convinced me. It's an honor to join."

I check my coat, and the hostess leads us back to a table set for six. She rests a hand on my back as she hands me my menu, her eyes bright with something: sadness, gladness, relief, apology. I smile at her.

As we sit, I admire Kathy's grace: the way her invitation was laced not with pity, but with sympathy, and maybe also with need. Kathy introduces me to her husband and to the other couple, her brother and his wife. She encourages me to sit between her and Penny, who shakes my hand with bright politeness.

"What brings you to Delmonico's tonight?" says Kathy.

"This is my mulligan. A chance to try again and get it right, since the last time I was here, I didn't quite."

"Oh dear," says Kathy. "Nothing too serious, I hope?"

"No, no," I say, not wanting to burden her. "Just a mistaken steak order."

The waiter comes to take our drink requests, and I ask for water, no ice, as it's already cold enough. "You'll have some wine with us, won't you, Lillian?" says Kathy.

"Only the tiniest drop. I strolled down here, and it's important to stay hydrated."

"I wish my mother understood that. She must be about your age, and she's forever dehydrating."

"You're supposed to drink eight glasses of water a day," says Penny. "We learned that in school."

"My granddaughter Lily told me that same fact last week when she was visiting for Christmas," I say. "I think you'd like her."

"If she's like you," says Penny, "I think I probably would."

"Medium rare," I say, when the waiter comes back to ask what we want for dinner, satisfied with my accuracy this time.

When the food arrives, I've almost forgotten that I've just made the acquaintance of Kathy and her family. They live in Brooklyn, but they love the whole city and regret its decline in the same way that I do.

"But we're not going to leave," says Kathy.

"For one thing, the pleasant people have to stay and balance out the cruel ones. And for another, it can't keep on this way."

"This Subway Vigilante," says her husband. "He's got to be New York City hitting bottom. We've held out this long. It's going to go back up from here."

"I hope you're right," I say. "And I think you are. I read an article the other day. About gentrification, of all things."

"I read that, too," says Kathy. "What's in a name?"

"That's from *Romeo and Juliet,*" says Penny.

"Right you are, Penny," I say. "Longtime residents call the neighborhood the Lower East Side. But real estate agents are renaming it the East Village to draw in new renters, so they won't be afraid of the rough reputation. So says the article."

"The part that floored me," says Kathy, "was when they quoted that one woman in her sixties who'd been there forever: $115 a month in a rent-controlled apartment. She said these young kids who moved in upstairs from her pay $700 a month for the same amount of space!"

"Ridiculous," says her husband. "But of course those kids call it the East Village, not the Lower East Side."

"So much is in a name," says Penny.

We chat about the things New Yorkers chat about — the constant low-grade lunacy of life in the city — but I am surprised to find, and I think they are too, that our stories emphasize the serendipitous, even the magical. Our tone is that of conspirators, as though we are afraid to be overheard speaking fondly of a city that conventional wisdom declares beyond hope. My long walks, I discover, have provided a rich reserve of encounters with odd, enthusiastic, decent people; I hadn't realized that I have these stories until someone asked to hear them.

The steak arrives and does not disappoint.

"Penny," I say. "I haven't heard that name in a while. It's lovely."

"Thank you, Ms. Boxfish," says Penny, with such manners. "It's short for Penelope."

"Oh, please, you may call me Lillian."

Penny looks to her mother for her approval, and Kathy nods. "Thank you, Lillian," says Penny.

"The nickname Penny makes me wonder," I say. "Maybe you've wondered too: Why doesn't anyone call their kids Nickel or Dime?"

Penny narrows her eyes, not sure if this is

239

a joke or a trick, wanting to keep the point in play. "Well," she says, "what names would those be nicknames for?"

"Good question. And you're quite right. Nickelope and Dimelope never became as popular as Penelope did."

"You're funny, Lillian," says Penny, laughing, and her mother laughs, too.

"I used to be," I say. "You know what else I wonder? I wonder whether anyone will know what a penny was when you get to be my age."

"Gosh," says Penny, very serious, very adult. "You're how old now, if you don't mind my asking?"

"Eighty-four," I say, lying as always.

"And I'm eleven," she says, sending her blue-eyed gaze to the ceiling as she mentally calculates. "So that's seventy-three years from now, right?"

"Correct, Penny," I say. "You are excellent at math."

"Her father's an accountant," says Kathy, winking at her husband.

"So that will be the year 2057," says Penny.

"Good grief," says Kathy. "That sounds so far away!"

"Lillian," says Penny, "I hope it doesn't make you too sad, but I have to say that I

240

do not think anyone will be using pennies at that time. It won't be cost-effective."

"They just stopped making them out of copper," Kathy's brother says. "They're using cheaper metal now. Zinc, I think."

"I predict that you are right, Penny," I say. "Though it does make me a tiny bit sad."

"Well," says Penny, "I have a penny collection at home, actually. And I think that if I know anything about myself, I will still have it even then. So it's not like pennies will be *completely* gone."

"That makes me feel better, Penny," I say, because it does.

I've been talking, I realize, and have made little headway on my steak. For a moment I fear I've once again let circumstances prevent Delmonico's from serving me a perfect meal. But it's still warm and still delicious, and I dispatch it with dispatch. I drink the last of my wine with the last of my meat, and when Kathy's husband looks at me and reaches for the bottle, I shake my head no and mouth my thanks. Not because I don't want more, but because I do.

I set down my water glass and feel overcome by something akin to Stendhal syndrome: a dizzy head, a thumping heart. I'm so touched by their kindness. Although a long series of dim and darker days has

241

tempted me to conclude that I inhabit a world on an ever-sewerward skid, here they are. Penny and her mother are just too much. I feel almost faint.

I excuse myself. To powder my nose, I tell them.

But I take my things with me.

I do stop in the lavatory, but when I am done, I do not return to the table. I go to the front, catch our waiter, and settle up. I pay the bill for the entire party on my Carte Blanche, and I leave without saying good-bye, because I'm not sure I can hold myself together, I'm so happy.

Back on William Street, I don't want to go home. I don't want to sleep because I want to be awake for this feeling — awake to see what happens next.

This, I am reminded, is why I love walking in the city, taking to the streets in pursuit of some spontaneous and near-arbitrary objective. If one knocks oneself out of one's routine — and in so doing knocks others gently out of theirs — then one can now and again create these momentary opportunities to be better than one is.

It's about 9:30.

When I first came to the city there were dirigible masts and chromium spires rising in every direction, pointing up toward the vault of heaven, ahead toward the world to come. I pictured them clung with honey-suckle and morning glory, eighty stories up. Everything was so pretty then.

Those spires were dreams before they were spires, and who knows what dreams still shelter behind the distrustful eyes I meet on these streets? That makes me think of my friend Wendy and her enormous Nikon, hunting Madison Square Park for signs of that kind of beauty. Wendy, whose New Year's Eve party is probably just now getting underway.

I figure Chelsea is a hair under three miles away as the crow flies, but I've never been inclined to let crows plot my routes.

15
NATURE IN THE ROAR

Even before our new baby was born, I became, for a time, an expert on crying.

I sat trying not to on Friday, January 16, 1942, vastly pregnant on the thirteenth floor of R.H. Macy's. It was my farewell party.

My office had already been emptied, and I'd be taking the last box of my things home with me that evening. Everyone from institutional advertising had turned out to say good-bye.

"Lilies for our beloved Lily," said evil Olive, my grinning enemy, presenting me with a bouquet of Orientals and fairly licking her chops at the prospect of my permanent departure.

I'd been sensitive to smells for the past eight months, but the mawkish white scent of the freckled pink flowers was especially nauseating. The obscene open blooms — flung wide, stamens dangling — served to make the room feel even closer than it already did, more wintry, the windows more emphatically locked. A gift of lilies was an aggressive move, always. Even cloddish Olive understood that.

"You really put a lot of thought into these, Olive. Thank you," I said, because it was mannerly and because it was true. The flowers were on the nose: odiously odorous and overly apt. Funereal, really.

"You look a vision, Lillian," she said. "Like a flower yourself."

What cloying falsehood. I looked absurd.

Still, I looked her in the eye and said, "How sweet of you, Olive. I have the women's department of R.H. Macy's to thank for making this particular silhouette possible."

I had always liked dressing — shopping and matching, creating a style. In the early 1940s, though, the fashions for women expecting a blessed event did not look or feel so blessed. Made to conceal one's impending maternity, they seemed designed to induce both embarrassment and regret. A popular maternity frock was called, with all its associations of blood and violence, the Butcher Boy: an unflattering mess with a flapping front of rayon crepe that the ads said would keep your little bundle-to-be as secret as a rabbit in a magician's hat. How unmagical. I saw it billed elsewhere as "a pretty holiday disguise." Why disguise it? It was a fact of life.

Yet there I sat, at a vacant desk in the copy room on my last day of work at R.H. Macy's, wearing a Butcher Boy but still looking unmistakably ready to burst.

Max had come up from the rug department on the seventh floor and stood by my side, the picture of beaming paternal pride.

Since we'd found out what was cooking, he'd been a paragon of consideration and attention. We joked that my new motto should be "Make hay while the muffin's in the oven," and that I looked darling sporting the halo he was so willing to set on my head.

Even prior to the pregnancy I had become one of the women to whom, for years, I had been advertising — those in charge of their households, each buying for her man: his crackers and milk, his collars, his pants, his cod-liver oil, his brace of lamb chops. But I didn't mind all that. I liked it. I did for him, and he did for me.

I would catch myself staring at him at the oddest times, still smitten: him standing in the fridge light in his undershirt, looking for a midnight snack. I was so ferociously in love that conformity felt like rebellion.

Before him, I'd thought myself singly blessed to be single. "Proud virginity" some newspaper profiles called it (although, although). These same profiles proclaimed that Max had "tamed" me, which grated, but to myself I said that I was going to be the exception that p'd the r.

Max wanted a baby more than just about anything, and I wanted Max, so we'd embarked on a tear of trying. We married in 1935, but I produced no child for seven years. I was, as the doctors had it, of advanced maternal age — even more advanced than my charts reflected because of my lying by a year.

I'd had three miscarriages — blood and violence indeed — before the being that eventually became Johnny took root. I half expected Max to blame me — for being too old, for not really wanting it, things I half-believed of myself — but he never angered, never wavered, never really doubted that I'd give him what he most yearned for.

When Johnny seemed as though he would come to fruition, I'd been so reassured and excited that I'd wanted to tell everyone, but I didn't.

Max and I decided to keep this one — the one that would work — a secret for as long as possible, both because we were so afraid we might lose him, too, and because I wanted to keep my job until the very end. I wanted to continue earning the money because I liked having it, and I wanted to keep working because it was fun, and I was anxious and needed something else to think about.

When I finally had to tell everyone, I made a point of fibbing. When friends and relatives asked when to expect the baby to arrive, I gave them a date two weeks beyond the one the doctor had given me. They still checked in ad nauseam — and in those days I was never far from nausea — but I was spared the final flurry that I'd seen almost all my friends caught up in, with mothers and mothers-in-law transformed into prosecuting attorneys: *Is it or is it not true, young lady, that you ought to have pushed forth the screaming bundle of joy by now?* The pressure I was under to produce felt more prying and presumptuous than any work deadline. When Johnny emerged a full fourteen days ahead of ostensible schedule, I was hailed as a hero. In the meantime, I just took in their advice with a grain of aspirin.

Someone handed around slices of chocolate cake from the downstairs café. We ate it reminiscing about the ads I had written over the past fifteen years.

Some of the girls who worked under me had made a few of them into a card, collaged and oversized, covered with copy on the front and signed inside by everyone in the department.

"This one's my favorite," said Chester, my boss, reading a postcrash one from November 3, 1932 in the *World Telegram:* " 'Nature in the roar,' it says, below a vintage Helen McGoldrick illustration of a crying baby. 'This is a brand new baby, hot off the griddle and very determined.' Still so funny, Lily."

"Not so funny that R.H. Macy's could find it in their hearts to keep me," I said.

"Dammit, Lily," said Chester. "I'm happy as hell for you two, but we're sure going to miss you."

"Chip, dear," I said, clutching both hands to my abdomen. "I know you're a man overcome with emotion, but language, please. Little ears! Snooks in here is highly advanced."

"Lillian, you're irreplaceable, you know that?" said Chester. "I'll keep the freelance pipeline flowing."

As much of a prince as Chester was being, one could only sugarcoat the hemlock so much. My career as I knew it was dying. Dead as of that day. To be reborn in a different incarnation, perhaps, but not here on the thirteenth floor. R.H. Macy's was kicking me out.

It wasn't personal. Every woman who got pregnant met the same fate. Maternity leave was unheard of; having one's job held was not an option, and the assumption was that a mother couldn't work anyway — not to mention that she shouldn't, what with having a man, her baby's father, to support the little family.

What else could I say but, "Thank you, Chester. And good-bye for now."

The end, now that it had arrived, threw new light on what had come before. All the reminders I had received over the past fifteen years that I was remarkable — the highest-paid advertising woman in America, et cetera — were now swept away by this final reminder that I was not. I had loved this place, and I had succeeded here, but my successes had done nothing to change it in any real way, no more than Clever Hans the counting horse had opened up opportunities for equine bookkeepers. All the articles that I had clipped and mailed home to my mother to prove that I was right and she was wrong now seemed to be saying something different: that I was a novelty, not a paragon. A freak. The exception that p'd the r, all right.

Max carried the box out, down to Thirty-Fourth Street, and I felt grateful for the falling snow because the flakes on my face made it less apparent that I was crying again.

If we'd had a girl, I'd have papered the room as pink as a Turner sunset. As it was, we had a boy, and went with blue — though when he was brand new I wrote him a two-line poem, "To a Baby One Day Old": "It seems a sweet absurdity / to call so small a morsel he."

He was born on January 25, 1942: little Massimiliano Gianluca Caputo, Jr. He was the second person on this earth with whom I fell, in spite of myself, into love at first sight.

We decided not to call him Max — too confusing — but to focus on the Gianluca component. And so in those early days he was Johnny, sometimes, and sometimes he was Gianino, and sometimes he was our Little John. He was fiercely and always ever after our son.

When they sent us home from the hospital with him, it felt like we were actors, the leads in a heist film. Like we couldn't be getting away with such outrageous treasure.

The first morning after our first night back in our Murray Hill apartment all together, Max and I sat up in bed, propped against pillows, staring down at Johnny, asleep in my arms.

"I don't know what I'm doing," I said to the baby's closed eyelids, which seemed impossibly thin, delicately veined. "This is . . . a person."

"You're doing great, Lils," Max said. "Think of it this way: In a lot of regards, this is no different than learning to swim — terrifying at first, but ultimately a matter of confidence. Jump in. You're doing it."

"I suppose," I said, and he put his arm around me as the snow fell outside.

We'd been afraid that Tallulah, an old cat by now, a grizzling ten, would resent the baby. But that first morning she hopped on the bed and sniffed him curiously before curling into a furred heap in Max's lap, joining us in watching the infant sleep. She seemed determined to steady all the nerves that needed steadying, which was to say every nerve of mine.

I was happy, of course, that Johnny was there. But childbirth had left me jagged, ripped. It was physically the worst experience that I had ever endured, and I had less than no desire to endure it again.

Max, on the other hand, was over the moon.

"I don't want to rush things, Lils," he said, stroking a finger down sleeping Johnny's cheek. "But you and I need to make more of these guys. They're great!"

At that point, with Johnny just days old, there was no need to fight about adding to our menagerie, so in my mind I said *no way, no how,* and outside I said nothing. I just kissed Max on the lips and turned back to the baby.

I came to like it, sort of, motherhood. And I instantly loved Gianluca, Gianino, Little John, Johnny. So much so that I could admit to myself that all my simpering girlfriends and workmates had been right: I'd never felt a stronger emotion.

But the other thing I felt — that no one had ever told me I might — was that as much as I loved him, I could never be totally sure that I wanted him around forever. I did not know if my life was categorically "better" for having him here.

Our days fell into a routine that was an unprecedented mix of the banal and the hectic.

The pregnancy had added volume to my statuesque figure, of course, but I lost the weight in no time — in sterilizing bottles and making the formula, in bathing him, little acrobat as he was, and in feeding him and not myself. Six ounces in twenty minutes? Never. He took forever to eat. Took the occasional after-breakfast snooze, the 1:30 rest.

I did like it when people came over to see him, although during his nap I wouldn't wake him for friends or even for relatives, not when he was all cozied in with his quilts and sweaters and booties, knitted by the hands of loved ones more domestic than I.

"He's not a diorama at the Natural History Museum," I'd tell them. "You can wait."

He cried a lot — a *lot*. The city sanitation crews would wake him, bouncing the metal trash cans on the concrete, infuriating him, and he, in turn, would infuriate the neighbors.

He was exhausting, unable to avoid and seeming to seek danger. If one gave him a stuffed animal with large-headed pins for eyes — common in those days — he'd yank them out and make to devour them.

Max loved Johnny, and me for producing him. But he, like his fellow fathers, had only the most perfunctory interest in the baby at the bassinet stage, leaving me to change and feed and nap and burp and quiet his screaming.

Before I had a baby, I obliged lady friends who insisted that I race from the office to see their darling offspring: There he was, asplash in his prebedtime tub, and there I was, being regaled with all his vital statistics, height and weight and pooping propensities. No conversation to be had when Baby was in the room. And I would grin through gritted teeth and compliment them: on baby's skin, smooth as a pale cherry blossom; or baby's precocity in the vocabulary department, demonstrable by such word pairs as "toidy seat." I pushed back my rising gorge at their feeble minds, unimpressed that their child's fondest wish seemed to be beating the backside of a frying pan with some chromium utensil.

After I had a baby, I was gifted with epiphanic understanding of where they'd all been coming from. Suddenly all my clothes were washable, and my sharply pointed jewelry had been retired; the only prickling was in my eyes from lack of sleep.

I understood, too, the competitive comparisons leveraged by motherhood. Was my baby as heavy as the baby next door? Did he get his teeth soon enough? What of speaking? This animal love turned even the most mundane events into monuments.

I worked from home and tried to glamour up by six, when Max got back from the rug department: powder and lipstick to paint myself the Fairy Queen of the Nursery, like in a storybook — but I'd as often be wearing, too, prune pulp and farina. At least little Gianluca always looked good: the handsome crabapple of his parents' eyes. I did find some dresses with buttons down the front that I could dive into without looking like I'd taken a stick of dynamite to my hair. I could never bring myself to let the baby yell while I made up my face, though, so many were the nights I was mostly undone.

I wouldn't say I was jealous, exactly. But I was intensely wistful every morning when Max would leave to go to R.H. Macy's, and when he would return home from there every night.

Wishing for something never made it so, and I never wished for Max to lose his berth at R.H. Macy's as I had lost mine. But inevitably the war came for us, as it had been coming for everyone.

Max was drafted and, like that, he was gone.

For a little over a year he had been deferred on account of our baby, but by the end of 1942 Uncle Sam could no longer do without him. He had to go to Italy because he spoke Italian.

So from early 1943 until late 1945 it was just Gianino and me, experiencing those formative years as an unstable duo. I spent all the time I wasn't raising Johnny freelancing and writing many more letters to Max than I received. Enduring darkness and blackouts both literal and metaphoric.

I felt like a different person without Max around. A worse one.

I was still doing the same job, ostensibly, as I'd always been doing: influencing people with kids and families. I was supposed to be pulling their strings with my skills. I knew that most ad writers followed a simple formula: If you have a worry, then they have a product; buy the product, banish the worry. I had never worked that way, and I wasn't about to start. But I understood it. More so now than ever.

With Max thousands of miles across the sea, maddeningly unreachable and maybe in danger, I felt myself vulnerable in ways I never thought possible. As if I'd spent every day for a long time at the shooting range but had always been secure, safe behind the barrier. Now I was walking amidst the targets, and I didn't like it. That analogy came up a lot in my mind as the war dragged on, inspired by one of Max's earliest letters from basic training about marksmanship practice.

He ended up in a noncombat position, thank god, as an American officer in the Allied Control Commission for Italy — executive director of the economic section.

That still put him largely beyond my reach. Our correspondence remained wildly uneven.

I would send, for example, a typical letter that read something like this:

Dearest Puppa:

I've been sending you V-mail letters every day and others, too, but they fill up so fast. So I have been jotting down things Gianino says that are new and funny and sweet, which I know you would want to hear.

This A.M. the first thing he said when I went in because he was shaking the crib apart was "Daddee, mail!" How he had that on his mind I don't know because all I've said about mail is that I'm writing Daddee and he can put a kiss in the letter. Anyway, now all incoming and outgoing mail must be kissed.

Tonight when I was feeding him dinner, he said, "Mommee, is Daddee all right?" just like that. And I said Daddee was fine and he put his darling little arms around me and his face against my cheek and said "Mommee so sweet. I love Mommee." What an intuitive little party! When I have made a point of being full of good cheer, he still knows he's got to pinch-hit for the greatest guy in the world.

I miss you more than it's possible to say. I'm hoping we'll both get a letter from you soon.

Love,
Mumma

In reply, I might get a love letter on an airmail sheet: *Just a quickie as I am leaving soon — I loved your letters. They are always wonderful. You are wonderful in every way. Will write you and phone you when I can, but it may be some time. I LUVE MY MUMMA.* If he was feeling effusive, there might be a drawing of a heart.

Often, I might get no more than an official receipt telling me he had received from me at his APO:

1. *Life* magazine

259

2. *Time* magazine
3. One carton Philip Morris cigarettes
   and one carton Pall Mall

That was the maximum amount of smokes a soldier could receive every two weeks. Max didn't smoke them all, but rather traded them around the country, he said, for various needs.

At any rate, this was a meager diet of love for me to live on for three long years, especially when I'd been so accustomed to a nonstop feast.

Max returned not long after V-E Day, arriving home in June of 1945.

It was a relief to have him back, but things were never the same.

It was not an abrupt or a radical change, just a different texture in the weave of our lives.

R.H. Macy's had not held his job, and so he began working for the government — a long-term contract, doing the kind of economic development tasks he'd been doing in Italy, only here in the States. This meant long train rides back and forth between Manhattan and D.C. Which meant fewer excuses — now that he was going there often, and I was lancing freely, and we had a child whom everyone in my family wanted to see — to avoid my family.

How I came to miss the relative privacy — not to mention the privacy from relatives — that I routinely enjoyed while breadwinning, even in my bustling and clamorous office, where I could shut the door and tell the receptionist to lie: "She's not in."

No one quite believed that freelancing and being a mother qualified as actual work.

Friends dropped by, thinking they were helping, but often they'd only take up the time I'd set aside to read or write. They thought I was lonely without Max. And I did miss him greatly, but that was not the same as being lonely.

"Gather ye hot dogs while ye may," I said to the few single girls left among them when they'd stop in.

Oh, they'd reply, *we're tired of the man chase. Tired of the rat race. We envy the pace of your relaxing life.*

That would make me long to caress them with an axe.

I never ceased in my attempts to spin the straw of drudgery into the gold of fun. I came to feel gratified at having a scrap of time large enough to write a letter or to pay the phone bill. To put a baked potato slurried with beef juice in Johnny's bowl, and a martini in my glass.

After Johnny was born, I was pulled by a tension between resistance and acceptance: wanting to hide the playpen sometimes, somehow, to pretend there was no infant on the premises. Why?

As ever, it was Helen who had the most sensible solution. She sent reporters from her women's magazines over to profile me and my happy little family.

In 1946, for instance, we were written up — Max and Johnny and me, all three — in *Woman's Day.* "The toddler pictured here is a strapping young gentleman of this decade's bumper crop of babies. As you probably know, Mrs. Caputo is Lillian Boxfish in public life, famous for her light verse and one of the best-liked contributors to this very magazine. It is still too early to predict Johnny's future, but if he shows a tendency to clutch a pencil and put marks on paper with an inspirational light in his eyes, we will keep you posted."

The attention did make me feel a bit better, like I existed again.

It was also Helen's idea to collaborate on another book, not unlike our etiquette guide, but this one with an eye, of course, toward the how-tos of motherhood.

So Now You've Done It: A Practical Handbook to Handling Baby we called it.

In my initial drafts, I wanted to tackle such burning questions as:

Why do people feel they need to have children to act like children? Why not eat Cracker Jack in the street if that's your pleasure? Why not scuff the leaves or romp in the snow? Cut out the damn middleman and do what you want.

In the end, though, we aimed at — and hit — the popular middle, offering, as the jacket copy said, to help the consumer enjoy their new baby: "Here, at last, is the book which treats babies not like bundles from heaven, but like a bundle from Macy's — something you've wanted in your home that always arrives C.O.D."

Thus was Johnny, both directly and indirectly, a well-documented and inspiring and much doted-upon child.

Max snapped endless photographs: Johnny in the pram; me in a fur coat, pushing him on a swing in our neighborhood playground; Johnny sitting on a bench, eating an ice cream; me holding him in my lap; Johnny at seven, perhaps, playing the recorder with some lady on the piano accompanying him, or the other way around.

As Johnny grew up, I wrote poems not only about, but with him, like "Leave Us Batten Down Our Belfries":

I dote on cats
And also kittens
But I loathe rats
And all their rittens.
I feel the same toward bats
And bittens.

I tried not to smother him. I'm not sure I succeeded. Wholesome neglect is not in my nature; if I decide to do something I don't hold anything back.

Max and I turned our hearts over to Johnny. Providentially for us he was a benevolent dictator. We called him Attila, our affectionate pet name, when it was just the two of us, so wholly conquered did we feel. He was a wonderful child, sensitive and kind and extremely musical from an early age.

And while I hadn't even been sure I wanted him at first, it hurt my heart slightly as he grew, inevitably, up and away — loving, always, but more and more independent with the passing days. Watching him grow, I sometimes recalled that party long ago on the Upper East Side, and my otherwise-all-but-forgotten date, Bennie, when he, looking out over the city, had spoken of "the way a crane creates, then erases itself, from the skyline." He'd been referring to how I, as a copywriter, created R.H. Macy's, but the same metaphor might easily have been applied to how I, as a mother, was creating my son.

Don't get me wrong — don't let my ambivalence distort the story.

We still had good times.

Max and I were still in love.

We had fun with Johnny. The carousel in Central Park. Root beer floats. Fireflies.

We spent a few weeks each summer at our place in Maine: family vacations at Pin Point, which Max and I had rented on our first out-of-town trip together, then bought back in 1938.

We'd take Johnny for a swim in the lake, then leave our bathing suits on the green lawn near the white house to dry: pastel remnants of a day well spent beneath a blue sky.

But also cold skins — old skins we could never quite put back on and feel as warm as we used to, as comfortable in.

16
BACK TO THE STARS

Any day you walk down a street and find nothing new but nothing missing counts as a good day in a city you love. People are forever tearing something down, replacing something irreplaceable.

Walking north on Church Street, away from Delmonico's, I can smell the Hudson River — cool and murky, full of hearty but toxic fish, shiny and reeking with fuel from the ferries.

I want to see the water.

I'm not on a schedule, and I've got the time. Wendy is likely not expecting me at her party at all, and certainly not at any particular hour. Even midnight is a negotiable deadline.

So I turn left on Vesey. It used to lead all the way to the water's edge, but not anymore, not exactly.

Now I have to cross under the wreckage of the West Side Elevated Highway. They

shut it down more than ten years ago —
shut down the whole highway! — after a
dump truck fell through it — a whole dump
truck, and a sedan right after it! — at
Twelfth and Gansevoort.

Walking the surface street, I cannot deny,
is scary: a bizarre no-man's-land. There are
people down here, not many, who are as
good as ghosts. In order not to bother or be
bothered by ghosts, you just act like you're
one of them. That's what I do.

And I say to myself — out loud, I mean, I
actually say it, because sometimes it is to
one's advantage to sound a bit crazy — the
sort of thing I always say when I am walking and need to remember to not be afraid.

"The city is a city," I say. "But it is also a
house. This city is my house. I live in this
city, and this part is being remodeled. The
ceiling of the highway has been pulled
down, and the floor's been extended, and
the water's farther away. But this is my
house. It is still my house."

Beyond the ruins of the elevated highway
the old waterfront is unrecognizable. For
one thing, it's not at the front of the water
any longer. I haven't been down here in
ages, but they're building a whole new
neighborhood, a planned community, a little
slice of suburbanoid life right here at the

edge of Manhattan's tip: Battery Park City, that's what it's going to be. Constructed on landfill. Three million cubic yards of it, or so Gian — who loves quantifiable proof of humankind's colossal ingenuity — told me last week while he was visiting for Christmas. Rock and soil and garbage excavated during the erection of the World Trade Center.

To my disappointment, I cannot get to the water's actual edge. The construction site is blockaded with fencing, chain-link here, barbed-wire there. All I can do is stare through the looped diamonds at the river beyond.

I've always been fond of the Hudson. It's the path by which ocean liners leave the city to take passengers across the Atlantic. That's how Max and I left Manhattan — twice — to travel together to Italy. The first time was the best: our honeymoon cruise.

It's windy here tonight, making me feel less ridiculous, more vindicated, about wearing the mink. I hold on to my hat.

When we took that first trip in the summer of 1935 — June, following our city hall wedding — our vessel carried us way down the Hudson, starting from the New York Passenger Ship Terminal near Midtown. The piers were new and blindingly white, the big passenger ships having just moved there from the Chelsea Piers — more toward Wendy's party, now that I think of it. When the ships got too big, Chelsea came to be used for cargo only.

Max had been so excited to show me Italy. I'd been so excited to see it.

Our second voyage, I'm sorry to say, was quite another matter.

"Hey!" someone shouts from across the construction site. "Hey! You by the fence! What do you think you're doing?"

I turn around to face my inquisitor. Running across the muddy wastes is a short, wiry man in an off-brand uniform: coplike, but decidedly not a real cop.

"Pardon me?" I say when he's close enough to hear me without my having to shout. "I was just looking at the river. Is that not allowed?"

He's breathing hard from his jog, in front of me now, looking me in the eyes as if to appraise me.

"It's all right as long as you're not going to jump," he says, his eyebrows furrowing into concerned blond caterpillars.

"Jump?" I say, and feel insulted. "To commit suicide?"

"People do," he says.

I look at him, then past him. "I'd have to

cut through the fence," I say. "And then the water's not more than ten feet below. If I were going to kill myself, I wouldn't do it that way. What a mess. The whole goal would be for me to die quickly, not to pass torturously of blood poisoning or god knows what months after the fact."

"Look, lady, I'm sorry I yelled at you," he says. "I'm just trying to do my job, you know."

He looks about thirty. Up close his expression is more sad than angry, and his speaking voice is softer, more reedy, having lost the edge it carried when he first yelled.

"I respect that," I say. "When people are committed to a job."

The blond caterpillars huddle again. "Are you making fun of me?" he asks.

With the streetlight behind me I can see his face better than he can see mine. "I most certainly am not," I say.

"It's not even that I'm that committed," he says. "I actually hate this job. I just don't want anybody killing themselves or otherwise getting in trouble on my watch."

"So you're a night watchman?"

"Basically, yeah. Security guard. Rent-a-cop. Whatever you want to call it," he says. "I don't have any, like, authority. And it's boring. Yelling at you is probably the most

270

excitement I'll have all night. And I don't particularly get off on yelling at old ladies."

"I have a name," I say. "Which is Lillian Boxfish. You?"

"Stu," he says. "Stu Koszinski."

"How did you end up with this job you don't like, Stu?"

Stu opens his mouth, about to tell me that he's working, that he can't talk right now. Then he closes it, realizing it doesn't matter. "I'm a Vietnam vet," he says. "I used to be in the navy. I kind of lost my footing for a while after I got back. Now here I am, guarding this construction site on the waterfront. Far cry from the high seas."

I think about telling him that this place is called Battery Park for the old artillery batteries they built to defend the city — even here, war is not so far off — but instead I say:

"Thank you for your service. I'm sorry you had to do it."

"Really?" he says. "You're welcome."

"I don't make a habit of saying things I don't mean, Stu," I say.

"A lot of people of your generation seem to think that 'Nam doesn't rate," he says. "You guys got the good war. I know all about that, so you don't have to tell me."

"I'd never tell you that. I hate all war. I

hated that war, too. My husband was in Italy from 1943 to 1945, and when he got back things between us were never quite as they were before he left."

"Me and my old lady got divorced when I came home," says Stu. "I never even get to see my kid anymore."

"Max and I divorced as well. Though by the time we finally did I don't think the war had much to do with it, at least not directly," I say. "I'm sorry, Stu."

"It's all right," he says. "It's not like it's your fault. It's life, right?"

"Yes, I think so," I say. "I think it's life. Do you want to know what job I had and hated most?"

"Sure," says Stu. "Fire away."

"In the summer of 1945 I was freelancing — I'm a writer — and I was saying yes to everything at that point, because Max had just gotten back from Europe and we weren't sure what was going to happen. You understand."

"I understand," says Stu. "Gotta make the money while it's there. Mind if I smoke?"

"Not at all," I say. "So I took a job writing limericks. You know what those are, Stu, don't you?"

"There once was a man from Nantucket?" he says, taking a drag.

272

"Well, the ones I was writing were for a family newspaper," I say. "But that's basically the idea. The Sunday *New York Journal-American* hired me to write limericks — just the first four lines of them, actually — at $10 a pop. A year's worth, so $520 for the batch."

"$520 for incomplete limericks — that's so much money," says Stu. "Times have changed."

"Don't get me started, Stu," I say. "This was for their 'Best Last Line Contest.' Readers would mail in their submissions to compete for the weekly prize. Would you like to play? It might cheer you up."

"That's good of you, Lillian," says Stu, "but I'm okay. I don't ever get full-on cheerful. And I'm not mad that you're here or anything. You just caught me in a moment of commitment to duty. Maybe I over-reacted. Yelled more than I needed to."

He doesn't need to explain or apologize. Now that he's relaxed, I can see something clearly in his eyes, in the way he's standing: He's terrified to be here alone. Scared of what the job makes him do and scared, too, of whatever made him take the job in the first place. All reasonable fears, I suppose.

"Oh, come on, Stu," I say. "Let an old lady show off. I'm proud as a peacock that I can still remember any of them."

"All right," says Stu. "Try me."

"Okay," I say, and then recite, "In a moment off duty, a cop / Told a motorist, speeding, to stop. / Said the arm of the law, / 'It may stick in your craw —' "

I look at Stu. He looks at me. "Then what?" he says.

"Well, then *you* write the last line," I say. "That's how it worked. That was the contest. Come on, Stu. Go for it."

Stu shrugs, helpless. "But I need you to take off your top?" he says.

"Well," I say. "That rhymes."

"Sorry," says Stu. "Sorry. Just free-associating."

"No, no," I say. "That's not bad. It wouldn't have won you any prizes from family newspapers in 1945, but nowadays who knows? One more?"

"Sure," says Stu, smiling, finally. "I got nowhere else to be."

"All right," I say. "A gang of young rockets from Mars / Shot to earth, like exploding cigars, / But when they inspected / Our World, they elected —"

"To turn and head back to the stars?" says Stu, crinkling his face in concentration.

"Stu, that's pretty," I say. "If I were the judge, I'd give you the blue ribbon."

"Thanks," he says, tossing his cigarette butt down toward the Hudson. "I better get back to work. Patrol the site and all."

"Of course," I say. "Thanks for playing. I should be going, too."

"Where you headed?"

"I'm going to a party. For New Year's Eve. Up in Chelsea."

"And you're walking?"

"Yes," I say. "But I'll be okay."

"I don't know if anyone in this city's going to be okay," he says. "But if anybody is, Lillian, I got a feeling it'll be you."

"Stu, that's the nicest thing anyone's ever said to me on a Hudson River construction site," I say. "Happy New Year. I'll shove off now. People are expecting me."

Not exactly true, not exactly a lie. But a thing it makes him happy to hear, and me happy to say.

I head back the way I came, east on Vesey, toward Church, thinking of planning and cities, of battlements and landfill, and how the solid rock upon which my success was built turned out to be a snow heap and melted, melted.

17
WHY PEOPLE DO THINGS

On postcards it never rains. Our honeymoon was like a postcard.

On June 20, 1935, Max and I boarded a transatlantic liner bound for Italy.

Lovely day, top sun deck, I wrote in the small travel journal I'd gotten for the trip — a wedding present from Helen McGoldrick and Dwight Zweigert.

Max and I had stood at the railing together, waving white handkerchiefs — more wedding presents — monogrammed with our initials: his the same as always, mine now with a *C* in place of the *B,* although professionally I would continue to go by my real name.

Our families — both his parents and mine, in from New Jersey and Washington, D.C., respectively — had waved back, presumably until we were out of their sight. They got along swimmingly, to our delight and surprise; they were going to lunch together after seeing us off.

We watched until Manhattan receded behind the rooftops of Brooklyn and the ship met the open water of Gravesend Bay.

Then we sat side by side on deck chairs, Max to read and me to write a bit more in the little blue book labeled LEST WE FOR-GET. Bound in leather, it had a gold lock, the kind often found on the diaries one received and was encouraged to keep as a child. Eminently pickable, those locks were just for looks; growing up, I always hid my diary from my older brother under the mattress of my bed.

There were no secrets, though, in this one — nothing dark to confess, just pure happiness. A document boring to anyone but myself, the author.

The least ecstatic thing I wrote as the wind picked up and the seagulls dropped away was *My one regret is that I wish I had met my husband sooner.*

Young Lillian Boxfish had been a scoffer at not only love but also vacations — if we lived better day-to-day, I often suggested, we might not be so desperate to escape — but now I was prepared to sup on my own words. For years I had heard ocean voyages described with implausibly rapturous superlatives, but this particular journey really did

277

prove itself magical.

Along with everyone else in first class, we dressed up each day and every night. I wore velvet shoes and crêpe de chine dresses and silk nightgowns with collars of handmade lace. It felt less like getting all set for a fancy fête, more like preparing to put on a play — just the way Helen and I used to do, draping ourselves in bedclothes at the Christian Women's Hotel — only with the whole ship for our stage and a script that we made up on the spot.

I looked forward to glowing wines and southern sunshine.

My frozen northern soul thawed. We were beautified by love.

The longest trips I took prior to meeting Max were delayed rides on the subway, the El, the ferry.

My mother had given me a book called *You Meet the Nicest People on Vacations: The Traveler's Fun Book* — to express her joy, I think, that I was finally taking time to relax. Normally such persistent insistence on a socially circumscribed definition of *fun-fun-fun!* would have annoyed me. But the title was right: We really were meeting nice people.

When we arrived, we found the land as

grand as the sea. The churches and domes, the streets and the railroads, the food and museums, the ruins and the expanse of the sun-drenched countryside.

Every cathedral we saw, every aqueduct and amphitheater, every great work of art delivered a shock: popping up where you'd least expect it, bigger and brighter than life — as if done up in an advertising style they always taught us to avoid at R.H. Macy's, a style that would come to be known as *hellzapoppin'*.

Crude but effective, these ads grabbed for attention in an atmosphere of vertiginous zaniness, presenting their wares in odd settings, absurdly out of scale. A standard example might show a gargantuan package of the product dwarfing a surrounding crowd of customers evincing their bug-eyed, spasmodic approval — exactly how Max and I felt standing in the shadow of, say, the Cathedral of Milan, or Michelangelo's *David*. Everything in Italy was hellzapoppin'.

If someone had asked him, years later, what my tragedy was, Max might have answered that I was a workaholic.

I might have answered that that was *not* my tragedy, actually, but rather was what kept me from tragedy for so long.

Even on our honeymoon I was working, if only a little. I brought books along — mostly for entertainment, but also for continuing education, because that, to me, was entertaining also. It was light stuff — one called *Women in Cosmetic Advertising,* for instance — and no more taxing than the women's magazines I frequently wrote for. The book even had a quiz, which of course I took, writing directly in the margins, because it was my book, and because I liked writing in my books.

Max and I were sitting on the terrace of our hotel in Milan, hometown of his parents. We had been traveling by rail all over the interior of the country.

I pulled the book out of my bag and set it on the table with our *caffellatte* and rolls with jam.

"Come on, Max," I said. "Let's play a game."

"All right, Lils," he said, used, by now, to my penchant for this type of fun; I was equally avid about comment cards and reader surveys.

"Try answering this list of questions about yourself, sincerely 'Yes' or 'No,'" I read aloud.

"I can't be anything but sincere when I'm around you, Lils," he said.

And then I read:

"One. Have you changed your hairstyle at
least once in the last five years?"
Yes for me. No for Max.
"Two. When you were feeling very 'down'
did you ever buy a new hat just to cheer
yourself up? (Did it?)"
Yes for me. Yes for Max. Our hat collections were quite formidable.
"Three. In a train, bus, or streetcar, would
you rather study the people around you
than read even the most exciting new
book?"
Yes for me. Yes for Max. We'd make up
stories about them together.
"Four. Did you ever speculate — just once
— on how false eyelashes would look
on you?"
Yes for me. No for Max. Though he never
thought I needed them, and I agreed.
"Five. Do you read 'Advice to the Lovelorn'
in your daily paper?"
Yes for me. Yes for Max. Especially now
that we'd found each other. There was
something gratifying in reading about the
lovelorn when one had reason to believe,
however mistakenly, that one would
never again be lovelorn.
"Six. Do you like women — at least as well

as you do men?"

Yes for me. Yes for Max.

"Seven. Can you think of at least one way to improve the appearance of each of your five best friends?"

Yes for me, excepting Helen, who looked fantastic, always. Yes for Max. He appreciated stylishness as much as I did. In Milan for one day, we'd already had him fitted for three bespoke suits. One just couldn't find as high a quality, even in Manhattan.

"Eight. Are you interested in why people do things? (Are you also interested in what they do?)"

Yes for me. No for Max, unfortunately.

"Nine. Do you think requited love should be the most important aim of most women?"

No for me. Yes for Max.

"Ten. Have you ever, that you remember, spoken to a stranger in an emergency, a shared emotion, a sudden excess of friendliness — and enjoyed it?"

Yes for me, a hundred times on this trip already. Yes for Max, to a considerably lesser extent.

"It's a ten-question quiz, right?" he said.

"Correct," I said. "That's it. Now let's

score it up."

And then I read: "Give yourself ten points for each of these questions you've answered with a 'Yes.' If you've scored a sixty, stay with us — you can earn a living at cosmetics writing; seventy, you should go up in the world if you enter the profession; eighty or above means that you have the makings of a good advertising woman!"

"Tell me, professor," Max said, "how'd we stack up?"

"I got ninety points," I said.

"I suppose you might have the makings of a good advertising woman," he said, and laughed.

"You got seventy," I said. "So might you."

As we finished our breakfast, I thought of how it was true: Max could be extremely persuasive. The only conflict we'd had on that trip, in fact, came from his attempts to convince me to do what I'd sworn I was unconvinceable on.

He brought it up again that afternoon, as we strolled through the public gardens. I was thrilling to the exotic flowers, everywhere in bloom.

"Lils," he said. "If you like this, you'll love living in Rutherford. We can have a garden of our own in back of our house. We can fill the whole front yard with flowers that are just like these. My pops can order the seeds."

Ever since we'd left the New York Passenger Ship Terminal, Max had been trying off and on to get me to agree that what we really needed to do was move to the suburbs.

Arguing against comments like these had gotten me nowhere, so I'd taken to simply ignoring them. "Let me take your picture by these roses," I said.

While I treasured the occasional rural retreat — I adored Pin Point, for instance, the place in Maine we'd rented together the previous fall — the suburbs had always seemed mealy and unresolved. I understood that their in-between-ness — neither town nor country! — was supposed to be their very appeal, but I didn't find it appealing. I always wanted either to *be in,* or get *away from* the city, not to just be *close to* the city. Were I off in the pastoral hills shingling my own roof or riding a horse, well then, what fun. And were I catching the subway for a night at the opera, well then, hooray. But in the suburbs I could enjoy none of those pursuits with ease.

As I snapped the rosy photos of Max for our scrapbook, I tried to convince myself, against my best intuitions, that I might be wrong. That perhaps the suburbs would turn out to be like ocean voyages, or Italian vacations: laden with suspicious superlatives, but actually magical. *But where is the shuffleboard in the suburbs?* my intuitions asked. *Where are the mysterious ports of call? The engaging strangers?*

Max smiled widely until I told him he could relax. He came to my side and put his arm around my shoulder, and I thought about how happy he made me and how badly I wanted to make him happy in return.

On the ship back to New York late that July, I conceded. A bad idea, I knew, but I had come to see that the only way out of this suburban scheme of his was going to be through it.

After we moved to our "cottage in the Garden State" as the real estate agent called it, I kept paying the rent on my place in Greenwich Village. Thank god I did, because the suburbs were god-awful.

I lost all my poetry-writing time to catching buses and trains. Worse, there was virtually no more walking, my beloved walking, to get to and from work — just the crushed five-minute dash from Penn Station to R.H. Macy's.

285

Without the walking, I was more exhausted than I'd ever been with it.

No one walked in the suburbs. Our neighbors noted this with pride, but it was nothing to be proud of.

Max and I were back to living in Manhattan within two months. Whether the bulbs he planted in the first weeks of our Garden State sojourn ever sprouted and bloomed I never learned, and I could never quite bring myself to care. What rescued me, I think, was Max's realization that he might not want to be within mere blocks of his parents any longer — after living under their roof his entire life — now that he had a wife.

On the day he agreed with me that we were, undeniably, a city couple, I think I was as happy as I'd been on the day I said yes to his proposal of marriage.

Because my abode was small, especially for two, we had to look all over again for a new place to reside.

We settled on East Thirty-Sixth Street in Murray Hill, a space that immediately felt like home to both of us: ten reasonable stories of sturdy red brick, with a doorman and an elevator and a live-in super.

We chose a three-bedroom, Max populating the extra two with future children in his mind, me mentally decorating the one with the best light as my in-home office. The building had quiet hallways and a burnt-toast smell on the afternoon that we happened to view it.

I associated that smell with comfort and safety forever after. Sometimes, in my darker hours, I would lightly burn toast in our toaster — from R.H. Macy's, naturally — and it would make me feel better.

Years later, I would come to wonder why I even had that memory of standing in the empty apartment, soon to be ours, Max holding my hand and me breathing in toast. I couldn't access that beauty — tangibly, it was as lost to me as that first trip to Italy: trivial and evanescent, but still so real.

18
SULFUR AND MOLASSES

I never like to walk back the same way that I came if I can help it, but sometimes I can't help it.

To get away from the waterfront I have to take Vesey again, but at Church Street I head north so as not to duplicate my earlier route down Broadway, and also because I need to keep west to get to Chelsea.

I bear left onto Sixth Avenue, now Avenue of the Americas, though nobody outside of travel guides really calls it that. The new name came just after the war, courtesy of Fiorello La Guardia, the mayor whom both I and Max's family's cherished above all others: I owing to his reform politics, the Caputos owing to his being Italian. "The Little Flower," they always called him, which is what his first name literally meant, and he *was* small and florid, five-or-so feet tall.

The buildings on my left fall away into

Beach Street Park, a triangle of darkness gathered behind the ghostly column of a plane-tree trunk. Across the street, the AT&T Long Lines Building blacks out the eastern sky, interrupted by a sifting of lit windows: devoted souls tending the pulse in the wires that speed voices around the globe — the voice of Skip's fare maybe among them, dealing with the shit going down in Tokyo. I quicken my pace until I'm among street lamps and shop windows again.

Oftentimes, what causes old people to become poor walkers is poor walking. One must bend one's knees. One must lift one's feet up. One must be unceasing. One mustn't shuffle.

As I move ahead, I notice that my gait has taken on an uncharacteristic glide, and I realize that it's trying to match the beat of the song I heard earlier tonight from the window of that Dodge in Murray Hill, a beat that's been playing unobtrusively in my head ever since. A disco rhythm, I suppose. I never warmed to disco — which always struck me as crass yet flaccid, all buildup with no payoff — but rap I like. That's because of the words, of course, which instead of being chained to some inane melody are freed to lead the rappers where they will, by way of their own intrinsic

289

music. So it seems, at least, to my untrained ear. Much of it is utter nonsense, to be sure. As with the best nonsense, some of it seems as if it were made up on the spot, and also as if it could be a thousand years old.

It makes me happy, and also sad, to think that this is where playful language is cherished now, and where the verbosity that I and my clever friends prized in our youth has gone to reside: the slums. Words don't cost a penny; during the Depression, they were all many of us had. I used them to make a fortune.

Later, people got richer, and they seemed to lose interest in what could be gotten for free. The way I spoke to them changed accordingly. I think back sometimes in near disbelief on my professional vocabulary of 1929, the ads of yesteryear that could never fly today. Our ads changed with the times, of course. Did the times change with our ads? Did the world change or did I change it?

The blocks around Washington Square Park are best avoided in the dark, and now's a fine time to commence my westward drift: I have a quick stop I'd like to make for auld lang syne. Left on Greenwich, toward Seventh Avenue.

At this moment — the last hours of 1984,

in a decaying city populated by bums and dope addicts and thuggish teenagers and the pistol-packing commuters who apparently shoot them for sport — it is difficult to believe that the residents of Manhattan ever did anything so refined as "call on" one another. It's harder still to believe that the making of these social calls necessitated the ownership of cards — calling cards — that they would present in order to announce a visit, or to commemorate an attempt at one in instances where the resident was indisposed or not at home. Upon such cards, various ornaments — roses, perhaps, or doves — often occupied a spot below the bearer's name. My Aunt Sadie Boxfish had forget-me-nots on hers. She always left me one on her rare visits to Washington, D.C., when I was a child, and I kept them all.

Aunt Sadie worked as a nurse at St. Vincent's Hospital, right where I stand.

She went to the school of nursing here, in fact. This is where she was "capped," as they called it, with her trim white hat, back in the days when horse-drawn ambulances still clattered over cobblestones.

In 1911 she had seen, but had not treated — they had been untreatable for being dead — the victims of the Triangle Shirtwaist Factory fire. Garment workers, she told me when she visited us the summer after that disaster, those were the victims. Trapped in a sweatshop, locked in by the owners, 146 people — 123 of them women — alive and at work and then suddenly dead. Some weren't much older than I was at the time: as young as fourteen. Most were under twenty-three. Most had burned to death. Some had kissed or held hands and then jumped from the windows and died that way.

The only time I saw my Aunt Sadie cry was when she told me that story. We were on a bench at the National Zoo, where we'd often go to talk outside of Mother's disapproving earshot; my memories of her tales are all incongruously accompanied by the hoots and howls of jungle creatures that we rarely actually got around to seeing. Sadie felt it was important for a young person like me to hear accounts of the injustices she'd witnessed, which at any rate were never far from her mind. Mother, naturally, thought that people of good character ought to limit their consideration of such things to policies that might prevent them, and not to dwell on the indignity of their miserable particulars. I, naturally, was entirely with Sadie on this issue — but in my typical fashion, what I took from her stories was often not what she'd meant them to impart. When I finally left home, my aim was not to bring succor to the oppressed, but rather to find adventure in the wilds of Manhattan.

Sadie was at St. Vincent's, too, when the *Titanic* sank, not much more than a year after the factory fire. A cold night for April, she said — the temperature probably about what it is tonight: a warm night for late December, but colder by the minute.

Ambulances pass in and out, their sirens wailing, and people on foot in various forms of distress walk or are assisted inside. Standing curbside, I watch them through the clouds of my own breath.

As much a listener as a talker, Sadie was the first person I remember encouraging me to write, treating my girlish verses with seriousness. I like to imagine her among the nurses who helped save the life of Edna St. Vincent Millay's uncle, thereby earning that poet her middle name. By 1953, when Dylan Thomas was brought here to die after his alcoholic self-poisoning, Sadie was long gone: lost in the flu epidemic of 1918, only fifty years old.

She was even longer gone in early 1955, when I was admitted briefly to St. Vincent's, before they handed me off to specialists. I hope her ghost was nowhere on the premises, since the sorry shape I was in was bound to have upset her. I'm glad I was too far out of my wits at the time to consider what her shade might have made of me.

"What do you think you're staring at?"

The voice — female, with a Spanish accent — comes from a small, wide figure leaning against a pillar just outside the sliding glass doors of the emergency room entrance.

"Oh dear," I say. "Was I staring?"

"You were looking right at me," she says. "What, you never saw a pregnant lady before?"

She is pregnant, it's true: Her coat is open at the front despite the cold, presumably because she is too rotund to zip it. She hasn't got a hat, and her thick black hair is curly and disheveled.

"Seen one?" I say. "I've been one. But I apologize. I was off somewhere else in my mind. Are you all right?"

"Not really," she says, clutching her abdomen. "I'm in a lot of pain. I'm about to have this baby."

"Oh my," I say, and step slowly closer. "Is anyone coming to help you?"

"The father," she says. "He dropped me off. He's trying to park. He wanted to drive, this being such a big occasion. Back when we were thinking this over months ago, I said we should just take the train. But with that vigilante guy on the loose, no way. Now Luis is trying to park, and I don't even know where he's at."

"Why didn't you just take a cab?"

"Lady," she says, "we got a lot on our minds right now."

"I suppose you do."

"I was crazy to have a baby," she says. "I hate this."

"It *is* awful," I say. "I only had one, and I still remember. But it'll be over soon. And do you know the best part? With a baby, you'll go crazy twice as fast."

I'm surprised to hear myself say this — I know it's the wrong thing; I'm not sure why I said it except that I think it's true — but her face, half-lit by the hospital windows, doesn't show bafflement or anger, only fear and pain. "What's your name, dear?" I ask.

"Maritza," she says.

"My name is Lillian. Does tonight's guest of honor have a name yet?"

"Yes," she says. "But it's a secret. *They're* a secret — one for if it's a girl, one for if it's a boy. Luis would kill me if I told you."

"That's okay," I say. "I understand. My husband and I, we were the same way. Didn't tell anybody until it was a done deal.

We called him Snooks while he was inside."

"We call ours Coco," she says. "Like coconut. Though he, or she, is a lot bigger than that now."

"I recall the feeling," I say. "I thought I'd get too big to fit in revolving doors."

"I know," says Maritza. "Thank god these ones slide open."

"Why don't you let me take you inside?"

"No!" she says, stepping away. "Then they'll check me in and Luis won't find me. His English is not so good as mine."

She doubles over and groans with the pain of a contraction. I hold her hand and rub her back through the puffy coat. "It's okay, Maritza," I say. "I won't let them take you back without him. But you'll be more comfortable inside. We can just walk up and down the hallway until he gets here. It's better to walk before they strap you down anyway."

"Are you sure?" she says. "I can't go back without him. Luis and I aren't married. We will be, but we aren't now. I think they won't send him to me because he's not my husband."

"We won't let them do that," I say. "I promise. We'll make sure he finds you, and you'll go together."

"You think I'm a slut for having this baby

296

when I'm not his wife?" she says, looking up at me.

I try not to show the shock I feel at hearing that word, try not to act old. "No!" I say, "That's ridiculous. Now come on, let's walk."

"Okay, Lillian," she says, face sweating, and she lets me help her inside.

The doors part for us, and we pass among the afflicted and their attendants, under the fluorescent lights. Maritza does a slight double take the next time she looks up at me in the unflattering antiseptic glow — a reaction to which I've become accustomed each time my wrinkles and my mottled skin betray what my strong voice and perfect posture conceal. "How old are you?" she asks.

"Eighty-four," I lie.

"That's way older than I thought at first," says Maritza. "You're the same age as my *abuelita*. But you don't act like her."

"Thank you," I say. "I think."

Doubled over again, she doesn't respond. I want to try to get her mind off what's worrying her: Luis's whereabouts, her pain, the pain to come. "Tell me more about Coco," I say.

"What do you want to know?"

"Well, it's exciting to have a child," I say.

"What are your plans? No, scratch that — let's not talk about plans. What are your *dreams* for the little person? What do you want for him or her?"

Her creased forehead shines brightly with sweat, but she manages a little smile. "It's silly," she says. "Luis says it is. But I want Coco to be the first baby born in 1985. You know, the New Year's baby."

"That's a good goal," I say, and look at my watch. "It's about 10:30. You're within sight of it, certainly. If you get this show on the road, Coco just might make it."

"Ma'am!" says a voice from across the room: the receptionist at the admitting desk. She has, I realize, been saying it for a while. "Do we need to get her to maternity?"

"No!" Maritza says, pivoting her belly away as if to protect its contents.

"We'll wait for the father, thank you!" I say with a cheery wave.

"Are you an angel?" says Maritza, squeezing my hand so tightly it hurts. "I'm so glad you're here."

"Good grief," I say. "Don't go delirious on me."

She looks past me to the sliding doors and relief floods her face. "Luis!" she shouts.

A thin man with a round face that makes him look even younger than Maritza has

298

just walked in, his dark eyes frantic, scanning the room. He sees us and sprints over.

He wears a leather jacket and a baseball cap. He takes off the latter and clutches it in his hands as he looks at Maritza and then at me, confused. She says something to him in Spanish and he nods to me, and I transfer Maritza's hand to his.

"I think you're all set to check in now, Maritza," I say. "Yes?"

"Yes," she says, holding on to Luis. "Thank you, Lillian."

"*Muchas gracias*, Lillian," says Luis.

"Of course," I say. "You're welcome. And good luck. Just remember, the first thousand diapers are the hardest."

Maritza laughs, then says, "It hurts to laugh."

Luis seems to have all but forgotten me. He's holding both of Maritza's hands now, his eyes sharp with terror and wonder; his car keys, I notice, still dangle between his fingers. I think about all the ads for engagement rings that I wrote over the years, mostly for R.H. Macy's but also freelance. *How are you fixed for diamonds?* they'd ask. *Diamonds are better than sulfur and molasses for sweethearts suffering from the megrims. We've seen one of our diamond wedding rings revive a young lady's drooping spirit in half a split second.* A time came when these ads stopped seeming funny to me, and I could no longer write them.

"Maritza," I say, "don't worry too much about what anybody's grandmother thinks. Do whatever you want. Anyone who tells you you shouldn't is trying to sell you something."

As I walk back to the street, I try to make a mental note to check tomorrow's papers and see whether Coco, born to Maritza and Luis, succeeds in being 1985's first sparkling new baby. It's nice to feel a small sense of investment in the future, even if it only lasts a few hours.

I have so little future left. And so much past.

19
A HORRID LITTLE GHOST

One leaves a sanitarium with a renewed enthusiasm for making oneself up.

At least I did, that early summer of 1955. But one must remain in the sanitarium for quite some time before one achieves such a transformation. Four months in my case: from bleakest February to greenest June.

The last poem I wrote before they sent me in was called "Blackout;" it went like this:

When life seems gray
And short of fizz
It seems that way
Because it is.

It eventually found a home in *Ladies' Home Journal,* accompanied by a cute illustration.

I wasn't kidding when I wrote it. Or so I gather; I don't remember writing it at all. What I know of that period I've had to piece together after the fact — à la that clever Lieutenant Columbo — from journals, letters, medical bills, interviews with eyewitnesses, and the few odd flashes that have come back to me over the years. Filling in, bit by bit, an ugly picture of myself. At once the detective, the victim, and the murderer.

The people around me, Max and Johnny particularly, had come to notice signs of trouble: my drinking, my distraction, my utter lack of pleasure in things — this last, I learned, called anhedonia, which to me sounded like the name of a flower Max never planted in the garden I never wanted. Max tried, in his graceless way, to snap me out of it with a series of increasingly tineared and desperate inducements that culminated in our second ocean voyage to Italy, about which the less said the better, but none of it was any use. I had become a stranger — dark and frightening — to the people I most loved.

Or so I gather.

So in I went.

Max checked me into Silver Hill, a residential treatment facility in the tranquil hinterland of bucolic Connecticut.

Severe depression, alcoholism, and menopause on top of it all: that was Dr. R's tripartite diagnosis, a three-pronged stab to

302

Max's heart and pride. I, evidently, was so far beyond caring by that point that I took in this assessment without interest, as though they were speaking of someone else — which, in a sense, I suppose they were.

Comprehensive psychiatric and addiction treatment services, those were what Silver Hill provided. I remember, for some reason, holding their brochure, which Max gave me to browse on the ride down from Manhattan that white morning in early February; it apparently declared that they had been restoring mental health since 1931 — the same year that I became the highest-paid advertising woman in America. Or so Max told me; I had no appetite for reading and simply took his word for it. I don't think he cared. I think he mostly wanted to give me something to hold that was not his hand.

Silver Hill was meant to be a hospital that didn't feel like a hospital but rather like a comfortable retreat in the New England countryside: quaint and comforting as a house in a snow globe. But only if one had really lost one's mind — only if it were gone completely, never to return — could one forget what it really was and why one was there.

February is the shortest month, and thank whomever for small blessings, because I've never been lower in my life. The Silver Hill staff tried their damnedest to fix me, with talk therapy, occupational therapy, and drugs — Miltown, Luminal, Thorazine — but I was so far down the well that they could not even reach me, let alone pull me up.

So they farmed me out. On the first of March they sent me to Greenwich Hospital — twenty miles southwest, almost to the state line — where I stayed for ten days. The location felt like an improvement: Even bedridden in my drab gown, brain scrubbed of every good and bad thought, I could feel myself closer to the city. Closer to the ocean, too; at night the open window sighed the cool breath of Long Island Sound.

The drawback was that they'd sent me there for electric shock treatments.

They didn't administer such therapy at Silver Hill.

Electroshock treatments are horrible — even though, indeed *because,* I can't remember having them. To their credit, the staff at Greenwich Hospital was advanced in its methods: scrupulous about strapping me down and fixing my mouth with a rubber bit to keep the seizures from breaking my bones or making me bite my tongue, considerate enough to give me a muscle relaxant — and a more sophisticated formulation, at that, than the blowgun poison some doctors still favored — along with a general anesthetic to spare me the suffocating horror of the muscle relaxant. Such, I'm told, are the measures they took for my comfort; I'm sure it's all true. But the treatments purged themselves from my mind even as they did their work — the way that cranes create and then erase themselves from the skyline, one might say — leaving me with only the faint nightmare recollection of lying in bed afterward, every muscle sore, with no notion of who I was, who I'd ever been, why I was in a hospital, how I'd gotten there, or what I'd be returning to when I left. If I ever left. If I'd ever been anywhere else.

But the treatments helped me when nothing else did. In time — and not much time, really — almost everything came back: my address and my phone number, the fact that I was married and had a child, Max's and Johnny's faces and names, my books, my fame, all my years at R.H. Macy's.

What did *not* come back were the days that had led me to Silver Hill — or, more to the point, the miserable person who I'd been in those days. In an almost-literal flash, the treatments had transfigured me. My healing brain's sentimental attempts to feel conflicted about this loss met with no success. No easy medical metaphor — they had amputated a wounded limb; no, they had cut out a tumor — seemed the right fit. The doctors' electric pulse was more like the clearing of an old attic, or the burning of a barren field: Rather than destroying a part of me, it had restored me to who I really was. Or who I imagined myself to be.

The counterfeit Boxfish — that crazy woman, that sorry drunk — was a mistake, a wrong turn, a missed stitch. Now she was gone, unraveled, with no stone to mark her grave, mourned by no one. Me least of all. She shadowed me for years, feeding off her inarticulate anger at the world, and when she saw that I was weak, she attacked. She sabotaged every effort I made to adjust my dime-bright expectations to my middle-aged maternal circumstances, and when the resultant shambles didn't satisfy her, she tried to kill me and nearly succeeded. So good riddance to her — the best of all possible riddances.

My only hesitation — the only thread of doubt in my vast tapestry of gratitude — has been the fear that, thanks to the treatments' extreme effectiveness at expunging my enemy from my memory, I might not recognize her if she ever came back. Almost all electroshock patients have follow-up treatments every few months or years to keep their symptoms in check; I never felt I needed them, and so I never did. Over nearly thirty years, of course, this fear has faded as the stakes have shrunk. If she comes back now to claim me — this tall, proud, husk of a woman, ending her days alone in Manhattan — then I can't see how the prize would be worth the fight.

Once the treatments were over I wanted to go home. I could have walked back to Murray Hill, I swore — an easy thirty miles along the Lower Post Road, a thoroughfare older than the Constitution, rambling through Port Chester and Rye, through Mamaroneck and New Rochelle, across the Bronx, over the Third Avenue Bridge into Harlem, past the homes and the businesses of every kind of New Yorker you can think of, straight down Lexington to East Thirty-Sixth — but of course they did not let me.

Rather I got shipped — alone this time, no Max, and certainly no Johnny — back to Silver Hill for indefinite "observation" and further rehabilitation.

For three months I hovered like an astronaut over my old life, my real life. I wanted so badly to return to it — but in my own way, on my own terms. The thought of friends seeing me in my current circumstances was abhorrent. Fortunately, few of them wanted to. I received a number of kind and thoughtful letters, but blessedly next to no requests to visit.

"If I may appeal to your expertise," I asked anodyne Dr. R as he made his rounds, "perhaps you can settle a question for me: Is crazy contagious? Some of my acquaintances behave as though it might be."

Dr. R, accustomed at long last to my kidding, took this in the spirit it was intended. "For the most part, no," he said. "Unless we're talking about something like syphilitic psychosis. And you can assure your friends that they're in no danger of catching that here. Silver Hill is a progressive institution, but only up to a point."

"Thank you, doctor. You've helped me win a bet with myself."

"A thing I *have* noticed," he continued, unable to avoid self-seriousness for more than thirty seconds or so, "is that encounters with people who are confronting their psychiatric issues often produce anxiety in people who are *not* confronting their psychiatric issues, precisely *because* they are not doing so. You might keep that in mind while you're reading your correspondence."

I shook my head in mock wonderment. "What a peculiar career you have chosen for yourself," I said. "Didn't your mother want you to become some *regular* sort of doctor? Like a podiatrist?"

"Don't get me started on my mother," said Dr. R.

My own parents were both dead by that time, to my great relief. My mother died in 1950; my father lost his will to live in her absence and followed not more than six months later to wherever it is that people who've died go.

Nowhere, I think, is what you'd call the place.

My older brother never came to visit me. He did write me letters, though: distant and condescending ones, because those were the shallow pools in which his small mind swam. When he sent me a clipping called "Mastering Your Impulses," about how alcoholics bring their problems upon themselves and need merely to "buck up" and "grow a spine," I never wanted to hear from him again, at least not while I was still inside. I sent him an envelope full of worthless plastic prizes that I'd collected from boxes of Cracker Jack — Dr. R was a psychiatrist, not a dentist — and I wrote my response on the backs of what the box called

309

a Zoo Card Animal Game: *You are acting no more sensitive than a stupid animal when you send things like that. I feel caged enough as it is. If that is all you can find it in your brain to send me, then I wish you'd refrain. I'll just see you when I get out.*

He did not write me anymore at Silver Hill, and that was fine with me.

Saintly Helen McGoldrick was the first guest I was permitted. She came in March, on a morning blue and bright with the muddy smell of spring. It happened to be Saint Patrick's Day — a Thursday, so she could avoid the weekend traffic — and she brought a bouquet of green carnations suited to the occasion. They reminded me of the potted four-leaf clover Max had gotten me two decades ago when we were first in love, their botanical luck long since run out.

I met Helen in the common area, where residents were allowed to have visitors. We could order coffee or tea and sit and drink it and pretend we were free: normal people joining friends at a café.

Anyone else would have lied, said I looked great, told me I was beginning to appear healthy again. Not Helen. "Lily," she said. "Your eyes!"

I welcomed her lack of pretense, though it was hard to look at her still-lovely face as it saw my ravaged one. "I know," I said, raising a hand to my cheek. "You're the only person I'm seeing until my eyes have recovered. The creases and circles are from the Thorazine. It affects some people that way. Others break out."

"Thorazine?" said Helen, leading me by the arm to a table. "Let's sit down."

"I meant to write you and explain," I said. "But I didn't have it in me. I figured I could just tell you in person, if you even want to hear about it."

"I do, of course," she said. "If you even want to talk about it."

"They only give shock treatments to patients with severe depression," I said. "And they sure had one in me."

A wispy, deferential presence — I was never sure what to call them; they were less than orderlies but more than waiters, and I'll bet if a patient suddenly pitched a fit their wispiness would firm up in a hurry — took our orders and brought us our cups, smooth and silent as a marionette angel.

"Ah yes, the forced charm of these hospital saucers reminds me," I said, and handed Helen a small wrapped package. "Open it."

"A leather coaster," said Helen, setting it

311

on the tabletop, then setting her coffee cup atop it. "With my initials. Thank you. They're training you to become a crafts-woman?"

"A slave," I said. "This whole setup is a racket. They're abducting middle-aged women as forced labor to finally break the back of the leatherworkers' union. I was go-ing to stamp a desperate request for help into it, but the clever bastards took away all the vowels. You'd have never made any sense of it."

Amusement and alarm spun across Hel-en's face like a dog chasing its tail. I laughed, for the first time in a long time.

"I'm joking, honeybunch," I said. "But don't I make a damn good lunatic? The coaster is the happy byproduct of my oc-cupational therapy. I'm made to stay pretty quiet here, aside from walking in the gar-dens and working on handicrafts. That's because of the Thorazine. They gave it to me in large quantities to keep me from get-ting too high after those shock treatments. They're weaning me off it now."

"I hear electroshock is a waking night-mare," said Helen. "I can understand if you don't want to relive that."

"Oh, I *do* want to talk about those, Helen. If I may?"

"Of course, Lily," she said. "That's why I came. It's been so long. I've missed your voice."

She took my hand across the table — probably mistaking the joy in my soppy eyes for anguish — and I let her.

"Here's the strangest thing," I said. "Whoever thought up those shock treatments ought to be canonized. For so long I'd been looking at the sky, and trees, and roast beef, and friends, and even though I knew they were beautiful, I could take no pleasure from any of them. And I'm not just talking about these past few terrible months, Helen. This was *years*. Now even a field mouse looks divine. The days are crowded with the good old reliable joys: orange juice and sunshine and Coca-Colas and crows and sparrows and blue jays and petunias. And I can feel that joy in my chest again, immediately. I don't have to work it out like a crossword puzzle."

Helen gave me a cautious smile. "Is that what the Thorazine is for?" she asked. "To keep the mouse mousey?"

"They can give me all the Thorazine in Smith, Kline and French's coffers," I said. "The mouse and I will remain in cahoots."

"Lily, that's wonderful. Blackened as they are, your eyes *do* have the look of your old self back in them. Will it last?"

"It's supposed to," I said. "I think it will. Dr. R tells me that I may well get *dejected* over crises in the future — the parakeet croaking or what have you — but I won't get *depressed.*"

"What a world of difference between those two words."

"It's almost been worth it to go through this horror," I said, "because I don't believe I can ever again look at the lowliest angleworm without rejoicing in its suppleness and complexity and sheer life."

"Speaking of worms," said Helen, "would you care to give me a tour of the grounds? Will they let you?"

"I'm not permitted to be alone," I said. "Not yet, anyway. But with you as my escort, they'll allow us to stroll around the Gardens of Insanity. Your timing's perfect, too. These drugs make it hard as hell to sit still."

She helped me to my feet, we returned our cups, and Helen signed me out with the front-desk nurse. We set out among the trees and walking paths and birdbaths; the air was clear and tinged with the loamy defrosting smell that follows a long winter. Thanks to the Thorazine I moved slowly, with stiff shuffling steps, but I didn't mind; it just meant more time to look.

On one secluded loop in the trail I halted Helen so we could watch a pair of eastern phoebes — elfin and gray, big-headed and fearless, pumping their tails like prizefighters — as they snatched black ants from a redbud's trunk.

"I wouldn't wish my troubles on my deadliest enemy," I said after they'd flown away. "Sometimes I think it would be better never to have known how beautiful the world is. Just to be able to pass calmly by rather than pay the admission fee for a ringside seat. But here I am, ringside again."

"If you had a deadliest enemy," Helen said, "which seems unlikely, then I can't imagine that person could manage to see any beauty in anything at all."

Unbidden, Olive Dodd popped into my head; I hadn't thought of her in ages. I recalled the harsh whistle she sounded through my halcyon days, and my wincing contempt for her, but I found that I could no longer feel it. In its place was a sad sympathy, a suspicion that she never managed any happiness.

I was about to ask Helen if she knew what ever became of Olive, when she spoke.

"You can tell me, if you want, that it's none of my beeswax," said Helen, taking my elbow to help me around a puddle in the path, "but has Max been to see you yet?"

"*Yet?*" I said, and laughed. "That's a good one."

"I'm sorry, Lily," she said. "I oughtn't to have brought it up."

"No, it's all right," I said. "It's one more thing I'm gearing up to face after I emerge from my cocoon. Max and I are getting a divorce."

"I'd thought you might be," Helen said. I could feel her eyes on the side of my face, but I couldn't look at her directly while we talked about that. "I'm sorry that's happening, Lily."

"We've been heading down that road for a while, as I think everyone who knows us knows," I said. And then, because it was clear that Helen was saying both that she was sorry *that* it was happening and asking more about *what* was happening, I added, "Even before Julia, Max and I had gotten stuck in a tiresome spiral. I got sadder and Max couldn't handle it and flung himself into the younger arms of his workplace subordinate. I found out and we tried to fix it, but I got worse — more drunk, more distant. He kept seeing her until finally I just broke and the rest is pretty well on the record. They're out and official now, at least,

316

and I can look at my situation honestly, as well as at theirs."

"Dwight and I thought you might patch things up."

"No," I said. "No. The new-girlfriend rift is sadly unpatchable. But do you know what's funny? Looking back, I can't understand how or why I suffered such intense melancholy when I found out about Julia."

"Well," she said. "It was frankly a snaky thing for Max to do. Taking up with her the way he did, with you in such a state."

"My reaction was out of proportion, though," I said. "That's my point. I can see that now. As much as I loved Max, as much as I still do, it's still not comprehensible that such an estrangement of affection could cause a person to literally shut down. To make them unable to pack a suitcase, or to get on a plane or train alone. Barely able to do it even with the aid of as faithful a friend as you."

"I should never have let you board that ship," said Helen, stopping in the middle of the path. "I could tell. I knew you weren't well. And look what happened."

"That incident, dear Helen, is something I cannot talk about," I said. "But it's not your fault. If it's anyone's fault, it's nobody's but mine. Even Max, blameworthy though he may be in other respects, isn't indictable on this count. Not really. Please don't forget that."

She was silent.

"Want to hear one more fun fact about Max's new lease on life?" I asked.

"Probably not," she said. "But all right."

"He called me up last week," I said. "The day I got back from Greenwich Hospital. And asked if I could fly to Reno."

"Reno?" said Helen. "To expedite the breakup?"

"Why else? I'm sure he thought I was just stalling when I said I couldn't go. He had the grand idea that I could take my 'rest cure' simultaneously with the divorce."

"Oh, good lord," said Helen. "Now that *is* a package holiday! He should put that in a letter to the state tourism commission. What a heel."

"I know, I know," I said. "And we *are* getting a divorce, I assured him. Uncontested. I accede to my abandonment. But I really just don't have the mind or strength or spirit to go to Nevada at this particular moment. Much less to cope with lawyers. I only have it in me to grapple with one overeducated professional at a time, and right now that's Dr. R. So Max has agreed to do it the slow, old-fashioned way, right here in New York

318

State, once I'm up to it."

"What a sweetheart," said Helen.

"Always a romantic," I said.

Helen's arm was now bearing an unfair share of my Thorazine-inflated weight; my legs had grown leaden, my mind fogged, given to repetition and forgetfulness. It's fun to be around someone who appreciates wit, but only to the extent one is able to be witty, and I was fading fast.

"How's Johnny taking it?" Helen asked.

"The Great Schism, you mean?"

Helen's voice snagged in her throat for an instant. "All of it," she said.

I slowed to a stop, bracing myself against a bench to still a twitch in my legs. "I try to console myself," I said, "with the notion that this will all be character-building for him. Johnny, fortunately, is thirteen years old. His intense self-regard will get him through anything. Helen, would you forgive me if I told you I need to rest? This delightful excursion has just about finished me off."

She signed me back in at the desk, then insisted on waiting — reading a book in the common area with a quiet cavalcade of nuts, drunks, and dope fiends drifting around her, a lone bloom amid rock-slide debris — while I took my nap.

Afterwards we had a late lunch together,

and then she had to leave to catch her train back to Manhattan. "I'll be back," she said. "As often as you'll have me. And I'll bring Johnny as soon as Dr. R says you're ready."

We hugged good-bye. As I watched her go, she in her smart traveling coat, I admired how impressive she had become. As a dewy youth she'd been lovely, as a successful illustrator she'd been elegant, but now her application of patience and poise had somehow made her *formidable:* the sort of figure one stares at on the street, trying to recall what she's famous for.

I realized, without surprise, that I had neglected to inquire after all the good news her recent letters had contained. Her young Merritt was out of the Army at last, in one piece, in fine spirits, sporting a chestful of medals from Korea. One step-daughter was sending her twins to high school, while the other — summa cum laude at Barnard, J.D. from Fordham, not, as they say, interested in boys — had hired on as legislative counsel for Senator Lehman and was helping to give that tub-thumper McCarthy his long-due comeuppance, much to her father's delight. Dwight himself was a dynamo at seventy-one, still bounding down the front steps every morning to his battle station at *The New Republic,* where he'd been the art editor now for a decade. And Helen had just gotten a letter "out of the blue" from her alma mater: They were planning a retrospective exhibition of her illustrations, maybe even a catalogue. *So your important work won't be forgotten,* they'd said. "Of course they'll *have* to feature your verses, too," Helen had written. "All my best doodles took root in your rhymes. We're a package deal!"

She was a damn good egg, that Helen Mc-Goldrick. Even though Silver Hill gave me analysis aplenty, her ear was superior to ten thousand psychiatrists, and I was grateful beyond words for her loan of it that Saint Patrick's Day.

If you can fool even your closest friends into thinking you're sane, then maybe you're not so crazy after all.

Dr. R was handsome, but devoid of threat. Blandsome. A generic doctor-ish set of good looks.

He was not much of a reader, it turned out, though his office was book lined. They were for show. I looked at them, their spines on the shelves, whenever I needed to break eye contact, so as not to appear too intense. It was early May, and I was angling for a change in my inmate status.

"With all due respect, Doc," I said, "I don't like therapy — talk therapy. I have a lot of friends, and I'm up to contacting them now. So I don't feel like I need to keep paying someone to listen to me."

"One of the key features of therapy, Lillian," he said, "is that the therapist is an outsider. Coolheaded and objective. Not your friend, but a trusted professional."

This I ignored.

"And occupational therapy," I said. "I liked it for a while, but now I can keep myself occupied."

This was accurate. After the shock treatments, I'd been able to start writing poems again. Tacking them to the wall above the maple desk in my room, like an inmate hash marking down the days. Granted, they were a bit fixated on gloomy topics, but they were poems nevertheless. The one I'd written that morning began:

Please, God, arrange to let me be
A ghost, if You will be so kind,
Just long enough to ease my mind.
A horrid little ghost — and there
I'll sit upon his bed and stare
Until his tortured eyelids prickle. . . .

My great subject during that period was my

unsatisfiable longing to draw sad, salt tears from the eyes of my erstwhile darling. Max would never cry over me, though, not ever again. I felt as though these poems represented progress — away from self-nullifying melancholy, toward a concrete and productive anger — but I wasn't confident that others would interpret them the same way, and I didn't show them to Dr. R.

"Lillian," said Dr. R, "I'm happy your old habits and routines are finding their way back into your life. But, again, occupational therapy serves a different purpose than your poetry, so we're going to keep that up, too."

"All right," I said. "I understand. And I am grateful for the chance to build up my handmade pot holder collection. But my industriousness has been such that I've even written a poetical message for you. Want to hear it?"

"Sure," he said, smiling.

I read aloud:

Dear Dr. Rosemont, W.G.,
This is the day you don't see me
Trying to do anything you don't want to see.
Congratulations! Now I'm painin'
To buy a few things in New Canaan,
So I'd consider it a boon
If I could go this afternoon.

I knew that they were worried about a relapse of my drinking, and about the collapse of my marriage making me feel vulnerable — and honestly so was I — but I wanted out. Just out for a while: the tiny responsibility of going by myself into the town and then coming back.

Dr. R laughed appreciatively, but the effort got me nowhere.

"Lillian, I'm afraid we'll have to keep you close by as much as possible, and under constant supervision for a little while longer," said Dr. R, steepling his fingers as they must have taught him to do in Serious Doctor School. "Because of the grave nature of the incident that brought you here. I'm sure you understand."

"Oh, Dr. R," I said, trying to force my lips from rictus to actual smile. "Don't let's live in the past. I've moved on."

"We have to keep you moving in the right direction, though, Lillian."

"Taking some small unescorted trips seems to me to be one of the steps that will take us in that direction, doctor."

"It is," he said. "In due time. But we're not ready for that yet. Who's the expert here, Lillian?"

That was how it had been going for weeks. I didn't want to leave Silver Hill permanently, not yet. I was actually enjoying it: the rest, the quiet, my recovered mental self. But I did want some freedom and a bit more privacy. Yet as much as I tried to persuade Dr. R to let me have more of each of these, he refused.

"Of course it's you, Dr. R," I said, trying to laugh with him.

"How about this, though: Your son's coming to visit you this Saturday, yes?"

"He is," I said.

Thirteen years old, he'd be taking the train all the way up on his own. It would be his first visit. Dr. R had suggested three weeks ago that it might be time for Johnny to be reunited with his mother, but I'd demurred; I had not wanted him to see me until I looked less shattered, until I could be sure I had the stamina to sustain a lifted spirit for a full weekend. I did not mention this to Johnny, although I had been writing him a letter a day since the middle of March — and sometimes two letters on eventful days: when a craft project had gone spectacularly well, when a crazy person had done something crazy, et cetera.

"We'll have a nurse take you two into town," said Dr. R with exaggerated benevolence. "For shopping, for ice cream, for a movie. Whatever you like."

I had always thought that the capacity to persuade was based on one's wit, cleverness, and skill. But when one is trying to convince one's doctor to let one out of a mental institution, it becomes apparent that persuasion actually has a great deal to do with the position of power that one occupies to begin with. No amount of wit, it seems, will get one out of an involuntary psychiatric commitment.

Choice is an illusion promoted by the powerful.

"All right," was all I said out loud. "That sounds like a fair compromise."

"There's a reasonable girl," said Dr. R, standing up and walking around his desk to show me out, back to my pot holders and my shuffles through the garden.

I was not a girl. I was fifty-five. At that point in my life, an old fifty-five. But I stood and thanked him and went to go pick at my institutional lunch.

By the end of my stay, though, I had to admit: It was a good shop they ran, and I was a different person again, more like I'd been twenty years before.

I wouldn't miss having doctors and nurses hovering around to remind me of all my pills and exercise appointments, but they truly had helped me.

The week before my discharge I felt ready to face even the least appealing tasks ahead of me. I'd been sending business correspondence, tying up loose ends.

I'd found, in my luggage, one of Max's old handkerchiefs, one my mother had embroidered for our honeymoon trip to Italy in 1935. I had it pressed, and I mailed it to him at his new address, the apartment where he'd moved in with Julia on the Upper East Side. I'd made the note out to both of them, because this was the new order of things, the rearranged way my life would have to be. I would not be rude. I would not shun or ignore them. Civility and courtesy were the refrain of my song in those days, more than ever.

It seemed to work, I guess. Max called to thank me, and to apologize for his hateful Reno request.

And Julia wrote me back at Silver Hill — on a card, no less. An American Greetings card featuring a child with eyes the size of asteroids surrounded by flowers and a swooping bluebird of happiness. She loved, as I would soon discover, kitsch of almost any kind: patriotic, religious, you name it. Her sentiments would always be highly sentimental.

With all you have on your heart right now, it was so sweet and thoughtful of you to take the time to send this! she had written. *I am sorry about everything, but I hope we can be friends.*

Friends, no. But I would not waste my exertions cultivating anyone as an enemy.

And as the years went by, I would have to admit to a grudging admiration for Julia and the way, during the long summers that Johnny would spend with them, first in Chicago and then in California, she threw herself into the business of stepmothering. She quit work completely after she gave birth to her daughter with Max, and from what I could tell, never missed her job or looked back, treating both her own baby and Johnny with equally doting attention. All the child-rearing paraphernalia that felt to me like rigmarole, she enjoyed. I missed Johnny dearly, of course, during these bouts of shared custody. They made me feel, at first, like the summer was a marble mausoleum, and I was left behind, dispassionately, for those months' entirety, interred and cold.

But once I came to see how much Johnny liked his trips out west, and how well Julia treated him, I let myself enjoy my time alone as well. Because that's the unspoken secret that had always troubled me in the first place: children can be so *boring*. Even the best of them. And their parents are *always* boring. But Julia was impervious to that boredom's effect.

My last night at Silver Hill — after dinner and before lights-out — I went for a walk alone around the grounds. They finally let me, being as I was departing the next morning and would then be on my own indefinitely.

Early June, the roses in bloom, all those blossoms like tiny mouths exhaling their perfume into the air above the path.

The moon was full, and under its light the hills did look silver.

I stood looking up at it and thought, without really meaning to, of Artie, my editor at E.P. Dutton, who had been dead for many years. Arthur Eugene Stanley, kind and courtly, who had published my first book of verse, *Oh, Do Not Ask for Promises* — though he'd wanted to call it *Frequent Wishing on the Gracious Moon*.

I wondered whether my life might have turned out differently if I had gone with that title instead, as Artie had urged me to. Whether there was another world in which I had yielded to his request, and whether in that world I would not be standing alone under the full moon at Silver Hill, contemplating the wreck of my previous twenty years.

But there was no way to know, and no way to go back. I could not revise. I had been who I had been, and so I largely remained.

20
THE GOLDEN STATE

Never in my life have I shown up at a party empty-handed, and I am not about to spoil my record tonight.

I need to get a hostess gift for Wendy, and something to share with her guests. I'm half a mile from my destination, so my prospects are diminishing quickly. This, perhaps, is for the best: When I have all of Manhattan to choose from I tend to dither, to hold out for perfection — but as any poet can testify, limits encourage both inspiration and decisiveness.

Around Jackson Square, near where Greenwich Avenue meets Eighth, I spy a grocery store and video rental place — a bodega? I'm never sure what qualifies — and make my way toward its door. The window is crowded with rows of cut flowers, a hand-labeled price taped to each vase; above them, a Filipino flag is framed by dozens of dangling multicolored plastic rosaries.

They remind me of Max's mother, who was very devout. And an excellent cook. When I was in the vaguely distinguished twilight of my career, I often got requests from the author-dieticians of women's magazines for favorite recipes to print in their "Culinary Corners." I always gave them one I'd learned from Mrs. Dante Caputo, including a risotto that was a real filler-upper.

In the old days I'd always arrange to bring something homemade to a party, but that's not an option tonight, and anyway there's no sense in being sentimental. In retrospect most of those bygone canapés appall: grisly assemblies of cocktail wieners and maraschino cherries and liver paste that a decade of war and privation barely managed to cast as indulgent. Instead, I walk up and down the fluorescently lit aisles, searching for some packaged treat that Wendy might like.

"You looking for anything in particular?" asks the clerk, a young man — in his late teens or early twenties, probably — with jet-black hair and tired eyes.

"Yes," I say. "Party foods. But I do believe that I have found them."

I pick up a bag of kettle-cooked potato

chips — a brand Gian and the kids brought back from Cape Cod that I've never before seen in the city — and a packet of Mexican *mazapan* with red roses on the wrappers, which I know will charm Wendy. I bring them to the counter.

"You know these aren't marzipan, right?" says the clerk as he gets ready to ring me up.

"Yes, I do," I say. "Thank you."

"I ask because the other day some guy bought them and came back in here mad, wanting a refund because they're made from peanuts, not almonds."

"How unfortunate," I say. "I love marzipan, but I've had these before and they're delightful. I read that they make them this way because peanuts are easier to grow in Mexico."

"I don't know about that," he says. "I just don't want to get blamed for anybody else's bad choices."

"Rest assured, I take full credit and blame for all my choices, good and bad," I say. "What's your name?"

"Cesar Julius," he says. "I go by C. J."

"I'm Lillian," I say, and point to the flowers in the window. "If you were having a New Year's Eve party and I were coming over, which of these flowers would you most want to see me carrying?"

C. J.'s eyes meet mine for the first time since I walked in. "Is that a serious question?" he says. "Like, do you want me to tell you what's popular, or are you seriously asking me what I would want you to bring?"

"I'm generally very precise," I say. "This is not an exception."

C. J. squints, then smirks. "Okay," he says. "Be right back."

He glides past me from behind the counter, disappearing into the aisles, and I hear a storeroom door open with a jingle of keys. For a moment I'm alone on the sales floor, peering between the rosaries at the massive art deco façade of the Greenwich electric substation and the red brick ziggurat of the Port Authority building farther on. They're both somewhat obscured by my reflection, which — thanks to backlighting and my broad-brimmed hat — appears faceless, headless, like an apparition out of M. R. James. This pleases me.

I scarcely have time to take in this view before C. J. returns, takes his spot at the register, and ceremoniously sets before me a glazed terra-cotta pot full of dirt.

He slouches against the countertop to gauge my reaction.

"That," I say, "seems to be a pot full of dirt."

"Yep," he says. "There's a bulb in it."

"Amaryllis?"

He grins. "You're good," he says. "It's a hippeastrum, really. Winter-blooming. But if you call it that nobody'll know what you're talking about, so it's an amaryllis. A Dutch amaryllis."

I slide off a glove to brush the top of the soil, and sure enough, my finger finds the pale green ridge of a shoot just breaking the surface.

"Don't get me wrong," C. J. says, "I like cut flowers and all. But it's New Year's Eve. Do you want to give a present that'll start wilting by tomorrow, that'll be dead in a week? Does that make you feel good about the future?"

He taps the terra-cotta rim. "Right now," he says, "this is a pot of dirt. But by the first week of February your friend will have a big bunch of flowers better looking than anything you see in that window. I'll throw in a little card that tells how to keep it alive, make it bloom every year. It's pretty easy. Now, if you and your friend don't want to wait a month to see some flowers, I don't blame you. There's lots of great stuff in the window, and you can take your pick. But —

to answer your question — this is what I'd want you to bring to *my* party."

"Sold," I say.

He wraps the pot in a cellophane cone with two loops of twine supporting the bottom, then finds a bag for my chips and my candy. "Speaking of your party," I say, wriggling back into my glove, "do you have one to go to tonight? Or is New Year's Eve's not your thing?"

"I *should* be going to a party," he says. "But I have to be here all night. It's my parents' store. I'm giving them the night off. But they don't really even want me here. They didn't work their whole lives just so I can do the same thing they're doing. I have a high school diploma, plus almost thirty hours at QCC, studying to be a lab tech. I speak three languages. English, Tagalog, and Spanish. I should be doing *something* else."

I'm at a loss for a response that's not false or patronizing. "It's a very nice shop," I say.

"It's not a nice neighborhood, though," he says. "My dad's been held up twice in the last year. I want him to sell the place, but they need the income."

"How long have they had it?" I ask.

"Since 1970," says C. J. "Not all at this location. They were in Queens for twelve years before they moved here. Lots of immigrant people work in Manhattan hospitals now, and they need a place to buy their stuff."

"That's a long time, since 1970."

"Too long if you ask me," he says. "We've been in the States for twenty years, ever since I was a little kid. We came when a lot of other Asian people came, after the law changed."

"I remember that," I say.

And I do, more or less. I remember Kennedy talking about the need for it — calling the old system of racist quotas *intolerable* — though it was Johnson who finally signed it. I used to be able to remember these things perfectly: Names and dates leapt to mind with no effort, along with a half-dozen rhymes, and maybe a pun or two. Now I find myself in a golden age of trivia — as evidenced by that board game Gian and all his friends love so much, with its polychrome plastic pies — just as my recall has started to fade: a gunslinger growing slow on the draw even as the Gold Rush is breaking out. The Hart–Celler Act! How could I forget? Emanuel Celler, Brooklyn's long-tenured hero! Defending the huddled masses in the shadow of Liberty herself!

C. J. is watching me from over my wrapped

337

parcels; I have let myself drift. "What's that you're watching?" I ask, diverting attention from myself, pointing at the small black-and-white television set on the counter behind him. "Dick Clark in Times Square?"

"It's about to be the *Tonight Show*," he says. "It'll be a rerun."

"Are you kidding me?" I say. "If you're short on holiday spirit, at least show some civic pride."

"What do you mean?"

"I'm still mad at Johnny Carson for moving his show to L.A. It was so adult when he was here in Manhattan. It was for grown-ups. It had an edge. Now that it's in beautiful downtown Burbank, or Bakersfield, or wherever, it just isn't the same."

"He used to do the show here?" C. J. says. "I never knew that. I guess I've seen some of them, those old shows of his. I don't always understand them. Maybe he didn't really have people like me in mind when he made them. Young people. Brown people. Anyway, I guess a lot has changed since then."

"That is true," I say. "A lot has changed."

"Well, I don't blame him for moving. L.A. is where the stars are, right? I'd go there myself if I could. That's where my family came in — on the West Coast, anyway —

338

but then we kept going, to New York City. I have no idea why. We should have stayed put. The Golden State. I've got a ton of cousins out there. I'm thinking of going back."

"Oh, C. J., I hate to hear promising young people say things like that. This city needs you."

"Lillian, no offense," says C. J., "but you just met me. I haven't been feeling so promising lately. To make our rent here, we've had to start staying open all night. My parents have to sleep sometime, so I'm taking a break from school to help. I'm scared for them. I don't want my mom or my dad working here alone in the middle of the night. If the neighborhood gets any worse our customers will stop coming. We'll just be here to get robbed. But if it gets any better the rent will go up. It's not a good situation."

C. J. is looking at the television, not really watching it. On the screen are crowds of people, laughing and waving, some holding hand-lettered greetings to the folks back home, others raising two fingers for peace. The volume is either off or too low for me to hear.

"Since you have a date with the Best of Carson, and I have a party to get to, I won't

339

bore you with the specifics. How much do I owe you?"

"Oh man, sorry," he says. "$10.55."

I remove eleven dollars from my wallet and in the process discover that a faintly alarming quantity of bills still remains inside. This, I realize, is the result of an error, one of my little lapses: I took out cash from the bank yesterday, having forgotten until this moment that I'd also cashed a check at the market that morning. Nearly a hundred dollars. Traipsing through Chelsea after midnight with such a heavy pocketbook seems like a foolhardy undertaking.

"Listen, C. J." I say, "Keep the change."

I hand him the rest of the bills left in my wallet.

He looks flummoxed, even a bit angry. "What?" he says. "No way, Lillian. I'm not going to take all your cash. I didn't tell you my story because I'm looking for charity."

"I know that," I say. "Come on, C. J. You'll be doing me a favor. You see, I'm walking from here to a party in Chelsea, and then home to Murray Hill."

"And so what? The cash is too heavy?"

"No, silly. I don't want to be carrying that much money on me. I'd feel too vulnerable."

He stares at me, open mouthed with

exasperation. "Lillian," he says, "that is the craziest thing I've heard in all of 1984. It's New Year's Eve! It's going to be pandemonium out there! What if you get in trouble and have to catch a cab?"

"If I get in trouble," I say in my sweetest old-lady voice, "I'll catch an ambulance. Now, look, C. J., I don't want to offend you, and I won't try to make the case that you need this more than I do. But come on — Happy New Year."

His gaze shifts from my face to the bills on the countertop. "All right," he says. "All right. If you insist. Thanks, Lillian."

"Thank you, C. J.," I say, taking one parcel in each hand. "I hope you do make it to L.A. eventually."

The little bell on the door rings as I step through it, out into the last hour of 1984.

21
SOLVITUR AMBULANDO

Among the many unsurprising facts of life that, when taken in aggregate, ultimately spell out the doom of our species is this: People who command respect are never as widely known as people who command attention.

For a time I commanded both. I attracted attention and held it. I wasn't famous, exactly — Henry Luce never threatened to put me on the cover of *Time* — but those who knew my work kept tabs on me, watched to see what I'd do next. After R.H. Macy's sent pregnant me packing, my devotees somehow grew even more passionate, distilling into a cult of hermetists eerily adept at spotting my freelance copy — to which, of course, my name was never attached. With my association with my long-time employer dissolved and my poetry collections on their way out of print, my following became oddly similar to those of the pseudonymous criminals from the outer boroughs who cover subway cars with bright, hyperelaborate, all-but-illegible graffiti: fans keen-eyed enough to recognize not only art but authorship. The Lillian Boxfish Society! Connoisseurs of the cast-aside! Taxonomists of trash! Secret agents of an aimless, harmless, bottomless conspiracy no one can unlock — me least of all. I once received a beautiful handwritten seven-page letter from a twelve-year-old girl on an Indian reservation in Idaho that made the observation — supported by a dozen examples drawn from twenty-odd years of poems and prose, ads and verses — that tropical birds appear with great frequency in my work. *They often have funny names,* I replied by way of explanation.

But I never garnered enough of either — enough respect, enough attention — to be invited to appear on, say, *The Tonight Show Starring Johnny Carson.* Even when it was still based in New York.

And this is a shame, because I can say without undue pride that I would have been *so good* as a guest on those national programs: *What's My Line?, Hollywood Squares,* all the rest. At a certain point in my career, at my quickest and cleverest, I even would have been great — but that point was long past when I appeared on TV for the very last time.

Although I never hit the television jackpot, over the years I did make several well-received appearances on local affiliates of the major networks: news programs, talk shows, the occasional bit of occasional verse during a Yankees or Dodgers broadcast. From the outset, though, that final appearance was different: a one-off for a public television program called *Where They've Been and Where They're Going,* which took as its underwriter-seducing ambit the discussion of particular industries and the most eminent achievers within them.

When the show's producer, Mindy, first called me, she pitched the appearance as an opportunity to talk about my storied background, as well as a chance for some of the notable advertising women who'd succeeded me to honor the trail I had blazed.

Her invitation came in the spring of 1980, an anxious season when seemingly every flat surface in Manhattan was adorned with a "New Yorkers for Kennedy" sign. I had, by that time, finally stopped writing copy. For years I'd worked on campaigns for Arrow shirts, Pabst Blue Ribbon beer, Martex fiber, Clairol, DuPont, Seagram's, Simmons Beautyrest, and Chef Boyardee — a lot of decent freelance clients in the 1960s and '70s — but I didn't need the money anymore: I'd saved a lot, invested wisely. And lately copywriting hadn't been bringing me joy. So I'd let it go. I didn't quit, per se; I just started saying no until eventually no one was asking.

Poetry still flowed out of me — an unstoppable effluence — so I continued to write greeting cards, which I'd taken up not long after I got out of Silver Hill, but even that felt more rote than satisfying. The neighborhood of verbal felicity in which I still resided had gone down, down, down. I kept living there — trimming the hedges, freshening up the paint — but everyone else had died or moved away.

So Mindy's proposition caught me at a moment of uncharacteristic vulnerability. I let my guard down, allowed myself to be swayed. Solicitousness and flattery are, of course, the classic methods for preying on the aged. This, I'm unhappy to report, is because they work.

Though I'd have preferred to walk — it was only two miles I didn't want to get windblown on the way, so I took a cab to the studio on the Upper West Side.

When I showed up, Mindy greeted me with compliments. She had a feathered and

345

blow-dried haircut and a propensity to exclaim.

"Miss Boxfish, right on time! Don't *you* look sharp in that scarlet suit!" she said. "Thank you for not wearing black, or navy blue, or white. You'd be amazed how many people ignore our directions!"

"They think they know best what will make them look good, I imagine," I said. "But I assume you know your business, and I've done this often enough not to second-guess you. In fact I think I was in this very same studio once before, almost thirty years ago, to be a guest on Betty Furness's *Success Story.*"

"Is that so!" said Mindy, who clearly had no idea what I was talking about, no clue as to whether Betty Furness was a person or a manufacturer of home heating units. "I hope we'll get a chance to talk about some of that fascinating history today! Now the show, as you know, is telecast from seven to eight — which means this morning we'll be shooting for an hour or so! We'll probably go a little longer, so if we need to edit or cut anything, we can! We'll have the material!"

As I wondered what might cause a person to sustain such apparent enthusiasm — an endocrine condition? cocaine? — Mindy waved over an assistant who took my coat and hung it up. The studio was air-conditioned to a meat-locker temperature, the better to prevent us from becoming sweaty and shiny under the lights.

The other guest panelists were Leslie Monroe, an ad exec who'd rocketed from the copywriter ranks in the glossy 1960s and was still in the game, and Geraldine Kidd — she *did* look young — who'd recently made a stir with a provocative shampoo campaign and was on her way up. We all met in the green room.

The show's host, Tuck Merkington, came back and greeted us; he was fresh from makeup, salt-and-pepper hair shellacked into an oceanic sweep above his leonine face. Like so many public-television people, he was a former radio guy, with a voice made for broadcasting: even his name sounded like an avuncular chuckle. He thanked us for coming, and Mindy marched us to the set to arrange us in our places, tasteful chairs arrayed in a semicircle that was part home den, part doctor's waiting room.

The tape rolled. Tuck ran through his introductions of each of us, then kicked off the discussion with a patronizing cliché: "Now, this program will no doubt be watched by a lot of girls who already have a toe on the first rung of the advertising ladder," he said. "I'd love to ask you on their behalf: What steps are taken by those who scale the heights?"

Geraldine Kidd, unfazed by Tuck's vapidity, jumped in. "Listen, ladies, here is where you stand," she said. "Advertising is no longer the dream job of every high-school girl. Radio, television, and public relations have passed it in the popularity race. This is all to the good for those of you who want advertising or nothing, because you really stand a chance to make it."

"Indeed," I agreed. "The same skills that I built my career on are as valuable as ever. If you write well, if you have creativity and good instincts about how to communicate with people, then you'll make progress. Once you get in the door, it won't take long before your talents are recognized."

"Well, creativity is always good," said Leslie Monroe. "But we should be clear that writing is no longer the advertiser's primary tool. As early as the sixties, when I got my start, whether you were making classy ads for Ogilvy or hilarious ones for Bernbach, the priority was always to deliver a complete visual statement. Graphic artists and copywriters had come to be regarded as equals."

348

"Certainly, visual impact has always been important," I said. "I always worked with talented illustrators, and they deserve more recognition than they get. But words are still key. No matter what first draws our attention, language is where we make our decisions. If you look at the first ad in English — by William Caxton, from the 1400s — it says that a volume of Easter rules is for sale at his print shop and can be had 'good cheap.' No matter how you dress them up, the basic principles of advertising are all already there in Caxton's ad."

"What a charming fact, Miss Boxfish," said Tuck. "Very typical of your famous style, as I understand it."

While I was trying to figure out what Tuck meant by this — typical how? — Geraldine Kidd piped up again.

"We all still get a giggle from the ads of Miss Boxfish's era," she said with a youthful toss of her youthful head. "I'm sure most of us remember our grandparents constantly quoting some of the famous Boxfish lines. And they were, to be sure, hugely innovative for their time. But over the years, the way we in the profession think about advertising — how it fits into a larger marketing plan — has changed a lot. For instance, and to respectfully take issue with something

Miss Boxfish just said, we now understand that the advertising that we remember from her heyday simply does not take full account of the way people actually make purchases."

"Really, Miss Kidd?" said Tuck. "How do you mean?"

And then Geraldine Kidd sat up in her seat, expertly angled her shoulders toward the "A" camera, and proceeded to demolish everything I had achieved in my career.

"First of all" she said, "the old ads *spoke* to people. They charmed them, won them over, laid out the case for the product. This kind of friendly persuasion can be delightful, but it also assumes that the audience has the linguistic aptitude to follow the argument, the sophistication to appreciate the wit. This style of advertising can't sell anything to people who don't have those capacities. Next, the old ads assume that it's the heads of households — educated and informed — who make purchase decisions. That isn't necessarily so. As often as not, the real decision maker is a child. I could cite other examples, but my point is that it is ultimately just not that important how much we enjoy a particular ad, or how much we're entertained by it. Do we remember the name of the product? Will we act on what we've been told? That's what matters. We can't value our own cleverness more than our results."

"I think we all know it was established early on," said Tuck with a wink, "that pictures of little children can sell just about anything."

Then Leslie Monroe spoke up — smiling, wresting the wheel of the discussion away from addled Tuck, reasserting her authority over the upstart Kidd — to administer the coup de grâce.

"That's exactly right, Tuck," she said. "And not *only* children. Animals. Music. Fire. Sex. Darkness. Loud noises. The odors of the body. We've known for fifty thousand years that these things carry a powerful emotional charge. I came on the advertising scene just as we were finally learning how to use them in a systematic way to reach and motivate our customers."

She pivoted in her seat — Lurex halter glinting beneath her cropped batwing jacket — and laid a small, lushly moisturized hand on my elbow.

"Lillian's writing from those early years," she said, "the late 1920s to the early '40s, is just *so* clever. So glamorous, in its zany way. So *fun*! And innovative! And that, I'm sad to say, is really the problem. There's only one Lillian Boxfish. Ads that tried to imitate

351

what she did — that used humor to appeal to people's sentiments and their reason — weren't as successful. Worse, they made it easier for the audience to spot the tricks, to learn the methods. Lillian's ads were stylish, but styles change for exactly this reason. My peers and I knew we'd never beat Lillian at her own game. So we cut in line. We got to the audience *before* they listened to her pitch, before they *thought* anything at all. We figured out that it's far more effective to appeal to fundamental emotions: envy, fear, lust. Animal instincts."

"Miss Boxfish?" said Tuck, theatrically inquisitive. "Your thoughts?"

Meeting Tuck's phony gaze felt unwholesome, like talking to a wax dummy, so I looked past him to Mindy, who was watching through the windows of the control room. Nothing in her unflaggingly upbeat mien suggested that this was going any way other than as planned; she displayed no concern that rather than honoring my legacy, Tuck and my fellow guests were painting me as the Neanderthal in their History of Man diorama. Instead of *Let's thank the pioneering women who came before us!*, their tone was more along the lines of *Remember how we used to wear hoop skirts?*

"My thoughts?" I said. "My thoughts are

that I am on this program by some mistake."

In the glowing window, beyond the cameramen, Mindy was shaking her head.

"I'm afraid I've arrived unprepared to defend my approach to writing ads," I said, "never mind the very concept of professional responsibility, or the practice of simply treating people with respect. Therefore I'm compelled to defer to the au courant expertise of my two successors. Please, ladies, resume the accounts of your efforts to unwind the supposed advances of civilization and return us consumers to a state of pliable savagery. Who knows, perhaps some young lady who watches this program will take up where you leave off and find a way to ease us all back into the trees with the orangutans, who I gather are deft hands at the fruit market. With luck and hard work, perhaps we'll even recover our old gills and quit terrestrial life entirely. Back to the sea! That Florida swampland Mother bought may prove to be a good investment after all. In any event, I wish you both luck in your quest. I will not be keeping track of your progress, however. My interests, such as they are, lie elsewhere. To be clear, it's not that I no longer want to work in the world that you're describing. It's that I no longer want to *live* in the world that you're describing."

Tuck Merkington looked at me, then at Leslie Monroe and Geraldine Kidd, neither of whom seemed to have anything to say to that.

My intention wasn't to be rude, but I couldn't remain.

I got to my feet from the sleek stuffed chair.

"Thank you so much for having me," I said, clearly and with courtesy, "but I simply can't stay. I have to be going. Thank you, Tuck. Thank you, Leslie, Geraldine. Goodbye."

Mindy intercepted me the instant I stepped off camera. She tried to convince me to continue the panel, but I declined every one of her exclamatory entreaties.

It's probably not accurate to say that I realized, as I unclipped my lavalier mic, wound its lead around the transmitter, and deposited both in Mindy's beseeching hand, that this would be the last act of my career in advertising. I had known already that it was over; I had allowed Mindy to leverage my vanity to convince me otherwise, to lure me — like a safecracker or an assassin from some silly film — into taking one last job. Never again: Henceforth I would say no to all similar invitations, though these were not exactly flying thick as locusts anyway. My public appearances since then have been limited to a few speeches at girls' schools for commencements or career days, occasions at which I was introduced only as a vague eminence, an old lady who used to be funny. All these events I have enjoyed tremendously.

Burning a bridge, as any tactician will tell you, sometimes saves more than it costs.

I asked for and received my coat from Mindy's cringing assistant, buttoned it over my absurd, optimistic, embarrassing scarlet suit, and headed outside into the late-March sunlight to set about walking home, knowing that only a walk — zigzagging among strangers on their own peculiar errands, setting my pace in counterpoint to my pulse, dissolving myself in the street — would help me feel better.

A motto favored by the ancients was *solvitur ambulando*: It is solved by walking. Sometimes, I might add, by walking out. I like to imagine that that irascible tub dweller Diogenes would have approved of my big exit, my stroll away from the rolling cameras, even if he spared no contempt for the career that brought me before them in the first place. Well, too bad, Diogenes: I make no apologies for a life that privileged

355

pleasure, poise, and politesse. Had your lantern light fallen on my face that bright March morning I could have told you, honestly, that I have never been dishonest. In any event, I daresay the brand of cynicism displayed in that television studio was not one you would have recognized.

The spring air — clean, substantial — refreshed me as I headed down Broadway and skirted Columbus Circle. The leaves were just beginning to stipple themselves greenly on the trees, and I thought for a moment of going into Central Park. At this time of day the Literary Walk, with its statues and elm trees, would be as safe as it ever got.

And the elms reminded me of Max, and of Johnny. The elm that we three planted as a family the summer Max got back from the war still grew, up at Pin Point in Maine. Max, stripped to his undershirt and suspenders, had dug its wide hole, then balanced the burlapped ball of roots in the middle; Johnny danced around the edge, waving his little wooden trowel, singing an elaborate tune he'd made up, the only lyric of which was *tree.* The elm was quite tall now, thirty-five years old to Johnny's thirty-eight. Our musical son, now a professor of music himself, lived only a few miles from it, more at home there than he'd ever been in the city.

I decided against the detour, though — mostly because I was hungry, but also because it would deject me to see the bronze likenesses of William Shakespeare and Robert Burns and all their illustrious and manly compatriots. In my moment of professional humiliation it might have been nice to take solace in the eternal realm of art — to burn with a hard gemlike flame, et cetera — but there, too, of late I had met only with frustration and defeat.

My final book of verse — a collected, not an original — called *Free with Purchase,* came out in 1968, by which time my light, dry style was well out of fashion, although the few reviews it received were favorable. R.H. Macy's even bought an ad in *The New York Review of Books* to help promote their sale of it, someone having decided that the accompanying illustration should be a chef with a tagline reading: "A book to give your hero or heroine — appetizing, easily digested, and nonfattening, it makes a savory entrée or dessert."

With my various disappointments displaced for the moment by the notion of savory entrées, I headed lunchward, toward the Horn & Hardart at Forty-Second Street

357

and Third Avenue, the city's last remaining automat, where I stopped in for a bacon, lettuce, and tomato sandwich.

When walking, I generally welcome courteous contact with strangers — the surprising confidences of letter carriers and construction workers, waitresses and beat cops being just the thing to jolt my busy brain from its unproductive churn — but my mood just then was too tenuous to recommend such encounters. Besides, the automat's coin-fed mediocrity seemed more in keeping with the spirit of the day, and there I could be confident of uninterrupted solitude as I sipped my tomato juice and looked out the window at the jittery parade of truants and delinquents, the lonely and the bored, all headed west toward Times Square. About ninety percent of the passersby, I estimated, were younger than I, most of them considerably.

Old, old, old — I had grown old. No longer did any even faint acquaintance rush toward me as I was grappling alone with a sandwich and a magazine. I'd bolt my food if my aging throat weren't so loathe to open and close as quickly as it used to.

For the longest time, I knew so many people in the city that I couldn't sit down in Midtown without at least one of them coming up to say hello, maybe even joining me. But little by little they had moved away, or died, or were being held prisoner — by caretakers, by their own bodies — someplace far from the street.

Helen, heartbreakingly, was among those I'd never see again. Like me, she'd been a Manhattan holdout, insisting, over her son's and stepdaughters' requests, on staying in the Greenwich Village brownstone where she and Dwight had lived for the duration of their marriage. Dwight, so much older, had died in 1965, but Helen had hung on until just last year. Her son, Merritt, had her shipped back to Birmingham, the old family plot, so there wasn't even a physical spot in the city where I could visit her memory.

I might have liked to get married again, too — to remarry as Dwight Zweigert had done. But after Max and I split up I was not exactly residing in the Era of the Extra Man, and between mothering Gian and keeping myself together and afloat, I had had little time for the exhausting business of being courted. To be sure, I was also not at the peak of my appeal to most men at that point.

I went back to the vending window, fed it cash, and got a slice of pie — warm apple with vanilla sauce — plus a cup of coffee: black, no sugar or cream.

When I got home to Murray Hill, I would write Johnny — Gian — a letter. I'd type it on my Remington, probably, or on my Hermes if the ribbon got to snarling. I was already composing it in my mind, taking it — as I often did — as an occasion for arranging my own thoughts.

Since 1960, when Gian left for college, I had written him a minimum of three times a week. A lot, I knew, but not as bad as I used to be. When he first left home I wrote melodramatic poems with titles like "To a Distant College Freshman," and I longed for the days when measles were the concern, not bouts of going steady.

From the morning that Max and I brought him home from the hospital, Gian had delivered the gratitude and terror that accompany the gift of a beautiful thing: the implicit charge that you, thenceforth, will be responsible for its care and upkeep.

I was not sentimental over him, though I was devoted, as he was to me. He understood my sense of humor. He got me.

For my latest birthday he'd sent me a dopey card with a half a dozen tiny cats on it that looked just like Phoebe; inside he'd written *You're more adorable than a basket full of kittens!!!* He'd led all three grandkids in drawing their own cat cards, too, and had mailed them all separately, thus ensuring that the postman was credited with a tour de force on the day they arrived.

I finished the coffee and rose to take my dishes to the dish drop, wondering which of us would vanish first: me or this automat.

When I typed up the letter to Gian, I decided, I wouldn't tell him about the television studio. Only about the Horn & Hardart, and about the walk, most likely.

I had leaned on him so hard for such a long time — in person, after his father left me for Julia, then in writing, after he himself left home for Bowdoin — that I strove not to do so anymore. We had held each other upright for years; now there had to be distance between us, only a little, if we were ever to learn to travel under our own power.

Even when he was a kid, Gian seemed to understand the absurdity of what his mother did for a living — how my angle was to take common things and reveal them to be strange and attractive, and to thereby relieve the monotony of advertising. The monotony of living, really.

I drew my coat around me and reemerged into the strangeness of Forty-Second Street.

361

The point of living in the world is just to stay interested.

22
As Good a Day to Die as Any

History is packed with poets more committed to memory than I.

Take, for example, Clement Clarke Moore, the "Bard of Chelsea," whose country estate provided the name and the entire territory of the neighborhood in which Wendy now resides. Though Moore himself is mostly forgotten, there's hardly a parent or child in the anglophone world whose ear doesn't quicken to the words of his single famous verse, even if they know it only by its first line rather than its proper title, "A Visit from St. Nicholas."

As I lurch toward West Fourteenth — tilted off plumb by my unbalanced burdens, the amaryllis pot proving heavier than I'd guessed — I'm struck anew by admiration for Moore's poem, which just last week, on Christmas Eve, I performed by heart for my visiting grandchildren. At the time I hadn't paused to consider the extent of its success, so complete as to be all but invisible in its vastness: Not only did it universalize its image of Saint Nick as a rosy and rotund whitebeard borne from chimney to chimney by flying reindeer, it also erased itself as the source of these notions, allowing them to seem ancient and true, like something everyone has always known.

It was, in a sense, the greatest print advertisement in American history.

Lily was so impressed with my delivery of the poem that she promised to be the one reciting it next year. I have no doubt that she will succeed in her memorization, though whether I will still be around and alive to hear it is a separate question.

" 'Twas the night before Christmas, when all thro' the house . . ." I speak the lines aloud as I turn at the spooky Beaux-Arts façade of the old county bank building, because the street beyond is too desolate and dark for total silence: the bulb of every shepherd's-crook lamppost has been cracked by some meticulous hoodlum. I fall silent again when I reach St. Bernard's Church, its steps crowded with bundles of fabric and plastic, some of which are trash, some of which are people.

On this night, at this hour, I am the only moving figure in the landscape, the only person who is not where she means to be.

I am almost to the party. The address that Wendy gave me is on the other side of Ninth Avenue, which is odd, because this is the last residential block between here and the Hudson: Ahead there's only the brick butte of the Port Authority building to the north, defunct factories and packing plants to the west. For the first time it occurs to me that she might be living — squatting — in a warehouse, and I wonder, if this is true, why she didn't mention it. I imagine her weighing the wisdom of telling me, thus risking my disapproval when I might not have any real intention of coming, versus *not* telling me, thus risking getting me lost in a perilous area on New Year's Eve. Did she really not want me to come?

At the end of the block ahead I can see the tracks of the West Side Line where they pass through the walls of the old industrial structures. I remember when they opened the elevated line in 1934: the West Side Improvement Project. What a brilliant idea it had seemed at the time, getting those freight trains up off street level.

I remember, as well, when the line closed in 1980. The last shipment they sent down the rails was a load of frozen turkeys, cargo that seemed like a punchline for a joke that no one could be bothered to write. Now most people seem to think it should be torn down, and I expect it will be, once the city finds the money. I wish they could leave it standing, fix it up, run trains on it again — or come up with some other function for it, though I can't imagine what that might be. Everyone is always too quick to discard things.

When I get to Wendy's block there are no marked addresses, only a cramped compound of interconnected brick buildings that stretches to all four bordering streets — and indeed beyond, by way of a pedestrian skywalk that spans the space above my head like a latter-day Bridge of Sighs. Some of the buildings are windowless; some that aren't are boarded up with graffitied sheets of plywood. Not one betrays so much as a flicker of light.

The stubborn insistence of the human body — even an old one like mine — on keeping itself alive is a source of increasing amusement for me. On this deserted street, my unreasoning heart and lungs have commenced their rote double time, my pupils yawn, and even my steady knees have acquired a quiver.

But like all impulses, the desire to preserve oneself can be mastered, controlled. And

I'll be damned if I'm going to walk all the way back to Murray Hill tonight still lugging this incipient amaryllis.

About halfway along the block, amid a line of boarded windows, I find a set of double doors propped with a mop bucket; from the bucket's handle rises a spray of helium balloons. The door opens — with a haunted-house groan and no small effort on my part — on a hallway lit at its far end by a platoon of votive candles. There's no buzzer, and from the music I can now hear pounding above, it's unlikely that anyone would be able to hear it if there were one.

Behind the candles a piece of pink poster board leans against the wall. *PETER'S N–Y–E PARTY,* I read as I draw closer — not Peter and Wendy's; just Peter's — *7TH FLOOR FOLLOW THE LITE!* Around the text, the poster is collaged with dozens of tiny hand-tinted prints of the same black-and-white photograph: the appraising face of a handsome heavy-lidded young man. Wendy's name may not be written on the poster, but the photo clearly announces her presence, reassures me that I'm in the right place.

The hallway extends parallel to the street in both directions, but more candles scatter to the left, leading toward what looks like a distant freight elevator. My hosts' trail is charming and romantic to be sure, but also entirely unsafe: the propped door and low light create a perfect workspace for muggers and rapists. I hate thinking this way but also can't justify partaking in plain foolishness; I pause to search my purse for my trusty penlight, click it on, and proceed.

The bluish oval that it casts discovers a ceiling veined by pipes, ducts, and conduits, none of which provides a good clue about what this place used to make, or store, or process. The walls show signs of having been whitewashed so long ago that the whiteness is all but gone; here and there there's a flash of some more elaborate adornment. At one point a pair of pale painted hands takes shape from the darkness, each holding a doubloon-like circle — one black, one white — in its long bloodless fingers, as if illustrating an occult ritual.

As I study the image, I spy words painted above it, and I angle my beam upward to read.

OREO SANDWICH, it says.

The shock of recognition almost jolts the light from my hand. At once I know exactly where I am, and I can't suppress a laugh — though I don't much like the sound of it when the echo sends it back to me.

This is the old National Biscuit factory:

an amalgam of packaging plants, store-houses, loading docks, offices, and industrial-scale ovens that has overflowed this Manhattan block since Teddy Roosevelt was police commissioner. In disuse now for more than a quarter century — ever since the whole operation trimmed its name to Nabisco and decamped, like so many of my other aging neighbors, to New Jersey — this was once the nation's snack laboratory par excellence, where wizardly denizens invented tricks that would change food forever.

No hyperbole, that. National Biscuit not only found ways to ship their empty calories halfway round the world with crunches undiminished, but also to make sure that somebody was already craving them upon arrival. With such a wide reach achieved, their products ceased to be mere treats and took on the status of institutions, as unifyingly uniform as any flag, oath, or anthem. These brick walls witnessed the nativities of Zu Zu Ginger Snaps, the Lorna Doone, Ritz Crackers, and, of course, my hated adversary, derailer of my New Year's Eve, that dark satanic sandwich, the Oreo cookie.

I suppose I ought to be pleased by the evening's serendipitous circularity, but I can't quite manage. While it's tempting to cast my long walk as an accidental mock-heroic — arriving at last in the lair of the beast that wrecked my dinner plans, defeated though it now may be by my powers of digestion — there's nothing but phantoms to counterattack. Aside from this painted wall, no physical trace of my enemy remains.

Anyway, this is silliness. If my enemy *were* on hand to be vanquished, what would it look like? A crisp morsel composited from sugar, flour, and fat? A bookish child in a TV commercial? An invisible pile of money, flashing around the globe in the form of Nabisco Brands stock?

Or would it just look like me? After all, no one *made* me buy those Oreos. Or did they? I imagine Leslie Monroe and Geraldine Kidd emerging from the darkness, glamorous and camera ready, reminding me with a cluck of the tongue and a pat on the shoulder that *real* advertising — not the primitive quilting bee I apparently mistook for my own copywriting career — is an inside job: *deep* inside our heads and hearts, the secret crannies where we hide ourselves from ourselves. Who's been more the mother to Gian in the years since I fell apart, vigorous me or dying Julia? How did my son get by when I was fogged with liquor, or rebuilding at Silver Hill? All my cherished memories of his smartness, his sweetness: how many other such moments slipped by me undetected? I can brood, and I can speculate, but I can never know for sure — although I *can* buy a package of cookies.

Nay, if I turn mine eyes upon myself, I find myself a traitor with the rest.

The freight elevator elevates me not into the party but to yet more blazing candles, these blazing a trail down a wide corridor toward the ever-louder music. The hallway is lined with prints of Wendy's photographs, alternating with canvases presumably done by her husband, all hanging unevenly against the bricks from thick steel wires strung between exposed pipes.

I'm no art critic, but even though Peter's paintings look accomplished — abstracted landscapes in an attractive California palette that reminds me of Richard Diebenkorn — I like Wendy's work better and think that she is the superior artist. Partly this is because Wendy's work pulses with rhythms and textures that I know well; it's *of* the city, while Peter's is simply *in* it. Or maybe my preference is even more straightforward: Wendy's images have people in them and Peter's don't. My biases always run against

371

the systematic and the stylized in favor of the mess and adventure of human life. It's the same with music: Gian is always chiding me about my inability to appreciate all the modern compositions — atonal, aleatoric, serialist — that he and his colleagues inflict on their students, the poor dears who a year ago were playing Leroy Anderson tunes in high school gymnasiums.

The music coming from the party, though, I enjoy. It's not like anything I've heard before. It sounds as if it's coming from inside a cave or a subway tunnel, a simple repetitive bass melody with the occasional crashing cymbal and distant, slightly yelpy voices repeating something about slipping in and out of phenomenon. I don't know what that means, but it feels evocative and exciting.

I emerge from the corridor into a vast central space.

A pair of bare bulbs and a Vaticanload of candles barely succeed in lighting the room, which is thronged with people, mostly men, a few women, all young. What little furniture there is has been pushed to the walls. Some people sit but many are dancing. A lot of the women wear lace tops, and skirts over capris or fishnet stockings. A lot of the men wear trousers that seem impossibly tight.

Both the women and the men wear interesting earrings. Everyone seems to have taken great care with his or her appearance, which I appreciate. I take off my hat and smooth my hair.

By instinct I make my way through the bustling darkness to the provisional kitchen — a hodgepodge of countertops and cabinetry, basins and hot plates, threaded with rubber hoses and extension cords — to set down my gifts. Here, too, to a person, the guests all have meticulous outfits and thoughtful haircuts. I am glad, as I always am, that I made a point of dressing up, as I always do.

The crowd parts slightly so I can reach the counter. Except for one young man — with a face like a jack-o'-lantern: snaggled teeth and too-wide eyes — who peels himself from a conversation to stand in my way.

"Who the fuck invited Nancy Reagan?" he says.

He strikes the high-chinned pose of a movie gangster and tries to stare me down. He is not bad looking, but his cheeks are gaunt, and he seems to be under the influence of something stronger than alcohol and holiday cheer.

For an instant I'm taken aback by this affront. Then habit takes over and I relax,

373

square off. I may be out of practice, but I have attended a lot of parties through the years, been challenged by many boors in many kitchens. Those old muscles still flex.

"When you're insulting someone," I say, "the trick is to be fast, specific, and accurate. Two out of three won't do. You fumbled the third. Please note that I am six inches taller, twenty years older, and more adventurously dressed than Nancy Reagan has ever been. Does every woman over the age of fifty who spends a little money on herself look like the First Lady to you? Or do you have some sort of fixation on her?"

"Fixation?" he says. "Yeah, I got a fixation. I fucking hate that shriveled-up old hag."

"Well, you won't hear me defending her. I voted for Mondale and Ferraro. I think it's high time we put a woman in the White House to do more than pick out china services."

"My, aren't *you* quite the activist," the young man says. "Are you running for office? Do you want us to sign your petition? Or did you come here to save us? Did you get us confused with those nice violin-and-opera queers from the Upper West Side?"

"I've come here," I say, "because Wendy invited me. What's your name?"

The challenge in his face is losing its edge, becoming plain sullenness. "What do you care?"

"I'd like to be able to complain about your manners on an informed basis."

"You should keep away from me, Nancy," he says. "I'm a scary homosexual."

"My name is Lillian," I say, shuffling my burdens to extend my hand. "Not Nancy. And I'm not scared of homosexuals."

"Jason, lay off," says another man, coming up behind him and touching his shoulder. "You're being an asshole."

Jason ignores him, and takes a sip of the pink drink in his clear-plastic cup.

"Haven't you heard, Nancy?" he says. "We all have AIDS. Aren't you afraid?"

This irritates me in a way his previous gibes haven't because it's exactly what I am thinking: *Does he have AIDS?* and *Am I afraid?* He certainly doesn't look healthy. As I try to remember what I've read about the disease, I can't help but steal a downward glance at my own exposed fingers, veined and pale against the dark.

I decide I'm not afraid. "It's my understanding," I say, "that I am in little danger of getting AIDS from you, if you have it to give. Or I *would* be in little danger, had your parents raised you to be polite enough to shake a hand when it's been offered."

The venom creeps back into his eyes. "You don't want to hear about how my parents raised me," he says.

He tips the last of his drink down his throat, flicks the empty cup onto the dance-floor, and passes his palm across his mouth with a theatrical slurp, pretending to lick it.

At least I think he's pretending.

"Okay, sweetie," he says, extending his arm slackly, like the pope presenting his ring. "Put 'er there."

"Jason," the young man behind him says, then he doesn't say anything else.

I am unable to suppress an exasperated sigh.

Whenever I encounter strangers on my walks through the city, I always try to provoke them to reveal something of them-selves, hoping they'll surprise me, jolt me out of my own head. I'm generally good at doing this. When I fail, though — when they brush me off or, worse, when they begin to perform, behaving like some version of what they think I want or don't want them to be — the results are terribly dispiriting.

I'm failing with Jason. Looking at him is like looking at a mirror, a haunted-house mirror that reflects everyone as a corpse.

If I don't take his hand, then I am what

he says I am, and he wins. If I do, then I'm only doing it to prove something and the encounter is just about me; he remains hidden behind his curtain of contempt.

But that is his right, I suppose.

And I hate to lose.

I step forward with a smile. "All right, Jason," I say. "Today is as good a day to die as any. Happy New Year."

"Holy shit!" he says. "Nancy's a fucking samurai!"

"Lillian!"

It's Wendy, who's caught sight of me and rushed over. "I can't believe you came!" she says. "I'm so glad you made it!"

Jason cries out and throws up his hands in mock frustration, playing to an imaginary crowd that's cheering him on. "Saved by the bell, Nancy!" he says.

Wendy glares at him, takes my arm with one hand and my parcels with the other, and steers me away. "Come on," she says. "Let's get you over here among people who can appreciate you."

She leads me along a wall of boarded-up windows to an enormous table of unfinished wood, nicked and paint-stained. She's speaking but I don't catch what she says; she's already begun to fix me a drink when I realize my right hand is still extended, chilled by the lack of what it never touched. I let it fall to my side.

Wendy leans toward me in the festive din of the year's final hour. "I hope you'll forgive me for being a bad hostess," she says. "I didn't realize you were here."

"That's all right," I say. "It's a busy scene."

"I'm sorry about Jason," she says. "He's really angry."

She is wearing a skinny black tie over her usual white top. It looks nice.

"I'm sure he has his reasons," I say.

"I guess he does." She pulls out a chair. "Here, have a seat. We can just drape your coat — which is fabulous, by the way — right over the back."

I sit, and take the cup she hands me. The mink brushes the base of my neck, like a shy pet I'm sheltering.

Wendy sits next to me, opening the bags I brought, withdrawing the potato chips and *mazapan* that C. J. sold me, brightening when she sees the candy, clutching it with both hands like a thrilled child. "I love these things!" she says. As I'd guessed she would.

Her fingers can't manage the knots that bind the amaryllis, and all her sharp blades are in the kitchen, but I don't let her leave, knowing that if she goes back there it'll be past midnight before I see her again. I pass her the Swiss Army Knife that I keep in my purse — the real thing, a 1961 model, not the upmarket renditions that junior executives affecting rugged resourcefulness have taken lately to carrying — and she uses it with ease and skill.

A few grains of soil have fallen between the pot and its cellophane shroud, but not many. Wendy peels the wrapping away, then looks up with curious eyes.

"Hope you like dirt!" I say.

She laughs. "Is it a bulb?"

"Dutch amaryllis, I'm told. If it turns out to be cannabis instead, I trust you'll forget who gave it to you."

"Amaryllis is a lily, right?" she says. "Lilies from Lillian! I can't wait for it to sprout. It'll remind us of you every day!"

I think — but do not say — that it puts me in mind of a different Lily, my granddaughter, who's a far more apropos analogue: a green shoot rather than a brown husk. Instead I just smile.

"Where did you find all this great stuff?" Wendy asks, placing the pot at the table's center amid empty bottles and abandoned cups, then opening the *mazapan*. "You must have been running around all afternoon."

"I made one stop," I say. "About fifteen minutes ago. At that Filipino grocer and florist on Greenwich, just south of Jackson Square. Do you know it?"

She shakes her head. "I walk by there all the time, but I don't think I do."

"The young man who works there, C. J., is a smart cookie and a class act. The bulb was his idea. If it gives you any trouble, he'll sort things out."

Wendy is aglow with gratitude, but also scattered, betraying every good host's concerns: new arrivals to be welcomed, refreshments to be refreshed, oddball guests to be moored with companionable others so she can attend to her duties.

"Don't let me ensnare you," I say. "If I keep monopolizing your time I'm afraid I'll get indicted for unfair trade practices. I fully expected to be a demographic outlier at this shindig by a solid half-century, so there's no need to fuss over me at others' expense."

"But I'm so thrilled you're here!" says Wendy. "I want to introduce you to everyone, so they can all see how great you are."

I can tell she means it, but even adjusted for drunkenness, her smile shows melancholy and worry out of proportion to the circumstances of an old woman's surprise arrival.

I peek at my watch: 11:20. "Well, nuts," I say. "I am, I fear, unequal to your ambitions. It's hours past my usual bedtime. I'd settle for an audience with that husband of yours, though. I admired his paintings on the way in and now I'd like to meet him."

"Ah, Peter," she says, looking away, looking at the crowd, looking but not really looking. "That's a good question."

I follow her gaze and scan the room, taking it all in for the first time. Noticing things I hadn't before. The atmosphere of clandestine liberty. Bodies dancing and slouching and clustering in strange combinations. The faces: open and vibrant, brooding and doomed. I notice that some of the women are wearing thick foundation, heavy eyeliner, prominent rouge. Then I notice that they aren't women.

"Peter's not really your husband," I say, "is he?"

"Ha," says Wendy. She actually says *ha,* like someone in a comic strip. "You caught me. Peter and I aren't married. We're not even involved. We're friends, really good friends, who wanted to live together. We're both artists, and it's cheaper this way." She shakes her head, frustrated. "That makes it sound like convenience. It's not only that. We're a team. We're just not a couple. Not in what I guess you'd call the regular way."

"You don't have sex."

She smiles, and — I think; it's hard to tell in this light — blushes. "Not with each other, no," she says.

For an instant I feel as if I'd been fooled, and then as if I'd been foolish — foolish to think I might have a place in Wendy's world, a world I've sentimentalized as a carefree bohemian carnival. I have been presumptuous. As is my wont. As I made a career of doing.

But when I've regained my footing, I find that this is not so strange to me.

"To be perfectly honest," I say, "I'm not sure how regular the regular way ever gets. These arrangements are hard to explain. But I'm your friend, so I'd like to hear more. Maybe we can talk about it sometime, if you want to. For now, though, I just have one question: Why did you tell me in the first place that you're married?"

"Lillian, I'm sorry about that," says Wendy, picking up another *mazapan* with her black-nail-polished hand and nervously breaking it into chunks. "I say it sometimes because it feels true. More true than anything else I can tell people, anyway. We live together, we love each other, but he's not my boyfriend. If I say he is, then people want to know when we're getting married. If I say he's just a friend, then people think

382

it's weird, like it's a problem, and they want to help me find my own place, or to set me up with some nice guy they know. And I don't want that. I'm with Peter. It's different, but it works for us. I feel like you get it, Lillian. But when I first met you, well, I didn't really know you yet, and . . ."

"You thought I'd disapprove?"

"Yeah, I guess," says Wendy. "I mean, I thought you might. I guess I didn't think about it at all, really. It's just the way I talk to older people. Gah, I'm sorry — that came out wrong!"

"It's all right," I say, taking a sip of the pink punch: vodka and grapefruit juice and something else, powdery and fake-tasting, Kool-Aid maybe. "There's no sense in pretending otherwise. I'm really old."

"I just mean that I'm used to talking a certain way to my family back in Ohio," says Wendy. "My folks and my grandparents. I can't always trust people's reactions. And I get tired of trying to explain to people who don't want to understand."

"I suppose I was never *quite* so unconventional," I say, "but I know what you mean. Suffice to say my family back home in the District of Columbia did not condone my Jazz Age enthusiasms."

"There's Peter!" says Wendy, rising to

wave and shout his name.

Peter — whom I recognize at once from seeing his tiny face iterated across the poster-board downstairs — turns and walks over to us. He looks to be Wendy's age, in his twenties, and extremely handsome, his dark blond hair swept up in a slight pompadour. He's wearing a crisp white shirt, unbuttoned plungingly, with its sleeves rolled partway up, and his pants are black: tuxedo trousers with a red satin stripe up the side, no less stylish for looking as if they were stolen from the dry cleaning of a bellhop.

Peter and Wendy. For the first time it occurs to me that they are accidental namesakes, with literary antecedents that are a perfect fit, right down to Peter's tribe of lost boys. Maybe *too* perfect: It's easy to imagine them embracing the coincidence as a role to play, a mask to hide behind. *Yes, you're right, we're just the way you think we are. Now leave us alone.*

"Wendy!" Peter says, and pulls up a chair. "Is this Lillian Boxfish?"

"The one and only," I say. "I've heard so much about you. It's a pleasure to finally meet you."

He glances over at Wendy and raises his eyebrows.

384

"It's okay," says Wendy. "She knows our terrible secret."

"Ah," says Peter, sitting down and sighing. "That's a load off. I hate having to lie. Thanks for coming."

"Thank you for letting an old lady crash your party," I say.

"Oh please," he says. "I like to hang out with all kinds of people. Most of our young friends act as if we're the first ones who've ever tried to live our lives differently. It's so easy for a kid to write off an old person — they can't understand this, they've never felt that, they no longer feel anything, they don't count anymore. I think it's small-minded. I wish there were more people over sixty here, to tell you the truth."

"That makes one of us," I say, and they both laugh. "If you want to turn down the stereo and organize a bridge tournament, please be my guest, but I can't promise I'll be yours."

"So," says Peter, "Wendy tells me you used to be a veritable Emily Dickinson."

"Hmm," I say. "You're in the ballpark. I've never been a shut-in — at least not by choice — and I still write."

"Wherever do you find a quiet place to compose your verses, Lillian?"

"There are no quiet places in New York,

dollface," I say. "You know that. But I write funny poems, and most humor starts from irritation. There's plenty of that here."

"They say oysters need grit to make pearls," says Peter. "Take this detritus, these obstacles, and make of them art."

"Better that than just a peevish oyster," I say.

Peter reaches for a *mazapan,* and I notice a tattoo — a tiny black anchor — on his inner right forearm.

"Nice design," I say, pointing. "Very nautical. Very classic."

"Thanks," he says. "My dad worked on the docks when I was growing up in Baltimore. Loved — still loves — the sea. He won't talk to me anymore. I never go back there, but I miss it. This was one of the ways I let myself say good-bye. But you don't want to hear about all that sad crap. It's New Year's Eve!"

"See, Peter? This is why Lillian is so great," says Wendy.

"Why? Because most geriatric types don't care for tattoos?"

"Kind of," says Wendy. "I notice the way you notice things."

"Peter, maybe Wendy has told you," I say, "but I spent a large part of my life writing advertising for R.H. Macy's. There's a surprising bit of trivia about their company logo that I think you'd enjoy knowing."

"The big red star?" says Peter, leaning in like a conspirator. "Do tell us, Lillian. Don't hold back."

I play along, looking theatrically from side to side as if in search of enemy agents, but the gesture feels wrong: false, or forced, as if I'm humoring children who are humoring me. I feel my mood swing, helped along by the pink punch, which I seem to have drained my cup of.

Peter and Wendy are kind, but I don't belong here. If I'm still present at midnight for the countdown and the kissing, then they'll want me to feel included, and that simply won't work. If I could feel fairly certain of being ignored — just a weird old lady people watching in the corner — then that might be fine. But Peter and Wendy will be so concerned that I have a good time that I am certain I will only be a disappointment to them.

"That star," I say, "comes from a tattoo that Mr. R. H. Macy himself got at the age of fifteen. Back when he was a sailor. He worked on a whaling ship out of Nantucket, the *Emily Morgan*."

This fact now sits invisibly between us, satisfied with itself. Daring us to take it up, to make use of it. It's impossible. Why did I tell them? What could Wendy and Peter possibly do with this information? With the news that an iconic red star recognized by every eye in the city — one that hung like a beacon over the best years of my life — was inked on the skin of a teenaged Quaker the same year that Queen Victoria took the throne? I've known it for more than a half a century, and I'm still not sure what to do with it myself.

"No shit," says Peter. "I had no idea that that's where they got the logo."

We sit in companionable silence, contemplating distances and durations, the beginnings and the endings of things. That's what *I'm* contemplating, at any rate.

"Can you please," says Peter, "please, *please* tell me the star was on his ass?"

"Love to," I say, "but can't. It was on his hand."

"Dammit," Peter says. "Well. Still a good story, Lillian."

And that, I figure, is as good a curtain line as we're likely to find. "On that note," I say, standing up, "I think I'd better be going."

"What?" says Wendy. "You just got here! Come on, stay."

"It's less than a half hour to midnight," says Peter. "At least ring in 1985 with us."

I hesitate, not because I'm reconsidering, but because I can't find my balance. The floor under my feet and the table under my hands both seem to be swaying — like the deck of a whaling ship, I think, or maybe a prosperous dry-goods store, afloat somehow on the high seas — and adrift in opposite directions. For a moment I'm terrified that I'll fall, a wet bag of splintered bone flung in the midst of everyone's New Year. I must be having a stroke, or suffering some other profound bodily betrayal: the final catastrophe that I've been waiting for. Then I remember that it simply has been decades since I consumed this much liquor in an eight-hour stretch.

I regain my poise. I conceal my distress.

"Well, that's just the thing," I say. "It *is* nearly midnight. And I am notoriously terrible at ringing out the old and in the new. Always have been. Now, don't misunderstand: You're both just wonderful. And this is a great party. Now that I know where you live, and how close it is to my place — not even two miles — I'll come visit again, if you'll have me. But I have a long tradition of ending years in my bathrobe to uphold, and I'm cutting it awfully close."

"All right, Lillian," says Peter. "I'm sure you know best. But we'll miss you."

"You'll let us get you a cab," says Wendy, "won't you?"

Before I can answer, Peter adds, "Wendy's right. The streets aren't safe this late at night. You should stay off them."

"I appreciate your concern," I say, and I do, although I also find it annoying. "But there's no need to get me a cab. As you young sophisticates probably already know, New Year's Eve between 10:30 and midnight is the best time in the entire year to catch a taxi. I'll just walk toward Penn Station and find something."

"No!" says Wendy. "Whatever you do, do *not* go by Penn Station. A lot of our friends have gotten mugged up there."

"Thank you, Wendy," I say. "I am grateful for the warning. Thank you, Peter. I'll be all right, believe me. I'll see you again soon."

I put on my coat, give them each a hug, and weave semi-steadily back down the art-filled hallway toward the freight elevator. As I walk out, the music on the stereo starts to affect me the way music only does when I've been drinking: I suddenly want to say *I love this song* to everything that comes on, and I start hearing messages that seem meant just for me. As I slide aside the elevator's scissor door, a man's pretty voice is crooning low, then singing high, something about how pretty girls make graves.

I am not a girl anymore. I haven't been one for a long, long time.

Whenever "everyone" is doing something, I seek to avoid it. But whenever someone tells me *not* to do something, that thing has a way of becoming the only thing that I want to do.

I leave the building and pull the metal door shut behind me. The soft clang of its closing comes back as an echo, ricocheting up and down the empty street.

23
THE BEST TECHNIQUE

On postcards it never rains. Our honeymoon was like a postcard.

Our second ocean voyage was not like our honeymoon.

It was more like a card with an appealing photo on the front — perhaps one hand-tinted in an age long gone: a hint that its rosy report is not quite current — but with a reverse scrawled with sprawling misgivings.

Max and I departed for Italy on New Year's Day 1955, just under twenty years after our first such trip together.

I knew it was a luxury to take such a vacation. The voyage was a gift from his favorite aunt and uncle, who'd prospered in the import business, and who'd noticed that we seemed to need a little time away, a little perking up. By *we* they meant me.

I had always been praised, in public and in private, for my love of fun — for seeming young forever, forever young.

But.

Happiness and a love of fun are not coextensive, and their relationship may even be divergent. If one were *happy,* then one might stay in with a book, say, and not go out hunting for fun.

As I watched the Manhattan skyline shrink away, Max and I were not holding hands, and no one was on shore to see us off. His parents were staying in our Murray Hill place to watch Johnny while we were gone for the month.

Gian, not Johnny, I kept having to remind myself. He'd be turning thirteen in a few weeks and had tired of the nickname. Baby-ish, he'd deemed it.

The symbolism of setting sail on New Year's Day was deliberately heavy-handed, handpicked by Max's well-meaning family.

The hope was that with a new year we could have a new start.

The idea was that I would be renewed by being in a newish place. It would still be wintry, but not nearly as much so as New York City at that time of year. A sweet thought on their part, but honestly, I might as well have been commuting on the IRT as floating on an ocean liner. It was all the same to me. Everything felt flat and feature-less.

Even during the weeks we toured the Italian interior under the still-robust winter sun, I was at my wits' fucking end, if you'll forgive the phrase, being in a place where the weather did not reflect my mood. I was raining; the sun mocked my sadness.

I have always loved the pathetic fallacy, in verse and in life.

For a long time I could remember almost nothing of this second honeymoon, which resembled the first the way an embalmed corpse resembles the lost beloved. My mind was a wreck then — my perception dulled, my perspective poisoned — and the electro-shock cure, when it finally came, swept away all my thoughts from this time, along with the person I was when I thought them.

But I left myself a path back: a travel diary, diligently kept. For years it lay forgotten at the bottom of my old steamer trunk; for years after I uncovered it, it remained unread. I feared it was a trap I'd set for myself: a trick by my old adversary to gain readmittance. I resolved to destroy it, but I never did, and then one Halloween, after a call from Gian and the kids — who were about to get a late start trick-or-treating after an hour of shaping Lily's hair into

394

buns above her ears, the crux of a costume I utterly failed to follow — I found myself in the mood for a ghost story, and I dug it out.

The diary made it clear that I had taken the trip as an occasion to crown myself Queen of the Mayhem, at least in my mind. My attitude was that of a saboteur: seemingly mild and compliant, biding my time, waiting for the moment to throw a wrench in the works.

The entry from when we stopped in Milan read: *When in the dumps, I hate the things that ordinarily I love.*

In Florence it was: *Down with bluebirds.*

In Venice it was: *Vivacious chumps declaring how great it is to be alive. And down with them, people who say the weather forecast should be "partly sunny" instead of "partly cloudy."*

The first time we'd visited Italy, I'd learned so much. The second time, it seems the main lesson was: Ennui dies hard.

Up until then, despite the vicissitudes of my position, I'd always felt invincible. But in Italy I had come to feel vinced.

This is it, I had written on an otherwise-blank, undated page, with regard, I believe, to my career, my marriage. *The stuff you see above you that looks like higher peaks may just be clouds. This is it. This is it.*

I guess I wanted *more,* and also didn't trust what I did have.

Stupid brain, I wrote.

By the end of the trip, Max didn't know what to do with me. Not that he'd known what to do before — he hadn't for a long time. How could he, when I didn't know what to do with — or about — myself?

That night, the night of what my various caretakers would later take to calling "the incident," we were shipboard again, shipboard at last, headed back to New York. We were having drinks with some new friends we — or rather Max, really — had acquired, a couple whose names I heard, then immediately forgot, and only picked up again when Max used them in our stilted conversation, conspicuously for my sake: Vivian and Herb.

What happened that night embarrassed Max irrevocably — both as it was happening, and in its aftermath, which was eternity, or at least the rest of our lives. He never spoke of it, not even as "the incident."

What's odd is that I've never forgotten it. Even as the days that led to and from it were scrubbed away by alcohol, madness, and electric shocks, its details have remained perfectly clear in my mind, gleaming like the bright scales of a fish arced over turbid water.

I've never told anyone this. I lied to Max, Gian, Helen, every doctor I've ever had. Myself most of all. The truth is, I do remember.

And it is up to me — not Max, not anyone else — to decide if I am embarrassed by it. If I am not embarrassed, well, then it is not embarrassing.

So here's what happened:

We were in the lounge when I finally scrounged up the will to do what I had been contemplating.

The conversation was about travel: places we'd been, how we'd liked them, and why.

Vivian and Herb were the relentlessly positive types. They had a theory that maintaining a positive attitude was the secret to successful travel.

Vivian was insisting that no matter how bad something was, you could always find one thing to praise about it. "Even if it's just something like 'Lovely salt, isn't it?' " she said, laughing.

"Or," said Herb, squeezing her knee, "if you're on a terrible bus ride, you can still find a way to fixate on the scenery. America the beautiful!"

"That's exactly right," said Max. "Why

couldn't we meet you two on the way over? I've been trying to explain this to my wife for a month! See, Lillian? Maybe you'll listen to strangers if you won't listen to your husband, eh?" He gave Herb a big, stagey wink. "Positivity! I'll drink to that!"

"I'll just drink," I said, and I drained my Manhattan, leaving the cherry skewered on its toothpick, lacking the appetite for even that much food.

I could feel Max's disapproval. It had been my second drink, and everyone else was just halfway through their first.

"Lily," said Herb, "you are a perfect social hooligan!"

His mirthfulness and forced familiarity seemed sincere and well-intentioned, devoid of Max's aggressive edge. Herb and Vivian were nice people. They had no business mixing with the likes of Max and me. I was about to show them that.

"Excuse me," I said, picking up my clutch. "Off to powder my nose. I'll be back in two shakes."

I had had my sea legs well under me almost from the instant we'd set sail for home, but I felt unsteady walking away from our table.

During my younger years there were moments when I'd find myself alone in my room for the first time in weeks, and it was time for a good cry. It's not as though I had never known sadness prior to that horrible year; it's that by then I no longer knew what to do with the sadness. How to get through it and then put it efficiently behind me.

That year I had become unable to cry. Just blank, blank. I felt like a white wall.

There in the bathroom, certainly, I felt well past tears, and made a point of not meeting my own eyes in the mirror. The minute you see yourself you're forced out of your head and into your body, forced to reckon with yourself as a thing that takes up space in the world, that others can see and react to, that has a story with a beginning, middle, and end that intersects with other people's stories. A mirror gives you perspective.

I didn't want perspective. It wouldn't help me do what I had come to do. For months I had felt increasingly out of myself — everything seemed to be happening *about* me, as opposed to *to* me, as if I were the still midpoint of a swirling cloud of trouble. I didn't want to be convinced that my circumstances were otherwise. I just wanted to be back in control, calling the tune.

Had I been anywhere there was a chance that Johnny would find me, I don't think

I'd have tried it. As it was, I'd finally found a good use for the voyage.

At the bottom of my clutch, kept hidden for weeks, was a razor blade folded into a dollar bill. I unwrapped it, held it to my left wrist, and cut, remembering as I did so a supercilious young surgeon I'd met at a party some twenty-odd years before, who'd told me — to shock me, I'm sure, with his callousness — that the best technique was not across but rather up the arm, vertically. Him I paid little mind, but his advice I filed away, on the off chance it might come in handy someday.

He wasn't wrong. I hadn't expected it, but the pain was astonishing — a feeling of total wrongness and distress that didn't even register as pain — and the mess was immediate. My hands went slippery, and I wasn't dexterous enough any longer to use my mutilated left to do the same to my right. I sank to the floor — clammy linoleum, the kind that was patterned to look like marble.

If I'd really wanted to be effective, I could have just jumped. Erased myself. Hart Crane'd off the ship, and that would have been it. It's ugly, I know, to admit that part — just part — of why I did it the way that I did was because I wanted Max to see me.

400

To witness, publically, how his affair with Julia had hurt me.

I tried to focus on my rage — my only source of warmth — as my teeth chattered and my head swam.

True, I had been no blanket-on-the-grass-in-the-sunshine picnic to be around during that last year we were together. But he didn't have to do what he'd done. Not the way he'd done it.

He should have asked for the divorce first, before sneaking around. But for all his seeming nonchalance and joie de vivre, this was one area wherein he lacked courage: He would never risk a loss without a contingency plan, without assuring himself of a soft landing — in this case, in Julia's much younger and less complicated lap. And now she'd be waiting to nurse him — and Johnny! — through this tragedy. Good luck, Julia! Can't say I didn't warn you.

Then the door opened, and Vivian found me. Crying, finally. Dress ruined. A bloody mess.

It is my understanding that because I had been gone a long time, Max had sent our new friend to fetch me. Typical Max! I could easily picture his gambit, outwardly concerned but actually cavalier, pushing off what ought to have been his responsibility with such charm that it would never have crossed poor Vivian's mind to say no.

Something's wrong, he would have said. *She never takes more than two minutes in the bathroom. Could you go check on her?*

And so Vivian unearthed the heap of me: such an embarrassment.

By the time Herb was sprinting for help and Max was manhandling me — crushing his thick thumb into my armpit, just the way the Army had taught him — I had blacked out, but I could still hear silly Vivian fussing innocently about, looking for jagged edges and smashed glass, trying to figure out what accident had befallen me. *I'm murdering myself, you moron,* I wanted to shout.

The shipboard medics rushed me to the infirmary, where the doctors stabilized me.

When we landed in Manhattan they checked me into St. Vincent's.

I wasn't glad that I hadn't died. And I wasn't sad that I hadn't. I wasn't anything.

Afterwards, when they were holding me, trying to figure out where to ship me next, making arrangements for residential treatment at Silver Hill, Helen came to visit.

She asked me — as a lot of my friends would ask, actually — why I hadn't told someone. Why I hadn't gone to one or another of them for help.

That was a fair question. It wasn't as though I hadn't seen it coming.

I had always cultivated a magpie mind: Any and every shred of life's ephemera could come to serve as an adornment, either for verse or for advertising.

For the past year or so, though, the only baubles I had noticed were articles on alcoholism and subjects of that ilk. I clipped and saved pieces on mastering one's impulses and preventing suicide. I hardly recall reading any of them, only collecting them: the expression of yet another unmastered impulse.

That afternoon — visiting hours, the end of January — Helen was sitting at my bedside. My left hand was under the covers because seeing it upset her too much: She had always been one to faint at the sight, or even the thought, of blood. But she clutched my right hand and looked into my eyes and waited for my answer.

Part of me wanted to ask why she, why they, hadn't *asked* me if I needed help. They surely had to have noticed. But I could not blame them — *did* not blame them, not really. I did what I did. No one else was responsible.

In a way, it was my own independence — I could see now, after the incident — that had caused the incident. The very compulsion that had driven my achievements for so long had somehow begun to work against me.

It had never been an effort for me to keep up my aggressive vivacity — until suddenly it was, and I didn't know how to get it back or what to do in its absence. And so I did not do anything, and I did not tell anyone.

The answer that I gave to Helen was:

"I have never cared for those who treat their friends as they would a charity ward."

"But we'd have *wanted* to help," she told me. "You know I would have. You know any of us would."

"I know," I said. "I know you would have. And you're helping now. And I'm grateful. And I'm sorry, Helen. What I did was incredibly rude, and I'm sorry for that."

She protested, but I knew I was right. My long, fine streak of charm had ended: I had jumped the groove, gracelessly scraping everything in my path. I had become boorish, embarrassing, but worst of all I had become *exhausting*. I was sure I heard a sigh of relief every time someone trundled me away into a cab or train, or took their leave of me through a hospital door.

I had even worn poor Helen out: Her re-assurances gradually waned in the face of my stolid despair. We were sitting in silence when we heard the Morse-code tap of sensible heels down the corridor. The supervising nurse appeared at the door, and visiting hours were over.

I was left alone again to think, and to listen to the traffic outside: a throbbing note appropriate to the irreparable wreck of Cupid's barque. An almost tidal-sounding score perfect for the choreography of the passage of time, a dull and dogged reminder that I was just like everyone else in suffering the injustice of chronology: I could only walk through it facing forward, going in that one direction.

24
A SECRET

Although I have promised Gian that if I am ever confronted by muggers I will not resist, this turns out to have been an untruth.

I do not discover my falsehood immediately after emerging from the party, but rather outside of Penn Station. It takes a few minutes.

Walking north to Thirty-Third Street, leaving Peter and Wendy's place, I pass numerous idling cabs, yellow and hungry like the golden Pac-Mans in those video games my grandchildren love. Single-minded, the drivers trawl the curbs, aiming to devour little ghosties like me. With just moments to go until midnight, every cabbie is waiting for a fare, all hoping that whoever drunkenly stumbles through their doors after ringing in the New Year will be a short trip: each seeks to pack as much earning as possible into this, the cabbie's busiest night of the year.

As I walk, I'm weaving a little — hard to say just how much — from the effect of drinking cheap vodka two hours past my usual bedtime. It makes me a target, but I want to be a target. A spectacle. A catalyst. Things used to *happen* around me.

It hasn't rained, but the sidewalks are as damp and gray as tombstones.

I arrive at Penn Station, by which I mean not Penn Station but the atrocity they erected in its place in 1968. I have walked by it hundreds of times since then, but the nastiness of the place still claps like a slap across the face. It is so ugly.

The old station, the one that stood when I arrived in 1926, was a Beaux-Arts marvel of pink granite and glass and steel that evoked not just travel by rail, but also travel through time: the splendor of an ancient Roman past, plus the possibility of a future where beauty and civic function are not just valued but understood to be in harmony.

I will not make it all the way there before 1985, but I have decided that I would like to walk by R.H. Macy's on my way back home. The last stop of the night.

Stay off the street, Peter told me. *Stay off the street,* Wendy agreed.

I am not going to stay off the street. Not when the street is the only thing that still consistently interests me, aside from maybe my son and my cat. The only place that feels vibrant and lively. Where things collide. Where the future comes from.

Where lights snick on and off in unreachable windows, like the ones above me. Even when the street is not majestic or momentous, it fascinates me. The lights that working people leave on after they go home: pies in a pie case bathed in bulb glow, the desk lamp burning in the funeral home, the hundreds of indistinguishable desks in fluorescent-washed offices, waiting for the next business day to restore their significance.

Footsteps to my left and a deep voice. "Hey, lady," it says.

I turn to face it and see three teenagers, three young black men.

"We're gonna need five dollars from you," says the voice. It belongs to the tallest one — taller than me but just as skinny, wearing blue jeans and a red leather flight jacket striated with glittering zippers. It's a handsome jacket, but too short for his arms, leaving his wrists bare to the midnight chill.

"Excuse me?" I say.

The kid to his left — shorter, but stronger looking — steps in closer. The third hangs back, his eyes darting from me to the street

408

to the sidewalks to the nearby buildings and then to me again. He seems not to want to be here, and his nervousness makes me nervous, snaps me partly out of my drunken overconfidence.

"Give us five dollars," the short one answers, "is what the man said."

His eyes are closed off, as impersonal and unwelcoming as Madison Square Garden looming beside us. He's dressed in an Adidas tracksuit; his tennis shoes have no laces. All three of them are shivering, dressed for this morning's warmer weather. They're a ways from home, wherever that is — across the Harlem River, probably.

Five dollars. This, I remember, was exactly the request that prompted the Subway Vigilante's act of violence, if the news coverage can be believed. I wonder whether these boys know this — whether they're referencing it deliberately, or whether it's just the standard protocol for muggings these days.

"You boys should be careful in this neighborhood," I say. "It's a dangerous area. And you don't know *what* people are liable to do."

The tall one and the short one exchange incredulous looks. "You're not understanding what I'm saying," the tall one says.

The nervous third steps closer to get a

better look at me. He's dark skinned and slight; his eyes — shrunken by the lenses of black-framed spectacles — are still frantically scanning our surroundings for any hint of danger, like those of a doughboy in no-man's-land.

"Yo," he says. "This is an old lady right here."

"I know what it is," the tall one says. "I got eyes."

"We ain't out here to fuck with old ladies, man," the nervous one says. "Let's go."

It occurs to me that thanks to my height and my bearing, someone who spots me from a distance in bad light might easily take me as younger and maler than I am, and this seems to be what my three challengers have done. Two seem set on proceeding regardless, but I think I see a hint of anguish in the bespectacled face of the third. A fear of consequences, probably — but it could also be recognition of some kind: an echo of a grandmother or a great aunt. With the vodka encouraging presumptuousness and leaps of logic, I cannot help but feel a sudden rush of affection for this boy, my reluctant champion, my bridge to safety.

I raise a wobbly finger to point at him. "You," I say, "look *just like* that young man

410

in the Oreo cookie commercial."

The three of them stare at me.

"Those glasses," I explain.

"Bitch is drunk or crazy," the short one mutters.

"We were just talking," the tall one says, "about the five dollars you gonna give us. Remember that?"

"Oh yes," I say. "I wish that I could."

"I think you can," says the tall one.

"I think you definitely can," says his short friend.

He has something metal in his hand — a knife, maybe, though it doesn't look like a knife. The men the Subway Vigilante shot were supposedly armed with sharpened screwdrivers, tools they planned to use to break into vending machines.

"Maybe you oughta just give us your wallet," says the taller one.

The third is silent, drifting away again.

For the first time it occurs to me that these young men might kill me. Or they could knock me down, which at my age might amount to the same thing, depending on how I fall.

If they kill me, they kill me. Gian loses both his mothers in one night.

If they don't, they don't. And I don't think they will. They seem like troublemakers, but not hard criminals. They're not violent or strung out. If they wanted to hurt me they'd have done so by now.

"Are you sure you want my wallet?" I say. "If a police officer stops you, how will you explain where it came from?"

"Lady, what the fuck do you think this is, *Let's Make a Deal*?" says the tall one, but his eyes hesitate in a way that his words do not.

"Look," says the short one, "we ain't discussing this. You can give us the cash, or maybe we just walk off with your bag. Right?"

"Yo, what the fuck, Keith?" the nervous one says, addressing his tall friend, who blanches to hear his name spoken aloud. "This ain't what we come out here for, man. This ain't the guy."

Keith flares, forgetting me for an instant. "They're *all* the guy," Keith says. "You been listening to all the same shit as me, man. Every cracker in five boroughs is calling up the mayor, telling him to give the keys to the city to this Charles Bronson subway-shooting motherfucker. We got to take our streets *back*."

"Yeah, but these *ain't* our streets, man," the nervous one says. "We in Midtown now."

Keith has already launched into the next

412

component of his diatribe before I begin to grasp what he's saying. "Wait a minute," I interrupt. "Wait just a minute. Are you boys out here *looking* for the Subway Vigilante?"

He's back in my face now, leaning in. "What we're looking for," he says, "is five dollars. That's all you need to concern yourself with."

I catch my breath, let it out slowly. "For your information," I say, "not *every* white person in the city approves of what that man did." Keith objects, but I raise my voice, cutting him off. "That man wasn't defending himself," I say. "He was a racist thug looking for trouble. What he did was disgusting, and I hope he goes to jail for it."

This just makes Keith angrier; I need to start backing down. Before he can say anything else, I slide my purse from my shoulder and put it in his hands. "Here," I say. "Take a look. Go ahead. It won't help you. After you see there's nothing of value, I'd appreciate it if you'd give it back."

He passes it to his short friend, who begins to rifle through it, dropping items to the pavement as he goes: my little can of Mace, my penlight, my Swiss Army Knife. "Nothing here," he says, letting the purse fall, showing the wallet to Keith.

"You're too late," I say. "I gave all my cash

413

to a guy at a Filipino bodega in the Village. I spent all I had on some snacks and a pot of dirt."

Keith is giving me a withering glare, outraged and unsatisfied. The short one's movements evince an injured heartlessness, a desire to do harm. Even the prudence of the third is being shoved aside by plain fear. If they kill me, I just hope that someone comes to my apartment and finds Phoebe quickly. Cats can live for a while without food, but I don't want her to suffer because of my recklessness.

"Okay," Keith says, pointing at my mink. "You got no cash, you can give us that coat."

"Man, what are we doing all this talking for?" says the shorter one. "Let's grab the coat and get the fuck out."

"I don't want no part of this, Darrell," the third one says. He's even farther away now. More a spectator than a participant. The chorus in a Greek tragedy. I think back to the Christian Women's Hotel, our bedsheet-costumed performance of *Antigone*. How little we understood then of the lines we spoke. *No man is so foolish that he is enamored of death.*

Tall Keith and short Darrell are squaring off, looking at me, then at each other, then back to me. Darrell tosses my wallet over his shoulder. It hits the ground with a slap. A decision is about to be made.

"Let's think for a second," I say, "about where to go from here. Your friend" — I nod to the distant third, the shortsighted chorister — "wants to let me go. Darrell here wants to pursue the assault-and-battery route and take my coat by force. But these are not our only two options. Let's keep this conversation going."

"We don't need this hassle," says the nervous one. "Let's just go. That coat ain't even real."

"I beg your pardon," I say. "It most certainly is real. I paid four thousand dollars for it in 1942."

"What's it worth today?" says Keith.

"I honestly couldn't tell you," I say. "I've never thought about selling it. Look, I'll give you the coat. But it's cold out here, and I'm old, and I still need to walk to R.H. Macy's tonight before I go home. I can't do that without a coat."

"That ain't our problem," says Darrell.

"I think we ought to swap," I continue. "You get my mink, and I make it home without freezing to death. That's the offer on the table."

Darrell is still ready to rush me — legs wide, knees bent, shoulders low — but

Keith softens, rocks back on his heels. His flood of anger has drained away, showing what's underneath, which looks like sadness. "Okay," says Keith. "We'll swap."

"Keith, are you fucking serious?"

"Shut up, Darrell," says Keith. "Give her your jacket."

"What?" says Darrell. "She ain't getting nothing from me, fool. What you giving away *my* coat for?"

"Because it's the shittiest one we got," says Keith.

"Hold your horses," I say. "No offense to your coat, Darrell — which actually looks both elegant and comfortable — but that deal doesn't work for me. This is a fur coat. In addition to being very expensive, it's extremely warm. As you've noticed, it's gotten cold tonight. Based on the fact that Darrell, who is in the prime of his life, is visibly shivering, I must conclude that a track jacket is not warm enough for an elderly person like myself. Plus the arms are too short. I want the flight jacket."

"Aw, fuck you, lady," Keith says.

I open my arms wide, feeling vulnerable, trying to seem confident. "Come on, Keith," I say. "This is your lucky day. A full-length mink coat in perfect condition? Free and clear, with no trouble from the law? You can sell it and buy jackets for the whole neighborhood."

Keith looks at me, shakes his head. "You're crazy, lady," he says.

But he takes off his jacket.

I do the same with my coat. The cold air rushes in around my armpits; I hadn't realized how much I've been sweating. It feels good for a second. Then my teeth start to chatter.

Keith puts out a hand to give me his coat, another to take mine. We swap. He drapes my mink over his shoulder, steps away. "Let's not be too hasty," I say. "We'd better try them on."

"Come on, man," says Darrell. "Let's get the fuck out of here."

"What are you scared of?" I say. "This is an honest swap. Nobody's in trouble."

Just as Keith puts on my mink coat and I put on his jacket, the clock must strike midnight and the ball must drop, because we can hear, all the way over here, all the people in Time Square roaring.

It's 1985.

The coat looks stunning on Keith, like it was tailored for him.

"You look like a pimp," says his formerly nervous, now visibly relieved friend.

"Thanks," says Keith.

"And *you* look hilarious," his friend says, using his chin to point at me. I am sure that he's right.

"Well," I say, closing the jacket's most functional zipper, "Happy New Year, gentlemen. It's been a pleasure doing business with you."

"No doubt it has," Keith says. "You're gonna run for a cop as soon as you get your ass round that corner, ain't you?"

"Why would I? There's nothing to call a cop about."

"Oh, right. This shit here was just a routine midnight street-corner business transaction between a fur-coat-wearing old white lady and three black dudes from the South Bronx. They're gonna have *no* problem believing that."

"Hmm," I say. "I see your point. You want a bill of sale?"

"Yes I do, actually."

"*Fuck,*" says Darrell. "Can we *go*?"

I take a moment to search the dark pavement for my notebook and a pen. The third boy finds them before I do, hands them to me, and then gathers the rest of my things as I write up the bill, returning them to my purse, returning my purse to me. The bag doesn't match my new coat, but that's all right.

418

"You know," I say, "I have a question for you boys, if you can spare another minute."

"Y'all are killing me," Darrell says, hugging himself, bouncing on the balls of his feet.

"As I've been walking around the city," I say, "I keep hearing this song. A rap, I think it's called. I'm wondering if you know it. It's not easy to describe. There's no chorus, per se. It involves a great deal of hipping and hopping."

"Aw, man," the third boy says. "I bet I know what *that* is."

"That could be anything," Keith says.

"At certain points," I say, "one of the gentlemen, one of the rappers, refers to a Holiday Inn. Does that ring any bells?"

This doubles all three of them over, even Keith. "This shit ain't real," Darrell says. "It ain't really happening."

"Could be anything," Keith says again.

"Damn, y'all," the third boy says. "She's talking about Sugarhill Gang! 'Rapper's Delight'!"

"I know what the fuck she's talking about, Winston," Keith snaps. His mirth is gone. He turns to me, plucks the bill of sale from my fingers. "You heard what the man said. 'Rapper's Delight.' Sugarhill Gang. It's from, like, six years ago. What you want to know for?"

"As I said, I keep hearing it. I like it."

"Ain't you got your own music?" Keith says. "Barbra Streisand, or the Carpenters, or some shit like that? How come white folks always feel the need to tell us how good our music is, like we don't know?"

"Just curious, Keith."

"Yeah?" Keith says. "Go be curious about something else. I bet there's real good Japanese music and Mexican music that nobody's listening to. C'mon, y'all. Let's go."

He takes a few long backward steps away from me, then spins — the mink flaring — and marches off. His friends follow a beat behind him. "You crazy, lady," Darrell shouts as he goes.

"I'm actually not," I say. "I have been. But I'm not anymore."

Just as the other two catch up with him, Keith stops, turns, walks back to me. He lifts an index finger in front of my nose. I flinch.

"You gonna go home and brag about this?" he says.

"I have nothing to brag about," I say. "And no one to brag to."

He gives me a hard, troubled look. "This ain't no more than what it is," he says. "Just

420

because you show us some respect don't mean we got no problem with you. The reason tonight played out like it did is because you had this coat, and because you made a good choice with it. Lots of folks, they wouldn't have that choice. You think about that before you go feeling too good about how you handled yourself."

"I understand."

"You don't understand shit, old lady. Maybe it ain't all your fault that you don't. But you don't." He looks me up and down, as if taking me in for the first time. "You best get on home," he says. "Before a *real* criminal shows up to mess with you."

"You best do the same, Keith. Maybe I'll come up and visit one of these days. The South Bronx, you said?"

Keith laughs. "Yeah, that's right," he says. "South Bronx. Hunts Point, Tiffany and Randall. You curious? You come on up. You'll learn a lot. You gonna wear my jacket when you come?"

I shake my head, tap my hand against the zippered leather over my heart. "I'm gonna wear *my* jacket when I come," I say.

The three of them walk quickly to the west without another look back. I continue east, toward Seventh Avenue, then down Thirty-Fourth to R.H. Macy's.

The jacket is still warm from having Keith in it, and the smell it exhales is strange, but strangely comforting: coconut oil maybe, and marijuana, and sweat. I forgot to take my gloves out of my coat when I traded it, so I stick my hands into the jacket pockets, and in the right one I feel a scrap of paper: a fortune-cookie fortune that Keith had been saving for me unwittingly.

You think that it is a secret but it has never been one, it says.

There are a few more people on the street now that 1985 is underway. Partygoers have begun to trickle from wherever they were to wherever they want to be, seeping like water into the cracks of the city.

I stand in front of the main entrance of R.H. Macy's, the one with the clock face and the caryatids staring at the now-closed A.S. Beck shoe store across Thirty-Fourth Street, the carved women acting as pillars for the World's Largest Store.

Hats and frocks and shoes and cold creams and perfumes and pots and pans — the parts and parcels of people's lives. I can't see all of these items through the plate-glass windows, but I know they're inside.

I am suddenly so tired, I think I may already be asleep. The structure of the city is the structure of a dream. And me, I have been a long time drifting.

A white-collar girl who came to New York and hit the top. The first kiss of the city — I remember it, and so many after. But nobody can remember the last kiss, the final hand-clasp. When one leaves for good, one cannot recall the leaving.

There have been so many times in my life when I found the actual world to be completely unsuitable. I have done my level best to remedy that, through poetry and through advertising, and I'm glad my efforts were appreciated.

I am proud that I fought so hard against the world, relieved that I made my fragile truce with it. I can greet it now, from time to time, as it really is.

And I'm glad that I've stopped by R.H. Macy's, but I know I can't stay. I look at my reflection in the plate glass: the same check-in I made sixty years ago, on my way to interview for the job that gave shape to my life. The face I have now is hardly the same. Neither is the city.

As I turn and walk toward Murray Hill and home and purring Phoebe, I suspect that we do not know any more than the people of the past did, but only think somewhat differently.

Walking East on Thirty-Sixth Street, my street, I can't see the moon anywhere, but I know it's up there.

Somewhere under it is Gian, are the children. Somewhere under it is Julia — or not. I think back to the handful of greeting cards that she and I exchanged over the years, and her unrealized wish that she and I be friends. I always wondered what else she wanted from me, having already taken Max. I kept my guard up. And she cared for my ailing ex-husband, my only true love; she nurtured my son, and helped nurture his children, even after Max was gone. She gave of herself joyfully, in a way I could never manage, could never conceive. What else could she have wanted except to make amends, to care for us, to help when she was needed? Why did that never occur to me?

So many careers and fortunes are made by expecting the least and the worst of people. And yet people are rarely so disappointing. The city has taught me that.

A long black car pulls up next to me, engine sighing, a bass voice booming from the window, "Lillian! Is that you?"

And even though the voice has yelled my name, I jump, shaking with surplus adrenaline.

"Skip?" I say, stopping as the car stops, to stare at his familiar mustachioed face. "What are you doing up in Murray Hill?"

"I dropped my trader guy off at some sex party, and now I'm taking the scenic route home," he says. "I barely recognized you in that b-boy jacket. What happened to the mink?"

"Oh, I met some young gentlemen. We got on the subject of outerwear and decided to switch."

"You gave up your mink for some cheap leather and zippers?" he says, leaning out to have a better look.

"Naturally," I say, striking a catalogue-model pose, hand to hip, gaze over one shoulder. "It's very figure-flattering, and besides — I've got other furs, but I haven't got one of these."

"Whatever you say, Lillian," he says, and I am grateful to him for not pushing it further. "But how about you let me get my 1985 started off right by doing a good turn. It'd be my honor to give you a lift home."

"Thank you," I say. "But to ensconce myself in a car when I've made it this far with my own powers of locomotion would be a defeat that would set *my* 1985 off on the wrong foot."

"What is it with you and walking, Lillian?"

Skip asks, and for an irrational moment I worry that he's going to shepherd me bodily into the back seat, but of course he remains behind the wheel.

"Skip, I'm quite weary and can't explain it to you properly right now," I say, and slowly begin to continue my walk. "But I'm not exaggerating when I say that walking has done no less than save my life. Plus, you'll be relieved to know that this is my street."

He rolls the limo forward, too, matching my pace. "That does make me feel better, but I'm going to go ahead and walk you home this way."

"If you insist," I say, and we proceed the final block to 22 E. Thirty-Sixth, me on two feet, him on four wheels. The distance is so brief that I almost let the interval pass in silence, but then I find myself saying, "Listen, Skip, would you like to meet up and take a walk some day? I can show you what I mean."

"Aw, Lillian, you don't have to prove anything to me," he says, stopping the car and shaking his head. "I don't mean to insult you."

"No, really," I say, extending a hand toward his window. "Give me your telephone number. If you do, I'll call you. We'll stroll."

He hesitates a beat before reaching into his tuxedo jacket and presenting me a card. "You know what? You're right. I sit on my ass in this limo all the livelong day. A walk could only do me good."

"Me too," I say, putting the card in one of Keith's many zippered pockets and stepping away. "And now I bid you good-night, as this building right here is my humble castle."

I wave and he honks once — a gentle salute — when he sees that I'm safely inside my own building, before accelerating into the night.

I reach my apartment door, and fit the key to the lock. Poor famished Phoebe greets me in the entry, mewling and rubbing her rounded skull against my unsteady ankles. From across the otherwise dark apartment I see the insistent blink of the answering machine's message light — the grandchildren wishing me a Happy New Year, Gian wondering where I was when the children called, Gian telling me that Julia has died.

Nothing that won't wait until after the cat has been fed. I take off Keith's coat and drape it over the back of a chair.

427

I turn on lamps, open drawers, set the opener to the rim of the can. Phoebe watches me from the floor, her pupils green and cavernous.

"Be patient," I tell her. "Or make yourself useful by growing some thumbs."

I owned that mink for more than forty years, more than twice the time I was married to Max. I bought it a month after Gian was born, as a way of proving that my life was still my own. For decades it rarely left my closet and never left the apartment. With Max away on business, with Johnny napping in another room, I'd drape it over the bed and run my fingers across it, conspiring with myself, reaffirming my status as an imposter, an agent provocateur. *You think that it is a secret but it has never been one.*

And then one fall day in 1966 — with my long-traitorous brain at last reconciled with my body, with Max dead, with Gian living on his own — I rediscovered that coat, shrouded in plastic at the back of a closet. I put it on. I stepped outside, and the world seemed to accept me as a person who ought to be wearing it.

And then I took a walk.

I walked with no objective in mind beyond a vague interest in finding an old-fashioned cream soda, and six hours later I was seeing

428

the sun set behind the Statue of Liberty from the upper deck of the Staten Island Ferry, watching as the faces of the strangers gathered at the rails were warmed and softened by the orange light, hearing them whisper and shout in four or five languages and a dozen different accents. It was the most clichéd scene imaginable — like the hackwork of Rockwell's most gauche imitator — and my practiced mind filled with needle-sharp couplets to skewer it.

I didn't write any of them down, though. I just stood still and watched, hoping that the tears on my cheeks could be plausibly blamed on the biting wind off the Upper Bay. *We've been here all along,* the world seemed to say, *waiting for you. What took you so long to find us?*

I put Phoebe's food in her ceramic dish, pour myself a glass of water, and take a seat at the table in the dim kitchen, listening to the dainty smacks of her cat mouth.

The message light flashes on, a red pulse on the wall behind it. Somewhere in the building a party is breaking up; from the stairwell I hear the drunken talk and stumbling steps of those who've given up on the ancient elevator. We drift — all of us — farther from the fraught spasm of midnight, settling into the fog of another year.

No one survives the future, of course. Over the years I have rushed it, run from it, tried to shunt myself from its track. That these efforts did not succeed does not mean that I regret them.

Now? The future and I are just about even, our quarrel all but resolved. I welcome its coming, and I resolve to be attentive to the details of its arrival. I plan to meet it at the station in my best white dress, violet corsage in hand. Waving as it comes into view, borne toward the present on its road of anthracite.

AUTHOR'S NOTE
AND SOURCES

The story of Lillian Boxfish is inspired, in part, by the life and work of the poet and ad woman Margaret Fishback, herself the real highest-paid female advertising copy-writer in the world during the 1930s, thanks to her brilliant work for R.H. Macy's.

Back in 2007, my best friend from high school, Angela McClendon Ossar, was earning her master's degree in library science at the University of North Carolina at Chapel Hill and doing an internship in the Hartman Center for Sales, Advertising & Marketing History at Duke University. As part of this job, she got to be the receiving and process-ing archivist for a recent acquisition: the papers of Margaret Fishback.

Angela, as the first person ever to work professionally with the papers (after Fish-back's son, Anthony Antolini, donated the material), quickly realized that Fishback was a figure — a poet, a protofeminist, a successful career woman, and a mother — who would appeal to me as a poet, a feminist, and a professional myself. She called me up and told me all about Fishback, and I was so fascinated that I applied for a travel-to-collections grant from Duke, which enabled me, in May of 2007, to be the first non-archivist or librarian to work with Fishback's archive.

I instantly felt a deep connection to Fishback — an affinity for her writing both of ads and of poems, and her overall sensibility — though she'd been dead since the mid-1980s. I knew that I wanted to do something to bring her story and those of others like her (this whole forgotten generation of pre–*Mad Men* advertising women) into the light. I gave a lecture at Duke about my findings, focusing particularly on Fishback's innovative use of humor in her ad copy for Macy's, but it took me a few years to realize what shape my project should take. At last, stuck inside during a blizzard in Chicago in 2013, I got the idea to combine my love of Fishback with my love of cities and *flânerie;* I resolved to write a novel that would bring these two affinities together. Now, almost exactly a decade to the day that I first set eyes upon the Fishback archive, the book has arrived.

To be clear, this is a work of fiction and not a biography of Margaret Fishback. The circumstances of the novel are my invention, and the attitudes and opinions expressed by Lillian Boxfish are entirely imagined. That said, I encourage everyone to read Margaret Fishback's collections of light verse, which are utterly charming and are as follows:

I Feel Better Now, New York: E.P. Dutton & Co., Inc., 1932 (poems originally appearing in the *New York World, The New Yorker, Life, The Saturday Evening Post, The New York American, Judge,* and *Vanity Fair*)

I Take It Back, New York: E.P. Dutton & Co., Inc., 1935 (poems originally appearing in *The New Yorker, The Saturday Evening Post, Harper's Bazaar, Life, Ladies' Home Journal, The New York American, The New York Sun, The World, Judge, Vanity Fair, Red-book, Buffalo Town Tidings, The Stage,* and *The Forum Magazine*)

One to a Customer, New York: E.P. Dutton & Co., 1937 (an omnibus comprising *I Feel Better Now* and *Poems Made Up to Take Out,* supra, together with two other volumes: *Out of My Head* and *I Take It Back*)

Poems Made Up to Take Out, New York: David McKay Co., Inc., 1963 (poems originally appearing in *Better Living, Collier's, Glamour, Good Housekeeping, Ladies' Home Journal,* the *New York Herald Tribune, Pictorial Review, Reader's Digest, American Girl, American Home, The New York Times, The Saturday Evening Post, The Wall Street Journal, This Week, Woman's Day,* and *Women's Wear Daily*)

I also recommend taking a look at her how-to books, including the one on etiquette, *Safe Conduct: When to Behave — And Why* (Harcourt, Brace & Company, 1938), as well as a humorous guide to parenthood called *Look Who's a Mother! A Book About Babies for Parents, Expectant and Otherwise* (Simon & Schuster, 1945).

All of the poems and advertisements that appear in the book attributed to Lillian Boxfish — as well as the letter on page 258 — were written by Margaret Fishback and appear here with the permission of her estate. Many thanks to Fishback's son, Anthony Antolini, for granting this permission.

Additionally, the "Women in Cosmetic Advertising" quiz is drawn from *Advertising*

434

Careers for Women, edited by Dorothy Dignam and Blanche Clair and published in 1939; Fishback's copy of this book was a part of her archive.

The employees of Thorndike Press hope you have enjoyed this Large Print book. All our Thorndike, Wheeler, and Kennebec Large Print titles are designed for easy reading, and all our books are made to last. Other Thorndike Press Large Print books are available at your library, through selected bookstores, or directly from us.

For information about titles, please call:
(800) 223-1244

or visit our website at:
gale.com/thorndike

To share your comments, please write:
Publisher
Thorndike Press
10 Water St., Suite 310
Waterville, ME 04901